Elizabeth Tuckett

Pictures In Tyrol And Elsewhere

Elizabeth Tuckett

Pictures In Tyrol And Elsewhere

ISBN/EAN: 9783741149368

Manufactured in Europe, USA, Canada, Australia, Japa

Cover: Foto ©Andreas Hilbeck / pixelio.de

Manufactured and distributed by brebook publishing software
(www.brebook.com)

Elizabeth Tuckett

Pictures In Tyrol And Elsewhere

PICTURES IN TYRO

AND ELSEWHERE.

FROM A FAMILY SKETCH-BOOK.

BY THE AUTHOR OF

'A VOYAGE EN ZIGZAG'

&c.

De omnibus rebus et quibusdam aliis.

SECOND EDITION.

LONDON:

LONGMANS, GREEN, AND CO.

Hallstadt

PICTURES IN TYROL

&c.

LONDON: PRINTED BY
SPOTTISWOODE AND CO., NEW-STREET SQUARE
AND PARLIAMENT STREET

PREFACE.

MANY READERS may possibly find in these pages something to remind them of old holidays, and wanderings of their own amongst the hills, or be led to see for themselves what pleasant haunts are to be found in Tyrol, or what mountains are yet to be scaled, and for such, these histories of very small adventures, pictures of busy and 'still life,' will stir the old sympathies and memories that make for many of us so pleasant a *cordon* round the Alps.

Two of the following papers have already appeared in a magazine from which they are reprinted by the kind permission of the Editor.

Those on the Ortler and Viso districts and the Suldenthal were originally written for the *Alpine Journal*, with many additional topographical and scientific details, which have been omitted here, and with their present illustrations, they are now given to the public in a slightly more popular form.

November 1867.

CONTENTS.

LIST

OF

ILLUSTRATIONS.

———◦◦———

BREAKING THE ICE

OR

MOUNTAINEERING IN AN OMNIBUS.

—————◆—————

'Peregrinations charm our senses with such unspeakable and sweet
variety, that some count him unhappy that never travelled.'
                                                    BURTON.

BREAKING THE ICE,

OR

MOUNTAINEERING IN AN OMNIBUS.

———◦◦———

WE left England early in May 1866, hoping to escape the cold winds that still lingered about our English spring, and to find the lower Alps in all their fresh beauty, never to be so keenly enjoyed as at the moment when the latest fallen snow seemingly melts away in an hour's sunshine, and changes, as by a magic touch, into flowers and greenness. The mornings and evenings are still clear and frosty, but when the sun is out, the midday warmth makes a pleasant atmosphere for travelling comfort; and as a rule, in spring, amongst the mountains, you find a climate that is quite perfect in its adaptation to your needs. Unfortunately for us, there was something wrong with the calendar on this particular spring we had chosen; the winter still held everything in a strong grasp, and we had a hard battle with keen winds and frost before our patience and the cold weather came to an end together.

Our party was composed of sufficiently divers elements

B

to afford constant variety under the most dismal circumstances, so that we were. never reduced to a dead level
mentally, and were fully prepared to find plenty of enjoyment from all the mingled delights that Nature and
Art, queer costumes, *patois*, unknown food, springless carriages, and constant variety promised us, and endless
amusement from anything of discomfort or misadventure
that would have to be greeted with either groanings or
laughter.

A very blessed gift is that same power of appreciating
the ridiculous aspect of every situation; natures, with the
lights and shades of their varied characteristics put in in
tolerably strong colours, are the pleasantest to do with,
and a keen sense of the ludicrous is generally balanced
by a sympathy and large-heartedness, none the less true
because somewhat deep and still. We may value neutral
tints in a landscape, but in a life such vague shadows only
serve as a foil to richer colouring, and such a use of one's
fellow-creatures is too dismal to be encouraged by the
most confirmed misanthrope. There was nothing vague
about our party: thoroughly fortunate in our companions,
our enjoyment in everything was as keen as possible, and
from the oldest to the youngest traveller, we set out with
the knowledge that in our journey we were to take, daily
and hourly, that 'step' from the 'sublime to the ridiculous,' which makes travelling such an inexhaustible
pleasure.

Charing Cross. A family party. Mrs C & D, niece & grandaughter
as travelling companions.

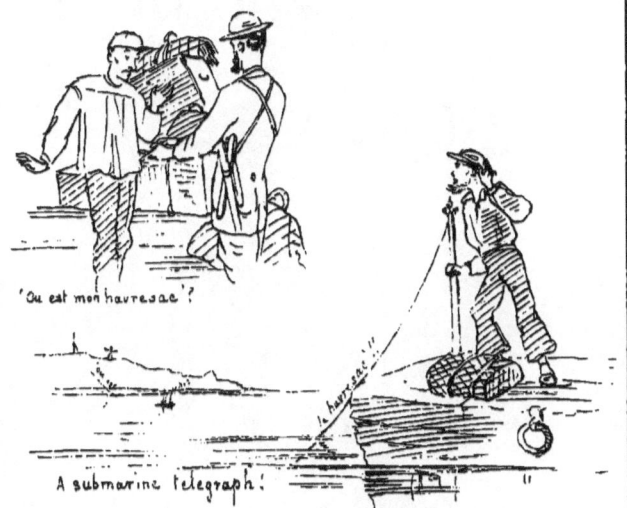

'Ou est mon havresac'?

A submarine telegraph!

Our stay in Paris was not to F. a season of uninterrupted repose. A particularly precious knapsack, carefully
packed with especial valuables for the mountains, had
been registered with the rest of our luggage at Charing
Cross, and the officials of the *Gare du Nord* declared it
was not to be found; a second journey to the station, and
yet a third, proved equally fruitless, though there was a
rumour that such a knapsack had been seen by some one
on the pier at Dover, and that, if not appropriated meanwhile, it might come by the tidal train; we had to start
for Basle in faith, trusting that a promised telegram would
somehow bring it after us. The twelve hours to Basle
were less wearying than usual, and we recalled, with
thankfulness as to the present, many gloomy memories of
heat and dust and discomfort in a long July or August
day on the same road. As it was, we read, chatted,
and talked, puzzled our brains over acrostics, sketched
people at the railway stations, and consumed a midday
meal at Troyes; after which we all went to sleep, and
woke up gladly to feel ourselves in Switzerland once
more.

Throughout our many wanderings we have always
been fortunate in small things, and found, as we moved
over our circumscribed part of the earth, that it never
grated on its axis, and the loss of that knapsack was a
terrible blow to our self-conceit; and we were brought
pitiably low by a further discovery, on our arrival at Basle,

where we took up our quarters at the 'Black Bear,'
wishing to get rid of civilisation and the 'Trois Rois' together, and where we found a pleasant welcome and clean
boarded rooms, primitive-looking bedchambers with rather
sloping floors, built regardless of architectural laws or
symmetry, each room being made up of angles, and having
no two sides alike.   However, like Samson's lion, our bear
contained many good things, and we were just sitting
down to an *Abendessen* of coffee and tea, honey, venison,
and trout, when F. entered the *salle*, and, amidst an
ominous silence, related disaster number two.   He had
just inspected his portmanteau, and discovered a case of
spontaneous combustion.   A large tin filled with vesuvians,
intended for his own delectation and that of his friends,
had come to grief; the contents had gone off—literally
blown themselves up, and words fail to describe the unutterably nasty state in which everything near them was
found, whether linen or literature.

Misfortune seemed to dog our footsteps, and it was
with an effort that we rallied our courage; but, recol-
lecting that it was highly reprehensible on F.'s part to
travel with such things at all, we all told him so, some
of the party adding valuable remarks as to the undesirable
habit of smoking in which the young men of the present
day indulge; after which we felt better, and were able to
attack the trout.   There was just time after breakfast
the next morning to visit the bridge; the old town looked

"Montez en voiture Messieurs et Mesdames"

very lovely in the bright sunshine, the river, in its swift steady flow, seemed the most lifelike thing about the place, and in its dreamy apathetic quiet all the vitality of Basle might have been washed down in that strong tide. The steep-roofed houses looked out with brown and white and pink faces amongst the trees; great rafts of timber and light boats floated down the stream; quaint-costumed peasants passed us on their way to market, driving carts drawn by a horse and a little cow, or by sturdy oxen; and women were at work washing linen in wooden-roofed barges moored to the shore, rinsing and soaking moist masses in the water, as the green waves swirled with a great rush against the planks.

Three or four hours by rail brought us to Schaffhausen, a very slow train affording endless studies of the country-people who thronged the little stations. At one of these we watched with much amusement a procession of men and women, laden with sacks, who had just descended from a third-class compartment; as they passed us, carrying their burdens on their shoulders, on their backs, or in their arms, each sack struggled and squeaked and wriggled in the most ridiculous way, and we thought pigs and peasants had all rather a hard time of it; little children on their way to school carried knapsacks strapped to their shoulders with the lesson-books of the day; and every traveller, male or female, was armed with a large coloured cotton umbrella. For the greater part of the way we journeyed by the river, passing many picturesque old towns and villages, the country looking most lovely with bright spring foliage shining against the dark background of the forest, *Schwarz Wald* in reality as well as in name. The fields were one mass of flowers, and the fruit trees were just bursting into blossom; here and there men were making hay in the fields; there was a freshness and lightness in the air that was very pleasant, and a delicious sense of coming summer.

At night we slept at the hotel above the Falls of Schaffhausen, feeling a little as though it were all a dream. We were evidently the first arrivals of the season, and the great empty house looked rather dreary. Somebody must be 'the first arrival' everywhere, so we made the best of it; and surely the most crabbed of mortals might well have been content, as, looking from the open window, the whole wonderful scene burst upon the view; the great green river, falling in one mighty mass over the rocks, lashing itself into a white fury, as it plunged and roared and struggled down the rapids, and then lying panting and still for a moment before it swept away again behind the hills. We saw it in a setting of softest tints of golden green from the wooded slopes and the garden beneath us, where a great Judas-tree threw its purple blossoms across the flow of the emerald water.

In the morning we ran down to the shore, and were

Pigs und Peasants!

Our Guard

Sketches from the train.

paddled in a long unwieldy boat to the opposite side, passing just near enough to the eddies to feel the faster rush of the water. We walked up through the woods, the Philistine belonging to our barge signalling an Amalekite with a prolonged whistle, who took us in charge, and marshalled us into a number of little galleries hanging over the water, and built out into the foam, across which a lovely rainbow had flung the glory of its colouring.

In the sunlight every bubble that burst upon the crest of the waves was irridescent and brilliant as a diamond, and deep down under the whiteness were shades of emerald and lilac and dark soft green, flecked and rippled with spray. The Amalekite rested near by, keeping us well within sight, but too accustomed to the scene and the appropriate emotions of the British traveller to be keenly observant of either. The roar was deafening, as the water dashed under the rotten old planks and flung a shower of foam over the gallery, drenching us in a moment if we ventured to the end, till, mazed and giddy, we were glad to retreat, and mount still higher into the queerly-decorated rooms of the chateau above. It had been a veritable chateau once, boasting all the dignity of age, and would be well in keeping with the scene, had not Philistines and Amalekites, and the other inhabitants of the land, hewers of wood and drawers of water, carvers and painters of the nineteenth century, combined to make

a stand there, and to prey upon the harmless stranger;
for which end you are led through odd little cabinets,
containing very bad studies in oil, and large collections or
carvings in bone and wood and ivory, until, with a sigh
of relief, you reach the courtyard and find a genuine
antique gateway and an old pump, and so wander round
to the bridge above the Falls, from which you look down
upon the river just making up its mind to the inevitable leap.

There was enough frost in the air to make a good fire
in the stove pleasant on our return, and as we gathered
round the lamp in the little *salon* lingering over our tea,
it was difficult to believe that we were only three or four
days out of England; our pleasant wandering life seemed
to have been going on for months, and we had already
reached a quiet atmosphere in which people speculated
dimly as to the chances of war. Count Bismark grew to
be little more than a myth, and we subsided to the level
of the agricultural population around us, peasants and
cows being about equally unconcerned as to the balance
of power in Europe.

A steam down the Lake of Constance brought us to
Lindau, where we landed amidst a crowd of natives
waiting to welcome old King Ludwig. The pretty little
town was alive with people; there were flags flying, and
green wreaths everywhere. A steamer, with its rigging
brilliant with coloured buntings, puffed up to the pier, and

The Amalekite at ease!

At the Pump.

Schaffhausen Falls.

The Philistines !

Schweizer Hof.

his Majesty landed—a cheery, kindly-looking old man, bowing and smiling as the eager spectators opened a path for him—and walked to the station, where a magnificent high-and-mighty, in blue and silver, Königliche-Baiern beadle mounted guard. The lake was lying still, and glimmering in the sunshine; the old towers and houses, black-roofed and high-peaked and picturesque, rose dark against the clear sky; the Lion of Bavaria, couched on its pillar, turned its placid face towards the water; and about its base pressed the kind welcoming people, and we eagerly scanned the sunburnt faces seeking for a Grindelwalder—the brave, sturdy, faithful, Christian Almer—who was to join us there, and give his good services for some mountaineering during the next few weeks.

Only two nights lay between us and Paris. A few hours in train and steamboat, and we had entered on a new life, as completely strange, un-English, unspoilt as to luxury, unhacknied as to rules and conventionalities, as any wayworn atom of civilisation could desire—even a little more so than was quite pleasant, in the matter of blankets and other mundane comforts. The Great City—that Kosmos of M. Victor Hugo, absorbing entire humanity into itself, according to the poet's utterances—rested infinitely far-off in an ideal atmosphere of its own. It is said that 'good Americans when they die go to Paris;' and leaving it to such faithful worshippers, 'sons of the soil,' and Transatlantic visitors, we were well content, though somewhat shivering, to dwell beyond its borders in a dim land—a limbo, if need were, M. Victor Hugo insisting on his fancy as to the world in general—full of great mountains and everlasting snow, simple natures, great quiet beasts, grass and flowers, and giant glaciers, *Stellwägen*, cows and fresh milk—innocent of the *laiteries* of the Pré Catalan and the *bergères* of the Bois-de-Boulogne.

Heavy rain came on, as our train slowly puffed and panted on its way, and with the rain a cold wind that made us shiver; and, worse than all, it began dimly to dawn on us that spring was two or three weeks behind its time here as well as in England, and that the Bavarian highlands and the accommodation they afforded were not exactly adapted to an inclement season. We did our best to believe we had not made a mistake, and to have faith each day in warmth for the morrow; but until we reached Ischl, nine days later, the prospect was not a brilliant one.

At Immenstadt we found a rather dirty little inn, but managed to secure some food, and then started, in two of the queerest shandrydan carriages, for a ten-mile drive to Hindelang. We passed through a broad valley rich in beautiful scenery, which we could enjoy even without the sunshine and in spite of the clouds, which did their best to hide everything but the road, as they came down

almost on the roof of the carriage. A great deal of fresh
snow must have fallen in the night, and the low hills and
pine-woods were thickly covered. We were glad when,
after due rattling of springs and boards (windows there
were none), our shaking vehicles drew up before an old
wayside inn, which, however, looked anything but promising. The rain was coming down heavier than ever,
and our last sight of the outer world showed us a stray
cloudlet that had ventured so low that it had actually got
caught in the shelter of a gable, where it hung, looking
rather ashamed of itself, and sighing for breath enough to
blow itself off again.

The whole situation was so deplorable that it was necessary for each member of the party to make an effort, and
rise to the occasion, which was nobly done; and leaving
the gentlemen to settle with the *Kutscher*, we rallied round
Mrs. C. as a forlorn hope, and set out on an exploring expedition. These great country inns throughout Germany,
Tyrol, and the Engadine, are all on the same pattern:
strongly built of stone or brick and often very large, they
wander over a great extent of land, the ground-floor
being devoted to kitchens, an entrance-hall with a wooden
table and benches for the peasants, and a *Stube* adjoining,
which answers to the bar of our public-houses. Making
our way to the staircase, we mounted to a long, broad
landing, or upper hall, with a vaulted roof and walls, all
whitewashed alike; the floors were clean, but very bare

and cold, and dark heavy doors led into the chambers. A *Kellnerin* explained to us that 'the *Wirthin* was out, and that the *Damen* must understand that the *Wirthin* bestirred herself in everything; consequently, when she was not there, it was simply chaos. Would the *Damen* kindly believe this, and adapt themselves to circumstances? There was a room':—pointing to an apartment with five large windows, a long table with eighteen chairs ranged around it, a big black stove, and two wooden boxes containing striped *duvets* in their respective corners,—'There were six travellers? Would not the *Damen* consider there was space enough for the entire party? They preferred several rooms? certainly they should have them then, but truly the chamber was very spacious!'

Appropriating the barrack to Mrs. C. and D. for the night, and arranging it as the *salle à manger* for the moment, E. and C. took possession of an adjoining apartment—the gentlemen being installed in rooms on the other side of the landing. A fire was ordered in the barrack stove, and we implored the people to give us some food as quickly as possible. But as we could see no signs of bed or nourishment, we sent for the landlord, and entreated him to make the servants hurry themselves. He was a large apathetic man, who echoed the *Kellnerin's* words:

'The *Wirthin* is away; the *Wirthin* sees to everything; without the *Wirthin* nothing can be done. She has all the keys; but, patience! she may return to-night, unless indeed she remains away till to-morrow.'

'But at least give us some food; tea and bread and meat you must have. We cannot starve because there happens to be no *Wirthin*!'

'Will the *Damen* graciously understand that there is no tea? There was some in a paper that a traveller left with us, but it is in a cupboard which is locked, and the *Wirthin* has the key, as I before explained to the *Herr-schaft*; also there is no teapot, which *gnädige Frauen* would in itself be a difficulty; but, patience—patience! may be the *Wirthin* will return, and then the *Damen* shall see!'

Utterly in despair, we took matters into our own hands. E. unpacked a small teapot, real Britannia-metal, her especial pride; Mrs. C. hunted out a packet of tea and some potted meat from the portmanteau; and then, with Christian's assistance, fetched some hot water from the kitchen below, which was boiled in a pan over a wood-fire, and dipped out with a ladle. Meanwhile a woman was induced to prepare some coffee and eggs, and slowly, and with many journeyings, a sufficient 'spread' was pro-vided; and we all gathered round the long table, and made ourselves very merry over our improvised supper. While we were feasting, the *Kellnerin* entered to arrange the beds and hunt up washing-basins, carrying on a frag-mentary conversation with us at the same time; her task

was nearly accomplished when one of the wooden boxes
gave way, or at least its bottom came out, and the bed
disappeared on one side; so with an exclamation of despair,
after puzzling at it in vain, she hurried away, returning
with a deaf old Oberland peasant, who had been busy
carting manure in the yard.   Their united efforts restored
order, but our attention had been meanwhile attracted,
and we noticed, with some dismay, that the bed-making
consisted in spreading one coarse sheet on the mattrass,
and placing a *duvet* over it.   It was freezing hard, and
we were stiff with cold and damp, and rather rheumatic.
' Where were the blankets ? '

' *Ach Himmel!* they had no blankets; there were the
beautiful *duvets*—what more could we want?   There was
not a blanket in the house; but when the *Wirthin* returned,
ah ! then indeed she would see to everything.'

The long room, and the long table, and the eighteen
chairs looked so unutterably melancholy when the feast
was over, that we had to dance in self-defence, while D.
played on a cracked old *clavier* that had been discovered
in E. and C.'s room; and our father entertained a crowd
of guides and peasants with a display of coloured lights
and magnesium-wire, and warmed himself at the kitchen-
fire.   The gentlemen fared but badly during the night,
but F. is impervious to cold, and one railway rug was
attainable, while the ladies entrenched themselves beneath
dresses and *duvets*.

The Kellnerin.

The landlord.

Hindelang.

Wonderful fun we had, if but little comfort. We carefully examined all our doors, and fastened them as well as
we could, to guard against extra draughts, or sudden gusts
of wind. Mrs. C. discovered a vast unfurnished apartment
beyond E. and C.'s, which seemed to have been shut up
through the winter, judging from the stuffiness of the atmosphere; and she returned announcing that it contained
nothing but an unpleasant smell! In fact, we had the
whole hotel to ourselves, so we barricaded that door also,
and then laughed till we were warm over the utter desolation of our rooms, and in the strength of that momentary
glow prepared to go to rest—such rest as it was. The
duvets were small and slippery, and if we pulled them up
to our chins our feet were bare; if we covered our feet our
shoulders were shivering, and we realised the unpleasant
sensation of cold water being incessantly poured down our
back. If one curled oneself into a ball, the *duvet* tumbled
off altogether, and of course it inevitably did so if we were
ever fortunate enough to fall asleep. But the longest
night must have an end; morning came, and brought the
Wirthin; and after a capital breakfast—which we had to
collect for ourselves piecemeal, as at supper, and which
was amusing enough in the display of crockery, no two
cups being alike—we felt equal to encountering the vicissi-
tudes of another day, and started at eight for Reutte,
driving in the carriages of the previous evening.

The cold was intense, with an east wind that would

have done Mr. Kingsley's heart good, but which was anything but cheering to ours, and we were glad to walk to
warm ourselves whenever we had the excuse of a hill.
The gleams of sunshine made the distant mountains very
beautiful, and the flowers were exquisite—gentians, cowslip
and oxslip, and little soldanellas starring the grass with
their bright colours.   At the frontier the gentlemen and
Mrs. C. descended to show their passports to two worthy
greatcoated Austrian officials, and then we rested for an
hour at a little wayside inn, eating bread and cheese, and
gossiping with the old *Wirthin* and her sweet-faced
daughter, who seated herself at our side, talking quietly of
the little interests of their daily life, and smiling placidly
while we sketched her.   It was such a good womanly
face, full of gentle modesty, and the placid content these
peasants seemed to have learned from the patient beasts
they spend their lives in tending, an ox-eyed Juno, grown
a thought less queenly from much milking of the kine.
Our fair-faced model had a sweeter if a lowlier name—
Filomena; and she wrote it, with a shy pleasure in her
own performance, under the little sketch, and then flinging
herself, in a sudden rush of confidence, upon E., hurried
her away from the little *salon*, with most persuasive
eloquence :

'Come, dear *Fräulein*, and see the house, and our dairy;
there is good cheese and butter, and the mother will be so
proud to show it you.'

We all followed, picking our way carefully across the somewhat dirty floor of an old stable, and reaching a clean cool room, where were many vessels ranged in order, filled with delicious milk, and a goodly store of cheeses in long rows. The old woman laughed with delight at our pleasure in it all, as we seized a tin bowl and dipped up some of the '*p'tit lait*' from the great boiler on the fire, scalding our mouths in attempts to drink it.

Then a cellar had to be visited, full of wood stacked in the corners, at one end of which was a tiny room, and a loom where Filomena spent many an hour weaving household linen, and singing like a bird that loved its cage, and knew it was still home for her, however poor and bent and old the bars might be. We had quite a little tender parting with these dear souls, and then a long drive to Lermos, where we were to sleep.

For part of the way the road made a rapid descent, bounded on one side by high rocks, amongst the crevices of which mosses and grass were springing wherever the earth could find a resting-place; lichens stretching out little hands, and grasping the huge stones with loving tenacity, working out slowly and patiently the great Creative will, preparing the tiny gardens where the spring flowers were to bloom later, and make the old hills beautiful with their sweetness. Even now there were blossoms shining in the grass, and as we ran down the hill there came a cry of delight from one and another as a fresh flower was

added to our store. A more adventurous climber would
be rewarded by a bright spoil of blue gentian and golden-
eyed cistus; and in some shady corner, which the sun had
not reached, there was still hanging a white fringe of
icicles, which glittered for a moment amongst the flowers
in our hands, and then trickled slowly away through
stems and leaves, making them shiver a little doubtless,
and leaving its traces in the pink finger tips that had
rashly grasped them, and hands grown cold and rosy in
the contact.

A wall bounded the zigzags on our right, and far below
there was a river dancing in the lightness of its heart—as
only mountain rivers do—because they know all the little
secrets of the hills, and are in such a terrible hurry to tell
them to the sea. What gossips the Naiads must have been,
and how dull they must have thought it to be swallowed
by a great overgrown stream, who was only bent on doing
its duty and going steadily on its way! We found many
villages lying near each other, large and prosperous, with
saw-mills and 'fabrics.'

At Reutte we stopped between three and four o'clock,
and while dinner was preparing, explored the curious
little town, where the houses are all set cornerwise to the
street, and are rich in coloured faces, pink and white and
pale green, and have queer little plethoric shops, with
bulged-out windows full of the strangest medley of goods,
specimens of coloured glass that have wandered here from

At the frontier.

p'tit lait! Schattwald

Munich manufactories, pipes and rosaries, and crockery ware, useful and ornamental. There was a charming stork in blown glass, with a great expenditure of yellow paint on its bill, in which was firmly grasped a '*kleines Kind*,' swathed in an extremely tight and uncomfortable manner, but held with wonderful skill by the admirable bird, who, proud of his trust, balanced himself conceitedly on one leg and surveyed the world at his leisure. Of course we secured such an interesting illustration of the habits of the country; but the bird had one disadvantage, he was undeniably brittle, and he and the baby were a great care during our journey, though we improvised a charming basinette among the frills in the border of Mrs. C.'s best bonnet, and had the proud satisfaction of bringing both nurse and infant in safety to England.

For the next few days we lived upon veal, eggs, and milk, unmitigated *Kalbsfleisch*, and eggs boiled and fried, in *Omeletten* and *Pfannküchen*, and *Mehlspeise*, the dinners being served for the most part in a most primitive manner, the supply of knives and forks, and clean plates, being very limited. A north-easter is a famous *sauce piquante*, and so we lived and flourished and enjoyed our calf, though it was not a fatted one.

The shandrydan and the cabriolet, which had brought us thus far, were dismissed, and we started in two *Postwägen*, with two gorgeous *Herren Postillionen*, and a flourish of trumpets, literal and metaphorical, each of our drivers

c 2

being provided with a horn, suspended from his shoulder
by a thick betasselled black and yellow cord. The road
was a fine piece of Austrian engineering, winding by a
gradual ascent round the hill side. We could see Reutte
far below us, and our track of the morning fading into the
distance: on one side lay the most exquisitely green valley,
and every turn disclosed another and yet another snowy
mountain gleaming in the light. The horses were fresh
and up to their work, and trotted on merrily to the music
of the horns which the two men were playing; the drivers
keeping time cleverly, with now and then an interlude of
jodeling, the echoes making wild work with voice and music,
and sending messages among the old mountains in a pleasant state of excitement, for was not the season beginning,
and were not the first travellers coming for a prey? As the
horses toiled up a steep ascent the men walked beside
them, affording us an opportunity of studying them quietly.
The leading driver was a very young man, well grown and
looking picturesque enough in his quaint dress, but with
the picturesqueness of an old album study, when young
men were drawn with long limbs, gracefully encased in
tight garments, with smooth cheeks on which was the flush
of youth and modesty, hair inclined to wave, with full-
orbed eyes, large curling lips, rosy as the cheeks, and a
nose somewhat long and drooping. Alas, for those days of
propriety and delicate sentiment! *Nous avons changé
tout cela*—-beards and muscles, a good honest appetite and

Balmoral boots have fairly extinguished them—our *Postillion* was the only live specimen we had ever seen of originals that must sometime have existed. Above the road stood a very fine old ruined castle, perched on the summit of a grand cliff amidst masses of greenery, and an amphitheatre of fir trees, tier above tier, swept away to our right, with distant white and blue hills filling up the picture. At a sudden turn a cry of astonishment broke from us; a mountain rose out of the trees, one great sheet of snow, utterly white, and dazzling us by its exceeding brilliance, except here and there, where a faint grey shadow flitted across it from the light clouds floating overhead. It looked like a great Easter cake for the little angels, with almond rocks somewhere hidden away in its depths, which were to be melted in the sunshine. Were there not some rosy fingers growing out of that cloudlet as we looked, floating nearer, nearer, and longing to begin already? Happy little angels! that only care for cake in German picture-books, and even then are never impatient; a snow mountain, beautiful and unearthly as it is, is too real for your ' immortal wonderment.' But there is a fresh light upon the mountain, a pink flush, that makes it look, oh! so nice, if only there was somebody to eat it. . It is more like a cake than ever, and it is such a very big one. Surely there are Dante's little spirits to fall back upon, who were so innocent and sweet, and whom he put into a mournful shadowy place, where the poor babies could do nothing but

sigh, and kept them far away from heaven because they
had never been baptized; which always made us unhappy
as children, when we read the story, and could do nothing
to help them.   We will fancy them now dwelling in that
cloud land, the ' poor little innocents,' who would not be
too good to eat the cake, and who would enjoy it so
exceedingly because they had never had very much on
earth.

We met droves of goats and meek-faced ewes slowly
wandering home from their pastures, or hurrying to quench
their thirst at a village fountain, jumbled altogether in a
queer mass of horns and impatient hoofs and frisking tails
longer or shorter, in their eagerness to reach the water-
trough.

As the evening was closing in we reached Lermos, pleasantly weary after our long drive, and all the exceeding
beauty which eyes and mind had been absorbing during
the day.   The hotel looked very unpromising, but profit-
ing by our recent experience we did not judge too hastily,
and when once the upper landing was reached matters
began to improve.   As before, there were the large rooms,
but they were better furnished, and if there were no
blankets, there were at least *couvertures* as well as *duvets*.
A fire was quickly lit in one of the great stoves, built half
into a corner wall, which was so thick that it had a cavernous depth of many feet, and piles of wood were heaped
in and blazed and crackled, we watching them from the

lermes.

landing through the small opening usually closed by an
iron door, and enjoying the sight long before any warmth
had penetrated the great pottery stove within the *salon*.
The tea was a peripatetic meal, as just outside our windows rose the great *Zugspitze* in all the rose glow of a
clear sunset, and we must perforce watch the light fading
and the cold shadows creeping up its side, though the eggs
were cooling, and the great bowls of warm milk were
bubbling most enticingly. Another very cold night, spite
of the large stoves, which, if your bed happens to be near
them, suffocate you with heat for an hour or more, and
then, as the wood burns low, a shiver creeps through the
room, and there is only a sense of heaviness in the air to
remind you of the departed warmth. The beds were narrow, and the sheets were cut to their *exact* size, so that it
was impossible to tuck them in anywhere, and the cover-
ings being made on the same principle, it was difficult to
make ourselves warm all over at once.

We were roused at an early hour by the goatherd's horn,
and watched from our windows the little beasts trotting up
to the *rendezvous*, obedient to the call. In German and
Swiss villages the same custom prevails; two or three of the
children are chosen as *Gans-* or *Ziegen-* or *Kuh-General*;
and armed with his long Alpine horn or whip, the little
herdsman summons his flock, geese or goats or cows joining him the moment their stable doors are opened, and
following him to the pastures, where they are allowed to

wander during the day. It is the prettiest sight in the
world to see them returning at sunset; each of the sensible creatures breaking away from the main body when
the turning towards its home is reached, and trotting off
to its owners.

We left Lermos soon after eight o'clock, starting in
bright sunshine which illuminated the little village, alive
with people and cows, whose cheery bells filled the air
with a pleasant music. This time we determined to try
a new conveyance, and rejoiced in securing a large
omnibus with windows at the side, behind, and in front,
space enough for two besides the driver, and for our luggage on the roof. When people and things were stowed
away, we felt rather like a band of strolling players, or as
though we and our van were somehow dimly connected with
a cheap-jack, or a merry-go-round. It certainly was an odd
and unromantic conveyance for a journey among the mountains, but we found it eminently practical, and as it was
impossible to procure anything like an ordinary close carriage, and equally impossible to drive in an open one, we
were thankful to secure our *Stellwagen* and four strong
horses, who carried us over the pass at a steady pace. It is
so hopeless by any words to describe the exceeding loveliness of everything that surrounded us, that one hesitates
to attempt a bad copy of a most perfect picture. Every
inch of the way was a study in itself, of jewelled moss and
fresh grass, dewy and sparkling, with soft heaps of brown

twigs and ground-ivy, amongst which pansies raised their
violet heads, and white flowers could nestle; each stone
was covered with grey or golden lichen creeping up to
meet the tufts of bright green ferns, which seemed to
spring out of the rocks; little streams made a sweet bab-
bling among the crevices and fell in delicious cascades over
the bigger pebbles, and floated away leaves and twigs and
broken stems till they disappeared in the great stream
which flowed beside the road. The trees were in the full
pride of their spring beauty, and the leaves were still too
young to have grown dusty; the sun turned them all to
gold, and cast long shadows across their stems and along
the hill side, and the passing clouds made purple shades
come and go, now deepening now brightened, in the thick'
boscage of the pines. The highest trees wore a light
powdering of snow that became them mightily, and the
hills were robed in fresh whiteness from a very recent
shower. But all the snow having fallen and turned into
beautiful white drapery for the old giants taller and
shorter alike, the sky was left to its blue, the sunlight had
everything its own way, and shone upon the little lakes,
deep tarns embosomed in the trees flashing with purple,
and blue, and emerald reflections of what earthly colouring who can tell?

At Nassereit, a picturesque little town, we descended
into the prosaics of life, and while the horses were changed,
we wandered through the winding street, making sketches

of the people, with a fine following of the *gamins* of the
place, to whom, when they had surmounted their first
awe, we evidently afforded the keenest amusement. There
was an oriel window, rich in diamond-paned glass, breaking the dead white surface of a wall, with women leaning
out, and showing bright-tinted kerchiefs and boddices
against the dark back-ground of the room within. From
many a little casement heads young and old peeped out to
watch our proceedings; from one a shrivelled nut-cracker-
faced old crone looked down upon us, a fit study for a
Murillo, with her deep wrinkles, and sinewy arms folded
lazily, a glorious bit of colour, from the deep orange folds
of the cloth about her head to the brown skin and the fiery
eyes, and one wandering old tooth which rested on the
lower lip: a very uncanny old woman, who might have
had a broomstick hidden under her bed! Nevertheless,
E. made a drawing of her, and held it up for inspection,
and the poor old soul nodded approval, which made us
charitably believe she might have a conscience; and then
we turned the old pump into a studio, but so many models
offered, it was difficult to satisfy them all. One beautiful
young peasant girl stood, with a pitcher balanced on her
small well-shaped head, round which the dark hair was
closely braided, her naked feet firmly planted on the
ground, the careless grace of her attitude and her grave
delight making a charming study. We distributed *Zwan-
zigers* and little German books amongst the people, who

Wayside sketches.

eagerly received our small gospels, under the very eyes of
their patron saint, who stood, wooden and stolid and very
gorgeous in the matter of paint and gilding, watching over
the consumption of water and the gossip of the town.
What an amount of scandal that poor old worthy would
have had to listen to, if he had been less hard of hearing
—quarrels, love-making, merry chatter, sad and tender
partings, all the chances and changes of this busy life,
must have been chronicled in that spot; and the poor
old image, very harmless in its way, held out its two
stiff old fingers, with the paint somewhat worn about
the joints, and blessed us all alike who passed beneath
it. The pious fellow-townsfolk had erected a tin umbrella, in the form of a double tea-tray, to keep the rain-
drops from its head, lest it should grow damp and cracky,
and moulder away slowly, as others did who were but
human.

The frost that had made everything so beautiful for us,
had done hard things for the poor cottagers; and as we
drove on we passed by many orchards, where they told us
sadly the apple-blossom had been all destroyed. This
next stage brought us to Ober-Miemingen, where we
were to dine, and here even our calf failed us. There was
a *Wirthin* within, who was the embodiment of the slow-
ness of the entire people.

'Ah! the Herrschaft are starving: that is grievous: but
then, dear heaven, what would they have—*Mehlspeise*

assuredly? It is not enough? Then, what else is there? Truly nothing, and I can but do my best.'

'Some meat, madame,' we answered, 'in just fifteen little minutes—and fried potatoes and eggs, *Ochsenaugen* and cheese, and bread, and beer, or some coffee, and per- haps a salad; but do not forget we are very hungry, and we must eat.'

'Ah, these Herrschaft—these travellers!' cried the Wirthin, 'it is *wollen, und müssen,* and *im Augenblick.* It is ever so, ever; but it is Freitag—there is no meat— the Herrschaft know it is a fast.'

'But, madame!' we replied, 'we are Protestants and English, and very hungry, and, according to our religion, when we are hungry we are to eat. Dear madame, send some one to look for that little calf, for assuredly meat is a canon of our faith, and without it our nation cannot exist. *Sauerkraut* is a dish highly to be commended, but the English stomach is inca- pable of being nourished by it. Is there not a little calf?'

Thus pressed on all sides, the good Wirthin gave way. If we were heretics, what did it matter? But she must have said an extra Ave or two over her frying-pan, to ease her conscience, and thus delayed the cooking, judging from the length of time we had to wait.

Once more in our omnibus, we journeyed to Telfs, where there were more picturesque houses and wooden saints, a great fountain, and a church tower, half spire, half dome,

Telfs.

a great brown bulb swelling out above the stone-work, with a slender rod ending in a gilt cross.   Large quantities of wood were piled up by the river, waiting to be carried down to the saltworks at Hall, and there was a churchyard full of quaint tombs, bas-reliefs, and rude frescoes.   Children were playing amongst the graves, and the Telfs' chickens making themselves at home on the grass, whilst one old hen was drinking solemnly out of a small cup of holy water, which was sculptured in the stone.   At Zirl our last omnibus was left behind, and, after a considerable amount of discussion and entreaty on the part of the gentlemen, a carriage was secured, and our luggage packed away somewhere about it, when the waiter announced to us that all was ready, and ushered us from the *salle à manger*, where we had been waiting, to the front-door. We seemed to have journeyed back two hundred years at the least, and to be living in some old-world story.   Such a chariot was waiting for us !   A dim old stage-coach hung between high springs and joints, and bars of wood and iron, sometime gilt and gorgeous, with two small windows to the doors ; very warm and comfortable within still, and well-padded and soft, if ever so moth-eaten.   We four ladies took our places with a gravity befitting the occasion ; the servitors placed their shoulders against the side of the vehicle, and heaved it up, and were thus enabled to close the door ; the gentlemen mounted into a cabriolet, and prepared to attend us, and slowly we were swung and rattled along towards Innsbruck.   A lazy content settled

down upon our spirits, that pleasant weariness that comes
so full of dreams.   One thought of all the little romances
that had lived and died within the shelter of our old coach
—the sweet faces, the patches and ruffles, the powder
shaken out of the fair curls, the little hands resting on the
window, or making silent talk to some bráve cavalier escort,
while a grim old duenna of a *Gräfin* slumbered in the
corner.   One could almost smell the patchouli, and realise
a dim presence there still.   A sudden lunge of the chariot,
a bump over a stone, and there was only nineteenth century dust, and the dull realities of modern travellers—D.
buried in the shadow of her hat, Mrs. C. asleep behind her
spectacles in a corner.   Perhaps some day we too may
grow legendary and poetical to our great-grandchildren,
and the prospective New Zealander will write the idylls of
the Alpine Club.

A shout from our driver, and vigorous indications of his
whip, directed our attention to the great cliff under which
we were passing, where, far above our heads, we were
intended to see the small cave and crucifix which marks
the scene of an old Tyrol story.

The Emperor Maximilian was as keen a sportsman as
any modern *Wildschütz*, and one fine morning, ever so
many years ago, he was led in the excitement of the
chase, to the very edge of the great Martinswand, and
while the chamois bounded away in safety, the less fortunate Emperor missed his footing, and, falling from the

The chariot waits!

"The poor dear Kaiser"!

rocks, was just able to save himself by clinging, with the tenacity of despair, to a small ledge of rock, where he hung helplessly, head downwards, in full view of his faithful subjects.   Nobles and peasants, priests and courtiers, gave him up as lost.   The spot was deemed simply inaccessible to anything without wings, and unless a special miracle was wrought in his behalf, a faithful son of the Church must perish.   Of course, a crowd was collected, and a holy abbot was summoned, who, kneeling on the ground on which our chariot and its heretical inmates were then halting, began solemnly chanting the prayers for the dead.   The poor Emperor, hanging by his eyelids meanwhile, and looking down from his elevation of more than 700 feet, must have been rather aggravated by the performance, if, in the awful agony of such a moment, he had any sight or thoughts to spare for earthly things. But help was at hand, and a brave huntsman, seeing from above Maximilian's mortal peril, cried to him to be of good courage, and to maintain his hold ; and with wonderful skill and hardihood, he swung himself down to the Emperor's side, seized him in his strong grasp, and clinging to the rocks with their iron-shod feet, they scaled the wall that seemed so utterly inaccessible, while the abbot chanted on below, and the people shouted ' A miracle, an angel has come to the rescue of the Kaiser ! '

Whether the abbot was put on the pension list for services rendered, the legend sayeth not, but to one, Zips of Zirl, sixteen florins were paid yearly—surely a not extravagant sum.

Of our two days' stay in Innsbruck there is but little to tell, but little to write about that would be new to anyone. It is a simple old town, with broad open streets, many handsome buildings, long arcades with shops hidden away in their shadows, and fruit-sellers hawking Verona cherries beneath the pillars.   There is a palace, and a public garden and *Caserne*, and many churches, a university and a museum.   Rows of trees make a pleasant greenery about the river, and rich woods skirt the hills, which form a perfect wall on most sides of the town—and from the windows of the houses, or the broad *Neustadt*, you look up to the great stone giants, and think that, standing on their summits, you could throw a pebble clear and straight into the street below; and it is from this outlook that hungry wolves are supposed to gaze when they come prowling round on market-days, licking their lips, and moaning in melancholy fashion at the fat little lambs below.

We lived in most luxurious comfort at the Osterreicher Hof, where an attentive· landlord and a good cook did their best to make us welcome.   One morning was spent in the Hof-Kirche, a church boasting very little beauty of its own, but rich in the grand tomb of Maximilian.   It was a proud thought of the old Emperor, that while his own image was sculptured, kneeling with hands meekly folded in prayer, about him keeping watch and ward evermore, should stand knights and kings and warriors, noble women, wives and mothers of kings, the dead whom he would do well to honour, and many who had touched his hand in life, or stood by him in his toils and triumphs.

A throng of mighty ghosts, silent and colossal, in all the pomp of royal robes and brilliantly-wrought armour, turned, as by a magician's wand, into rich bronze images. We could have lingered long recalling the history attached to each great name, and marvelling at the skill which made the robes fall in soft folds and showed the ermine at their edge, the gold and jewelled embroidery, the ripple of the hair, even the delicate lace over the clasped hands, the fine chain armour, and the helmet with its plume—all wrought out in the metal by a master's hand. Two of the most beautiful of the figures are our own king Arthur, a most peerless-looking knight, and Theoderic, leaning on his sword. There is poor *Joanne la Folle* and her handsome husband, Ferdinand the Catholic, burly Godfrey of Bouillon, and 'Frederick with the empty purse,' somewhat the scapegrace of the party. The sides of the tomb are covered with minute bas-reliefs in ivory, illustrating the life of the dead Emperor. Births, deaths, marriages, battles, and treaties— all are rendered with wonderful beauty and truth. Near the door of the church is the grave of Hofer, marked by a tomb and a marble statue. The Austrians, with tardy

D

justice, buried him in triumph, and sought to forget that they had sacrificed him. Near by is a cenotaph to the Tyrolese who fell fighting for their fatherland. It is not pleasant to have all one's ideas of right and wrong suddenly disarranged—and for the last few years Italian sympathies had been part of our very creed of faith—and here, in Austria, the divine right of kings and the tenderness of a paternal government smooths for us the angry feathers of the old double eagle, and we almost forget the cruel beak, the grasp of the talons, and the long agony of Italy.

It is well to see things with the eyes and minds of different peoples and races; you learn to have a horror of prejudice and preconceptions, and to feel more and more how little you really know of other's hopes and wishes and lives, and the modes of thought from which actions slowly grow.

We were breathing somewhat of a war atmosphere at last.* The town was full of soldiers, and regiments were being hastily sent on to the front. Officers and men strolled about the streets in lazy security, smoked and chatted; there was music, with blasts of trumpets, as *Jäger* or *Grenzer* started for the frontier: but there was little excitement and no enthusiasm; the men we talked to still seemed sceptical of the possibility of a war between the German peoples—with Italy there might be, but Italy would soon be crushed, and then there would be peace;

* Our journey was made during May and June of 1866.

and meanwhile the troops still passed to the front. One morning we were roused between three and four o'clock by a burst of music, and saw from our windows the long train filing through the street, with mounted officers muffled in great grey coats, men in full marching order, and baggage wagons, on one of which was stretched a poor sick soldier, that made one think, with a shudder, of the coming death and misery; hands were held in a tight clasp, and sunburnt soldiers kissed on either cheek by friends amongst the crowd, and here and there a woman turned away to sob; but, on the whole, things were conducted in a business-like manner, and with the customary German phlegm.

Just outside the town is the cemetery, *God's acre*, as the Germans name it, where there is much good sculpture and fresh flowers, and beautiful creepers wreathed above the graves. We made two expeditions to Schloss Ambras, once during this first visit to Innsbruck and again on our return two weeks later. The drive is a charming one, when you have once got over the dusty road immediately outside the town and begin to ascend, with rich wooded hills on one hand of the broad valley of the Inn lying at your feet. The view from the old chateau is quite perfect when the sunshine is flooding the whole scene with light, and before summer has come to melt the snow from the nearer hills. We stood long on the high broad terrace where Ferdinand and Philippina must often have lingered

in the early days of their happy married life, whispering
sweet words to each other, or speculating as to possible
forgiveness in the future, as they looked down on the old
palace (now buried beneath Maria Theresa's *neuer Hof*),
and thought of the direful anger of Kaiser and father-in-
law. Here their fair young sons grew up to that stately
beauty which so touched the old man's heart, when Philippina flung herself at his feet, that he pardoned them
all, and blessed and provided for them on the instant,
the mother and her young margraves going home content.
It is strange to see how all the old stories and romances
of Tyrol centre round this fair-faced woman, who must
have been as good and wise as she was beautiful, guiding
husband and children with a tender hand, and teaching
those rude knights and squires and people of the baser
sort, what home life and love might be. For thirty years,
the legends say, the Archduke lived happily with his
Burgher wife; and the quaint, beautiful poem—very
rarely to be read, alas! in those fierce days—ended in the
sculptured figures on a tomb, and a memory very tenderly
enshrined in the hearts of the people. Philippina Welser
was the daughter of one of the old Augsburg citizen
princes, and the sweet face that looks out at you from
the picture is patrician in every delicate line and curve,
and winsome enough to make even a royal lover feel the
world well lost for her dear sake.

Apart from the exceeding beauty of its surroundings,

there is a good deal of bathos about Schloss Ambras at the present day. The public are only admitted to the great hall, once gorgeous in decoration, and celebrated for the beauty of the collection of rare armour, paintings, and gems stored there by Ferdinand, one of whose prudent successors has despoiled the place. The marvels are all to be seen in Vienna, and there is very little left except a few old Japanese erections, some ludicrous oil-paintings of dwarfs and giants, and a ghastly array of wooden horses, grey and roan, black and piebald, waiting in their stalls for the armour and the trappings that may never clothe their poor old sides again. There was a stout porter in blue livery, who was *custode* of the great bare hall, and lived there happy in his implicit belief in the whole affair, and vegetating on a decayed reputation. Worthy old servitor! We regarded him with boundless respect and admiration as he solemnly marshalled us from one old stand of *bric-à-brac* to another, expending a limitless treasure of description on the Japanese pagodas, in voluble German, to which Mrs. C. lent a most attentive and conscientious ear, the rest of the party pretending not to understand the language, and adjourning to the horses and the dwarfs. We found a little bed, very mouldy-looking, and entirely in keeping with the rest of the furniture, with old banners falling to decay draped about it, and here the porter slept every night, and sleeps still probably, keeping watch lest the Prussians, or the Free-Lances, or the Turks should

carry off his wooden stud for heavy cavalry purposes, and
where no doubt he snores in peace (being somewhat
apoplectic) after his supper of beer and sausages in the
little tea-garden establishment outside the gates, and
dreams that he is High Steward, and that Ferdinand and
Philippina are waiting to receive a visit from the Königliche Kaiser, and that there will be great feasting in the
land.   In this age of scepticism an embodiment of a great
faith is very awe-inspiring.   We felt he conferred a favour
on us when he accepted with dignity a gratuity at parting,
in the form of a two-florin piece.

One evening we drove to Berg Isel, a pretty little
wooded plateau, the shooting-ground of the Jäger regiment, containing a sort of *restauration* and a beer-garden,
where we and some of our English friends sat under the
trees round a little table, drinking lemonade to the music
of violins, and realising the simple pleasures of a primitive existence, enhanced to the worthy burghers by the
additional possibility of Jäger bier.   We did our duty in
going to the Museum, but being, some of us, only acquainted with the *ologies* to a limited extent, were not
much edified except with the Hofer relics, which were
very touching things to see.   Amongst all the old dry-
as-dust collections, the products and practical good things
of Tyrol, the tin plate amulet, the last letter ever
written by that strong hand, the medal of St. Michael
which he wore on his breast when they shot him down—

even the old green braces, the vestiges of the peasant's dress he gloried in—are kept as the most sacred of treasures.

That spendthrift Frederick, Count of Tyrol, whom we saw in the Hof-Kirche, looking solemnised, as befitted the occasion, and staring gravely through his bronze mask, was a heedless fellow enough when living; and when twitted by some shrewd townsfolk as to his empty purse, covered the roof of a great oriel window looking on the street with plates of gold, the whole conceit being valued at a cost of some 30,000 ducats, for which it is more than probable the royal prodigal never paid. *Das goldene Dach* stands there now, a little dimmed by time, but still resplendent, for the admiration of *valets de place* and wide-eyed tourists.

We climbed on to the roof of our hotel, and walked across it, steadying ourselves on the rough edges of the tiles, and watched the sunset light up the snow-hills like a great illumination; and then, after one more night amidst civilisation, we started by train for Wörgl, passing through a station gay with green wreaths and banners in honour of the Emperor. The costumes of the people charmed us everywhere. On Sunday morning at Innsbruck we saw them at their brightest at a musical mass in the Hof-Kirche: the women in low-crowned hats with gold and silver tassels, gay-coloured silk kerchief or boddice, and white chemisette. They are a good-looking

well-grown race. Peasants from more distant districts
were mingled with the town and country people; and we
watched many a picturesque old dame busy with her
rosary and prayer-book, in a heavy cap of sable, very
handsome in effect, but uncomfortably hot one would
fancy to the wearer. As the train moved at the usual
sedate pace, we were able to secure many hasty sketches
of people and things. Very beautiful was the scene:
chateaux crowning the wooded hills, cloisters half hidden
among the trees, churches with slender spires, coloured
now deep red, now emerald green, according to the taste
of the parishioners, cosy little villages nestled at the foot
of the pine woods or on the summits of the lower slopes,
the long lines of rail running close to the swift-flowing
river, or crossing it over the many bridges on our route.
We were travelling on a Whit Monday, and, though de-
barred from the delights of ' Clubs' on the march, or
holiday-making Foresters at home, we found each little
station crowded by peasants in brilliant *festa* dress, waiting to start or watching for travellers. A *convoi* of
soldiers passed us; the men looked in good heart, and
there was a faint attempt at cheering from them and the
people; but generally, during their transit, the troops
seemed packed into huge vans destitute of windows or
any openings in place of them, in which they were penned
like cattle.

While we waited in an empty room at the Wörgl sta-

Château Frohsburg.

Sketches from the Railway.

tion, our father and F. hurried to the posthouse near by
to secure a carriage. This apartment strongly resembled
similar ones in England. There was a table and two or
three chairs, and one of those long lists of trains, framed
and glazed, on the walls, which you feel helplessly bound
to read through from end to end. Altogether, the resources at our disposal were of a negative kind. There
was nothing to be seen from the window but some super-
annuated trucks, no provisions of any kind to be found
on the premises, nothing but the table, the chairs, and a
thorough draught. But we had a certain supply of food
with us. A tin of biscuits, which were to be kept for an
emergency, and some potted meat—prepared in anticipa-
tion of a journey in the Dolomites, where, according to report, *Mehlspeise* forms the sole subsistence of the inhabitants. This same potted meat gave us the greatest anxiety.
It might only be eaten in limited portions till the Dolomites were reached; and it had become evident to every
one that it would not keep. A large number of tin pots
had been prepared, filled, and hermetically sealed with a
preparation of resin ; but the resin cracked, and then
melted, and then became a dust, imperceptible and deadly,
which insinuated itself with sticky persistency into everything within its reach. We had carefully packed the tins
in one side of a portmanteau, with cakes of preserved
soup, bibles and picture-books for presents, a bottle of
ink, a supply of chocolate, and a packet of arrowroot.

The state of that portmanteau when the arrowroot ran
out of a hole in the paper and joined the resin, it were
vain to try to describe in words.   One at a time the pots
were extracted, and the contents handed round ; but with
the escape of the resin the air had got in, and there was
a layer of blue mould on the top which was anything
but appetising, and which Mrs. C. daily eliminated with
unfailing perseverance, affirming that from constantly re-
siding in a damp county she was accustomed to such
emergencies, and fully prepared to meet them.

Meanwhile the gentlemen returned with an enormous
Stellwagen, which carried us on for the next three stages,
stopping at Elmau, where we dined, and painted flowers,
while the horses rested, gossiping with a pleasant *Kellnerin*,
who kissed our hands most gratefully when we gave her
a German gospel; for strong Roman Catholics as are all
the people of Tyrol, we have never had one refused, and
often our little books have been accepted with the greatest
delight.

The days when a *milord anglais* drove through Europe
with valet and courier to interpose between the wind
and his nobility, are happily over.   Our countrymen and
women, when they travel, have begun to discover that the
despised peasantry of the land are often as good, if not
better company than people they have left at home ; and
travellers in search of a new sensation enjoy roughing it
for a few weeks amongst the mountains, and are rather

bored than otherwise by grand hotels and a good *cuisine.*
But if we have come back to the archaics and the sim-
plicities of life, it is still only somewhat because fashion
affects primitive manners, and Marie-Antoinette has a
new *petit trianon.* We are no nearer, in reality, to the
hearts and lives of the people; and this we were earnest,
in our small measure, to achieve. It was easy for Mrs. C.,
who has an unlimited knowledge of the language, in every
shade of patois, to condole with the good *Frauen* over
the sickness among the cows, the father's rheumatism,
or Madeleine's love affair with a *Wildschütz.* Ordinary
mortals, whose talents are less brilliant, have to eke out
their remarks with smiles, or compassionate gestures ; but
it was pleasant to see how quickly a sympathy grew up
between you and the people, and to feel that you could
face the cold wind again all the better, for their warm
kindliness, which had so stirred your heart. Travelling
with a limited amount of luggage, there is little to give
away, but small things seemed to make them happy.
English knives or scissors, bright money, to be worn as
a charm by happy-faced little children, proud to show
the '*Königin von England,*' books always a delight,
pleasant pictures, and essays, and poems written for that
especial class. A 'British Workman,' or a 'Band of Hope,'
is a great prize to those Germans, who are eager to learn
a little English, from the *Kutscher* to 'boots' at the
hotels ; and, above all, the bibles are very welcome ; and,

in lone mountain homes, who knows what store of blessing and comfort and peace they may have brought to weary hearts.

We had been driving all that day from Wörgl through a pleasant valley, well cultivated and sprinkled with cottages and hamlets, and everywhere the Whit-Monday festivities went with us and met us, brightening all the road. There were quiet gatherings of the people at favourite trysting-places; in one village a little country fair was being held, the entertainments at which were restricted to beer, or very sweet strong coffee, sold at the *Wirthshaus* near by ; but there were three stalls with crockery and hardware, and leather harness, bright silk handkerchiefs, and long straw cords, plaited and twisted in some neighbouring district. We patronised the *Hutte* to the extent of some cords, and a few feathers with eagles' beaks, set in Tyrol fashion. There was a crowd of old men standing about smoking and talking, but the strength of the nation had been carried off to the wars, the conscription telling heavily in these thinly-populated districts.

Once more we slept in a country inn, where, however, the *Wirthin* was 'to the fore.' A brisk, pleasant woman, who managed her household with spirit and good temper, gave us good homespun linen and a capital supper, prepared by one or two cooks in a great vaulted kitchen, whom we watched at their work, as they stood round a

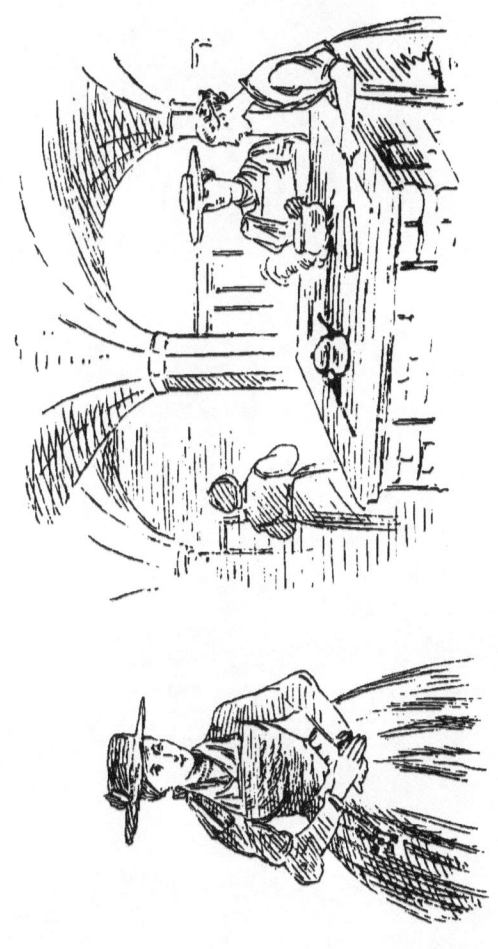

low stove about five feet square, in which were little ovens, and *on* which at pleasure a fire could be lighted. The *Hausfrau* carried her keys slung at her girdle, and wore a dozen petticoats, to judge from the size of her skirt, which she assured us was guiltless of crinoline, and 'all solid.' Our rooms were most comfortable, spacious, handsomely furnished, and exquisitely clean; we had a very good *Abendessen*, with meat and eggs and coffee, breakfast of the same, hot or cold baths, fires in all the stoves, and for our party of seven (including the guide), the whole charge was only eight *Gulden*.

There was the same battle the next morning between frost and wind and sunshine, and, of course, it was two to one against anything like warmth. We set out for a good tramp, leaving Christian and the luggage and the omnibus to follow us, while we *jodeled* and shouted to the echoes, ran races for the benefit of our half-frozen feet, and gathered great branches of ferns and flowers, masses of cistus, and gentians as large as the finest garden blossoms in England; there were myriads of heartsease, golden or purple, making large tracts of land brilliant with their colouring; country carts and carriages, marvellous to behold, passed us, and droves of goats and cows, their drivers resting under the trees. We climbed a very steep hill, which brought us to the frontier; the wooden bars painted black and yellow were left behind, and Bavarian white and blue appeared in sight. There were

polite officials, who graciously permitted us to enter the
little kingdom, dignified characters who would not con-
descend to ask for our passports, but greeted us with a
wave of the hand, which said as plainly as words, ' pass!
pass! our souls are too big for the meanness of mistrust;
consider yourselves saluted, and spare us the necessity of
removing our pipes in order to speak to you!'

We rested in the inn near by; warmed our frozen limbs
with hot mulled wine, a capital invention, as the sour red
wine of the country, which it would be utterly impossible to drink except during the greatest heat of summer,
when warmed and well sweetened, is very good, and serves
as a capital luncheon with fresh bread, which we could
almost always procure. From the high ridge on which
the *Wirthshaus* stood, we had a glorious view of the plain
we had just crossed, little valleys, wooded hills, and distant
mountains, with the soft powdering of yellow green over
the landscape, which comes when the first sunshine has
touched the boughs in spring. The long grass in the
fields waved in the wind, with white and grey lights and
shadows upon it, as the clouds passed across the sky, and
in contrast to the golden beeches, each tiny leaf looked
blue and emerald through the glitter of its frost and dew.

The divisions of these inland countries are always
strange things to contemplate when Nature has not herself
arranged the boundaries, and thrown-up a great wall, like
the Pyrenees, or formed a natural moat like the Rhine.

Mrs C complains of the cold!

Here, at Melleck, one seemed to go up stairs into Bavaria, so sudden and steep was the ascent of the hill on the summit of which the frontier was marked out. Austria lay below, secure in her possession as owner of the ground, while little *Baiern* appeared to have contented herself with a lodging *au premier*. But a half-hour's drive dispelled our illusions. Valleys and hills once more stretched in broken undulations around us, and there was nothing to tell us that we were now under the dominion of King Ludwig, except, indeed, a fresh collection of family portraits in the inns on our route.

We had become intimately acquainted with the Emperor and Empress in every possible attitude and costume, and could tell at what particular date the Kaiser had begun to shave, when he married, and the different fashions of the beautiful Kaiserin's robes and jewels. It was pleasant to see with what affection and loyalty the people everywhere treasured these pictures, and how much some of the very poor peasants must have expended on such memorials, which were always hung in the place of honour, with, among the better class of innkeepers, a portrait in oils, magnificently out of drawing, and in which the artist had given a minute attention to the family gems, ignoring such trivialities as features or expression; fine old *Wirths* and *Wirthins*, with any number of chins, smiling and rubicund, with one eye fixing you with a glassy stare on your entrance, and their hands complacently folded over their capacious waists. Here and there, in quite out-of-the-way places amongst the mountains, we have seen some fine studies— a 'Good Shepherd,' or a 'Madonna,' full of pathetic beauty, that make one wonder how they ever reached such poor little nooks and corners of the world. Perhaps some young artist, travelling to a great city, where he was to gain fame and bread, may have lingered at the wayside inn, and painted a picture for love of the soft-eyed model he had found there, or for the more prosaic reason that he was himself without a *Zwanziger* wherewith to pay his bill!

But meantime, on this 22nd of May we were journeying on our way towards Berchtesgaden, the horses trotting on briskly, eager to reach Reichenhall, the end of their stage, the old *Stellwagen* and the seven travellers lumbering behind them. There was something to us infinitely comic in thus wandering over the mountains in an omnibus, our preconceived notions of Tyrol travelling being based upon Swiss experiences, as far at least as the ladies of the party were concerned. All the good roads, which are to be found everywhere in Austria and Bavaria, make the style of locomotion of course utterly different to anything we had considered properly 'Alpine.'

The country through which we passed was wonderfully beautiful, the scene changing each moment as the good broad road wound leisurely round the hills. Now and then we turned suddenly into a narrow gorge, where grand cliffs towered above us, the pines clinging to their sides, while

St. Johann

we looked down through a foreground of soft grass, bright
with flowers and studded with stones covered with moss
and ferns, to the clear green water splashing over the
pebbles far below, and shining between masses of foliage,
acacias, larches, and firs, which clothed the foot of the
hills with endless shades of colour. The villages were
very Swiss-like, with their broad roofs and pretty wooden
balconies. We drew up at a big overgrown hotel in
Reichenhall, to which the saltworks, for which the place
is famous, bring, no doubt, many guests, mercantile and
others. Here we had to wait for two hours while something in the shape of a carriage was hunted out, *Stellwägen*
having apparently ceased out of the land, as far as they
related to private enterprise.

We whiled away the time by translating the last *Allgemeine Zeitung*, and trying to discover some glimmer of
fact and reality amongst the cautious fogginess and wonderful word-transpositions in which a German editor delights.
If language had been given us to conceal ideas, truly a
high and mighty Prussian or Austrian newspaper contri-
butor would come out as a *double first* in a competitive
examination, and Monsieur Talleyrand, if he had only
lived long enough to know him, might have requested
the pleasure of shaking hands with him, on his having
attained to such a rank in literature. A walk through the
streets proved utterly unexciting, and the shops, if possible,
more so. Dinner and a heavy snow storm occupied another

hour, and before we left we were much interested in watching a strange and motley procession, ecclesiastical in the
matter of priests and candles, but apparently combining
every grade of citizen and citizeness who had any pretensions to piety.   It is sad to realise the inevitable truth that
superstition and scepticism go hand-in-hand.   Those who
did not take part in the demonstration sneered at it rather
scornfully.   There were men who carried tapers, little girls
in white and blue with wreaths round their hair, supporting a platform, on which a great Madonna sat enthroned,
a mighty show of banners, images of saints, then trumpets
and the Host under a canopy, and priests, nuns, and
acolytes, rubbing their chilled fingers as they told their
beads, or chanting lustily.   Bread was given away to the
people, and old women, looking pinched with cold, and
with very red eyes and noses, hobbled on, each with a
long flat loaf under her arm, and covered, poor old souls,
with the heavy snowflakes which fell thicker and faster as
we drove out of the town, hastening on our way to pleasant
Berchtesgaden and a week's wandering amongst the valleys
of the Salzkammergut.

NOTES

ON

THE PASSAGE OF THE OLD WEISSTHOR

WITH

THE ASCENT OF THE SIGNALKUPPE.

———+———

> ' Look what streaks
> Do lace the severing clouds in yonder east.
> Night's tapers are burnt out, and jocund day
> Stands tiptoe on the misty mountain tops.'
> SHAKSPEARE.

> ' Here we go up, up, up!
> Here we go down, down, down!'
> NURSERY RHYME.

NOTES ON THE PASSAGE OF THE OLD WEISSTHOR,
WITH THE ASCENT OF THE SIGNALKUPPE.

———◆———

ON JUNE 15, 1861, accompanied by two friends, C. and W., and with the trusty J. J. Bennen and Peter Perrn as guides, I crossed from Zermatt to Gressonay by the Lys Joch, an account of the first passage of which by Mr. W. Mathews appears in the second series of 'Peaks, Passes, and Glaciers.'

The 16th being Sunday, we spent quietly *chez Delapierre*, and, on the following day, crossed the Col Valdobbia to Riva. Thence we proceeded to Alagna, and in the afternoon went over the Col di Moud, a pass between the Moudhorn or Cima di Moud and Tagliaferro (7,467 feet in height by the sympiesometer), to Rima at the head of the west branch of the Val Sermenta, and so to Rimasco at the point where the valley divides. Here, at the little albergo, we found good intentions in abundance; but paving materials make poor fare, and, without disrespect to our worthy well-meaning host, I must confess that the quarters are not a Capua, though, of course, good enough for Alpine Clubbists.

E 2

On the 18th, a delightful stroll of two easy hours in the
early morning by the side of a clear, flashing trout-stream,
which descends the left or east branch of the Val Sermenta,
brought us to Carcoforo, where, to our surprise, we came
upon a most cozy little *cabaret*, kept by one Pietro Ber-
tolini. Good wine, milk, cheese, honey, bread, and two
beds are to be obtained, and, what is far better, great
civility and real cleanliness, as far as our observations
went. Our object being only to reach Ponte Grande, we
determined to enjoy ourselves at our leisure, and so contrived to while away an hour in a second breakfast, and
two more in the most lazy and luxuriant ascent of the
grassy slopes of the Col d'Eigua, the summit of which we
gained soon after twelve. The height, by a sympiesometer
observation, comes out 7,394.8 feet, agreeing very nearly
with Studer's determination, 7,382. The view from the
pass is a very lovely one, but ten minutes' climb to a rocky
summit on the south-east is well worth so trifling an effort.
Monte Rosa is seen rising almost due west in great majesty,
and in our subsequent passage of the ridge which connects
it with the Cima di Jazi we derived great benefit from the
observations which we were here able to make. On the
north-east side, at a point several hundred feet lower, the
Col di Barranca, at the head of the Val Mastalone, is passed
on the right, and the path then continues down through a
succession of lovely scenes, the beauty of which can hardly
be surpassed. Ferns in profusion, magnificent rhododen-

drons and wild laburnums in full bloom gradually gave place to walnuts and chestnuts of royal dimensions, vines, and maize, whilst fine pine-woods crowned the heights, 'in silent vigil, keeping watch and ward' over the happy valley. In such spots the traveller's object is not so much progression as loitering; and, instead of boasting that we accomplished this distance in such and such a remarkably short time, I feel a greater pride in saying that after spending an hour and a half on the summit, we contrived to while away four more between it and Ponte Grande. A fast walker would probably accomplish the distance from Rimasco to Carcoforo easily in an hour and a half; thence to the summit of the pass in an hour and a half more, and down to Ponte Grande in two hours and a half, or five hours and a half in all. We found excellent quarters at Ponte Grande in the hotel and *pension* of the same name, and on the 19th strolled up to Macugnaga, devoting an hour or two *en route* to a pretty complete exploration of the Pestarena gold mine. This is worth a visit, but I must not here attempt a description of its really extraordinary galleries, or the marvellously cumbrous machinery, groaning, creaking, straining and wheezing in the bowels of the earth. As an illustration of the antiquated state of things,* I may just mention, however, that the ore, instead of being crushed by stamps, the water-power necessary for which is close at hand in any

* Written in 1861.

amount, was all broken by hand, in a dark, dirty room, where three or four grimy and wretched-looking objects were seated before piles which they were slowly and laboriously reducing to smaller dimensions by blows of a hammer.

We had originally intended to return to Zermatt by the Weissthor pass as now usually taken to the north of the Cima di Jazi, but I had long been anxious to lay the ghost of the *Old* Weissthor if ever the chance came in my way; and as Macugnaga was a better starting-point for the attempt than Zermatt, it was resolved that we would at least make the attempt, wind and weather permitting.

Our reconnaisance from the summit above the Col d'Eigua had led us to the conclusion that, in the actual state of the *névé* crowning the ridge, a passage would be most easily effected at a point in the long rocky wall connecting the Cima with the Nordend, not far from the former summit. From our point of view the Jazi glacier was hidden, but just above where we knew it must be, a broad *couloir* ran up for a distance of 1,000 feet or more, slightly bending to the right. It then divided, sending up (if I may be allowed such an inversion of ideas) a branch to the left of considerable width, and a second and narrower one to the right. The first continued without a break to the summit, but there the overhanging masses of *névé* appeared likely to give much trouble, if not bar

Reconnoitring.

5.45 a.m. their complexions begin to suffer!

further progress, and we therefore turned our attention to
the second and more northerly one. Half-way between
its commencement and the sky-line it again bifurcated,
and there seemed every reason to hope that its left arm
would afford the means of gaining the crest. As the
ascent proved, this is yet another instance of the great
utility of a careful examination of a doubtful route beforehand ; for, though I will not venture to assert positively
that in no other way than this could our variation of the
Old Weissthor have been accomplished, yet the rapidity
and ease with which it was done were mainly due to
our having previously made ourselves familiar with the
ground.

Arrived at Macugnaga, we lost no time in making pre-
parations for the morrow, and were ably seconded by
our host of the Moro. On inquiring for some one to
take our knapsacks round to Zermatt over the Moro, we
were informed that there were two or three men then
working in the inn who had also a great hankering to accomplish the Old Weissthor. How long this desire had
existed on their part we did not inquire, but it was soon
arranged to our mutual satisfaction that two of them
should come as porters with us to the summit, whence
we could easily manage the knapsacks among our own
party, whilst they returned by the New Weissthor. The
pay was to be fifteen francs for the two, we finding
provisions for one only, as the other came less because

we needed him than because his comrade did not like returning alone. The names of the men were Jean Baptiste Andermatt and Bartholomée Burgner, of Saas, and both, I may add, acquitted themselves to our entire satisfaction.

Monte Rosa withdrew behind the clouds towards evening, and as there was therefore nothing particular to detain us and good reason for retiring early, I must plead guilty to having turned in at the unconscionable hour of seven o'clock.

At 12.15 A.M. on the 20th we were up, and though a haze hung over the valley, which was black as pitch, it somehow *felt* like clearing up, and I had a comfortable sense that we should succeed. Breakfast was soon dispatched, and at 1.25 we wished our host good-bye, and under the guidance of the men of Saas, one of whom carried a lantern to be 'left till called for' at the Jazi Alp, traversed as rapidly as circumstances would permit the beautiful meadows above Macugnaga. The hamlet of Pecceto was soon reached, and the bridge over one branch of the Anza was successfully hit by our leader ; but the waste ground at the foot of the *moraine* led us into difficulties, and in the deep darkness, the lantern served only to make confusion worse confounded. The men declared at length that we were where the bridge *ought* to be; but there, before us, was the roaring stream with only a few bits of logs sticking up through its turbid waters.

It was vexing to meet with a check so early, and for some time it really did appear as though we should have to wait for daylight to extricate ourselves. After poking about in various directions, however, each man following his own devices, we at length effected a passage at the point where the stream quitted the glacier, though not without sundry immersions and hearty laughter. Spite of the delay thus occasioned, we gained the summit of the 'Belvedere' (which is close to the spot marked '*Beim See*' in the Schlagintweits' Map) at 3, and crossing diagonally the northern arm of the Macugnaga glacier, formed by the union of the Nordend tributary with a portion of that from the Höchste Spitze, reached at 3.20 the path leading along the summit of the lateral moraine, just where the 'struggle for existence' is becoming too much for some unhappy-looking fir trees picketed out here on the outskirts of vegetation. The mists now rose, disclosing grandly the vast amphitheatre so well known, yet so impossible to describe in adequate language; and every minute gave fresh assurance that, so far as weather was concerned, we had everything to hope.

Leaving the Rofelstaffel *Alp* on the right, we arrived, at 3.40, at the bottom of the slope of the Jazi *Alp*, facing the glacier of the same name; and scanning the great wall before us, were glad to perceive that our distant survey appeared to be entirely confirmed by a closer examination; whilst, as now seen, the slope seemed less formidably

steep than when viewed from a higher point. Striking off
at right angles to our previous course, we soon entered
upon the Jazi glacier, which was covered with firm snow
and *débris* of avalanches, and afforded excellent footing.
Having reached some rocks a few hundred feet above its
foot, we halted at 4 A.M. to take a second breakfast and
watch the hues of sunrise spreading over Monte Rosa.
Ten minutes and a keen appetite sufficed to lighten
considerably our provision-sack, and we were soon again
under way. Nothing could be more perfect than the snow,
nothing more exquisitely beautiful than the scene; the
guides caught our enthusiasm, and all bending to the task
with a will, we ground steadily upwards, the slope increasing from 30° to 35° and 40°, till 4.45, when a clear stream
coming down from the cliffs of the Cima offered a temptation that was not to be resisted, and we revelled for a few
minutes in the unlooked-for luxury. We were now working
up the broad *couloir*, filled with snow and avalanche
débris, which, as it descends, gradually spreads out like a
fan, and is transmuted into the Jazi glacier, of which it
supplies the *névé*. To the right were the cliffs of the
Cima, all adrip with streamlets. Next came the re-
entering angle of the vast mountain fortress, of which
the Cima may be termed the bastion, and the ridge connecting it with Monte Rosa the curtain; whilst immediately in our front, and at no great height above us, was
the point previously described, where the main or trunk

couloir divides into two smaller ones, of which the left hand and broader one appears to run up without a break to the crest of the pass, whilst its companion subdivides about midway.

The first point of bifurcation was reached at 5.45, when the sun struck us, and, as the fresh snow was very dazzling, we again halted for a few minutes to put on spectacles, &c. The slope here was about 40°, but became steeper as we advanced, and was ploughed up by two immense furrows or avalanche-shoots, six or eight feet deep, and four or five wide, evidence of the fire of stones which, no doubt, goes on here as soon as the sun makes itself felt. Even at this early hour, a puff of snow or a few splinters of rock would break away above and come flying down; but here the furrows proved of real assistance in limiting the lateral deviation of the falling masses, and by keeping to the ridges, the risk was much lessened. I have already mentioned the streamlets from the Cima di Jazi. These are really quite a *spécialité* of this pass, and, I need not say, a most agreeable one. At 6.30, after another bout of steady climbing for three-quarters of an hour, the slope increasing to 45°, another bright, sparkling stream came rollicking down on our right; and as there was a strip of shade here, and human nature could not resist the united attractions of this sheltering rock, delicious water, and a view of such exquisite beauty, we fairly cast prudential considerations aside, and perched

in various unbecoming attitudes, scarcely more suggestive
of *otium* than *dignitas*, with the intention of thoroughly
enjoying ourselves. Time flew by, and it was half an hour
before we could effect a start. At last, however, we were
off at seven o'clock, and the *couloir* becoming increasingly
steep (I measured 47° with the clinometer), whilst, from
the greater softness of the snow, the footing was less
secure, we occasionally quitted it for the rocks on one or
the other bank. Our party being a large one, seven in
all, our progress was slow, as the rocks were much disintegrated, coming away in the hand, and requiring great
care on the part of those in front. Everyone knows how
much time is consumed when every other step is a
'*mauvais pas*,' and all have to wait for each. We had,
however, gained a great height by this time; it was still
early, and there was no great hardship in having to pause
every half minute for some backslider below, and employ
the time in endeavouring to digest the details of the
glorious *cirque*, to one of whose walls we were clinging.
I have no note of the exact time, but I think it must have
been considerably after eight o'clock, when we found ourselves at the point where the *couloir* again divided. *I*
was strongly in favour of keeping up the left arm, but
Bennen, who had had a touch of his beloved rocks, and
was not to be cheated out of a good '*Klettern*,' maintained
that we had better keep up the '*Scheidewand*,' or rock
dividing the two branches. I was in too contented a

"Grinding steadily upwards."

"Otium cum dignitate."

Pounding the snow.

Bennen takes to the rocks.

frame of mind to contend with him, and though privately
I believed him to be wrong, it was probable that nothing
worse than loss of time would result from our taking
the track he proposed, whilst the scramble would prove
a pleasant contrast to the treadmill monotony of a prolonged couloir-grind. So, at the rock we went. It was
steep, frightfully steep I might say, were it not that in
truth there was nothing really frightful about it, but hand
over hand we climbed steadily up it till, turning a corner,
I ran into Perrn, who ran into Bennen, who came to a
stop and looked puzzled. Right and left of us were the
two branches of the *couloir* at a considerable depth
beneath; the ridge up which we had been coming had a
facial angle of about 60°, and just in front of us an
adventurous bit of snow had quitted its parent plateau
above, and crept foolishly down the very edges of the
'*Kamm*' on a voyage of discovery. To attack it *en face*
and walk over its back was simply impossible, and there
seemed so little chance of turning it by a flank movement, that I began triumphantly to rally Bennen, and
insinuate that if he had let himself be persuaded by me
and stuck to the *couloir*, we should have been on the
summit ere this. He was not to be baulked, however, in
this way, and at once made a dash at the right side of the
slope, cut, kicked, and stamped his way to a bit of projecting rock, and after repeated fruitless struggles dragged
himself up it by sheer force of muscle or magnetic

affinity.   Securing a footing, he then helped Perrn to
follow, and the two having anchored themselves firmly
and reported that the summit was only a few yards
above, I followed, and leaving them to assist the rest of
the party, loosed the rope, passed on, and found myself in
another minute face to face with the Matterhorn.

It was some time before the whole party were landed on
the ridge (9.30 in fact), and very curious it was to watch
them hauled up one after another from space.   Meanwhile,
I set up my barometer and reconnoitred the *couloir* a few
paces to the S., which presented no difficulties of a serious
character.   Even Bennen admitted that he was out in his
judgment, whilst I conceded that I was thoroughly satisfied
with the variety and excitement of the course we had
taken, though it probably cost us at least three-quarters of
an hour of additional work.   As it was, we had been eight
hours *en route*.   Now, I think for various reasons there
can be no doubt that this pass presents less difficulties
when taken from Macugnaga, than it would do if attacked
from the Zermatt side, but *in the state in which we found
the snow*, I believe it would have been perfectly easy, after
traversing the first 500 feet with care, to glissade down the
remainder of the slopes to the Macugnaga glacier.   In this
way, an hour would probably have sufficed to effect the
entire descent, and two more would be ample to allow for
reaching Macugnaga.   As the summit of the pass could be
reached in about four hours from the Riffel if the snow

The last three minutes.

Science and Shivers.

were in good order, it will be seen that seven hours would suffice, under favourable circumstances, to effect the passage. Thus, had we quitted the Riffel as early as we had started from Macugnaga, we might have arrived at the latter place to a half-past eight o'clock breakfast. To one, however, suddenly reaching the brink of these tremendous precipices after traversing for some hours gently undulating snow-fields, the first impression would be unsatisfactory and startling, and I do not therefore much wonder at the Zermatt guides, who are most familiar with the aspect of things as seen from the Cima, being discouraged thereby and reporting that the glacier had ' fallen in.'

We spent $1\frac{1}{4}$ hour on the summit in the highest spirits, then bade adieu to our porters, who went merrily off to return by the New Weissthor, waking up the echoes with their jubilant *jodelings,* and at 10.45 started ourselves for Zermatt. My barometrical observation gives for the height of the pass 11,976.3 feet. A. Schlagintweit makes his col 11,870.3, whilst M. Bétemps puts it at 11,733 and the New Weissthor at 11,851, and Plantamour makes the highest point between the Cima and Monte Rosa 11,862 ('*Mesures hypsométriques,*' page 5).

The day was still before us, the sky almost cloudless, and there was no occasion for hurry, so we strolled leisurely down, halting every now and then, and at 2.30 reached the Riffel, and Zermatt shortly afterwards. The total time was thirteen hours, during only nine of which, however, we were actually *en route.* I have made no allusion to the view from the summit, because, being extremely similar to that from the Cima, it is familiar to most mountaineers.*

On the 21st we lounged vigorously, strolling up to the Riffel in the evening accompanied by another Englishman who had designs upon the Cima for the next day, whilst we were bound for the Lyskamm, or some similar ascent, Kronig, however, whom he had engaged, was anxious to be with us if anything of a novel description was in hand, and his employer gradually catching the infection, it was soon settled that we should not separate.

At 12.20 on the morning of the 22nd, we got away in glorious moonlight,—and following our tracks of that day week, reached, for the second time, the Lys Joch at 7.40, having had shade up to seven o'clock. The wind was

---

* Later in the season Professor Tyndall effected the passage of the Old Weissthor from Macugnaga to Zermatt, accompanied as usual by Bennen, and has given an interesting account of the expedition in his 'Mountaineering in 1861.' On this occasion, however, the direction of the Filar instead of that of the Jazi glacier was chosen for the attack. The ice appears to have been soon quitted for the ridge of rocks to the N., by which the summit was gained after a most exciting climb of four hours. At times it seemed as though further progress were impossible, and Bennen would pause in discouragement; but this was only momentary, and returning to the charge their efforts were ultimately crowned with success. It is dangerous to criticise the proceedings of two such veteran climbers, but I would venture to hint that their proficiency as cragsmen may have led to their preferring the rocks to the adjacent *couloir* or slopes of snow and ice, and that these last would possibly have afforded greater facilities whilst involving less risk.

blowing a gale, and after a careful examination it was
decided that the long *arête* of the Lyskamm, narrow enough
at the best of times but now heaped up and rolling over
with the fresh and uncompacted snow, was not to be
thought of under the circumstances. Some of the party
were already suffering from the cold, and poor Mr. ——
having neglected to provide himself with properly nailed
boots, was constantly performing eccentric manœuvres, the
most successful of which consisted of a *pas de deux* with
Kronig, who, in his endeavours to hold up his slippery
employer, invariably came in for a share of his misfortunes.
Before, however, finally giving in, we worked our way for
a distance of some few hundred yards towards the Lyskamm, and then halted in a slightly sheltered depression
of the ridge to secure a second breakfast and decide
where we should next bend our steps. Remembering
that, under similar circumstances, Mr. Stephen had made
a dash at the Zumstein Spitze, I at length suggested
that we should attack the Signalkuppe, which, so far as I
know, had never been ascended before from the Zermatt,
and only once from the southern, side, when in 1842
Gnifetti, curé of Alagna, arrived with seven companions
on the summit, after three ineffectual attempts in previous
years. No sooner said than set about, and at 8.30 we
were once more in movement. At 8.45 the Lys Joch was
again reached, and gently ascending over the great *Plateau*,
or ' *Krone*,' between the Zumstein, Signal, Parrot, and

F

Ludwig, summits of Monte Rosa, we soon found ourselves at the foot of the final pull. This was rapid, but by making first for a sort of snowy saddle connecting the Zumstein Spitze and Signalkuppe, we avoided the steepest places, and, the snow being besides in excellent order, there was no sort of difficulty.

If, however, poor Mr. —— had been in trouble before, he was here fairly posed ; Kronig was knocked down so many times as to cause anxious reflections on the probable state of his knees, and at one time we had serious thoughts of abandoning our unlucky comrade to his fate. He, however, struggled so gallantly, was so perfectly good-tempered, laughed so heartily at every fresh capsize, and showed such innate pluck and vigour, that we could not allow him to fall a victim to his defective shoeing, especially as we had persuaded him to attempt what otherwise would never have entered his head. What, however, with laughter, blustering wind, and driving snow, it was not easy, with the best intentions, to know how to assist him ; but at length, leaving Bennen and Perrn free to cut or pound steps, and Kronig to bring up the rear and pick up his Herr as often as was needful, we three fairly put our-selves in the traces, and by main force dragged our helpless friend sometimes on his back, sometimes on his face, now on one side, and now on the other, but always up-hill, as far as the rocks just below the summit, where he at once found his legs again. It was 10.15 when the summit of

Down again!

Excelsior!

the Signalkuppe was gained, and ample was the reward. We could now look over the Lyskamm, which we overtopped by 75 feet, the altitudes being respectively (according to the Federal engineers) 14,964 and 14,889 feet. This I can confirm to a certain extent by an observation taken on our way back, with a portable level which, after I had descended what I estimated to be 50 or 60 feet, showed the Lyskamm to be still slightly below my station. The wind blew furiously, but the sun shone out, and the thermometer, sheltered behind the rock, indicated as high a temperature as 1° C ($=33^\circ.8$ Fahr). Nothing, however, is less to be relied on than the readings of this instrument in determining what I may perhaps call the amount of sensational or physiological cold, and by the time I had secured a sympiesometer observation, obtained a specimen of the summit, and had a good look at the glorious view, it was voted that 'this house do adjourn.' Of the view I need not speak here, as in its general features it resembles that from the Höchste Spitze, differing from it, however, in one remarkable particular. To those who are familiar with the atlas to the Schlagintweits' work it is well known that the Signalkuppe, the fourth in height of the summits of Monte Rosa, stands at the point where the chain makes a sudden bend, the north arm comprising the Nordend, Höchste Spitze, and Zumstein Spitze, whilst the southern includes the Parrotspitze, Ludwigshöhe, Schwarzhorn, Balmenhorn, and Vincentpyramide. The direction

F 2

of the former is N. 20° W., of the latter S. 13° W.   The
Signalkuppe is thus the salient of a very obtuse bastion
whose N.E. and S.W. faces command respectively the
Vals Anzasca and Sesia, whilst to the N.W. its reverse
rakes, between the Lyskamm and Höchste Spitze, the
entire length of the Gorner glacier, and on the S.W. the
basin of the Lys glacier and the lower portion of the
Val de Lys.   In fact it is, as a glance at the map will
show, the real nucleus of the whole system, which has as it
were crystallised out from it, and it will be at once seen
that this gives it great advantages as a point of view.
The Höchste Spitze of course conceals a certain portion of
the horizon ; much less, however, than might be supposed,
for as far as my memory serves me, the Dom, Täschhorn,
and other summits between them and the Nordend are the
only important absentees, and these happen to be less interesting features perhaps than most in the panorama.
The Zumstein is projected against the Höchste Spitze and
the lateral deviation of the Nordend is not sufficient to
cause much loss.   At 10.30 we commenced the descent,
and after several halts amounting in all to one hour, and
some little difficulties caused by masked crevasses into
which one or other of the party was constantly sinking
through the now soft snow, we reached the Riffel at five,
and strolled down to Zermatt in the evening, well satisfied
on the whole with the turn affairs had taken, though of
course there was a tinge of disappointment at having ' shot

at a pigeon and killed a crow,' aimed at the Lyskamm and struck the Signalkuppe. '*Non omnes omnia possumus,*' and so the pleasure of vanquishing the Lyskamm was reserved for future comers. Who they were I need not say, as an account of the expedition will be found in the first volume of the second series of ' Peaks, Passes, and Glaciers,' but I may be allowed to terminate this paper with warm and hearty congratulations on their success.

SKETCHES

IN

BERCHTESGADEN AND THE ZILLERTHAL.

———+———

' 'Tis best, where'er we are, to follow still
The customs of the country.'
PLUMPTRE's *Sophocles.*

' When many a merry tale and many a song
Cheer'd the rough road, we wish'd the rough road long:
The rough road then, returning in a round,
Mock'd our enchanted steps, for all was fairy ground.'
JOHNSON.

SKETCHES FROM BERCHTESGADEN AND THE ZILLER-THAL.

COMPARATIVELY few English travellers know the charm of an early spring in the mountains. People who have been living through an Italian winter are eager to cross as quickly as possible into more familiar regions, and reach town for the season, and a few hours in a lumbering *vetturino*, with some shivering comments on the chilly blasts that sweep down upon them as they hurry over the St. Gothard or the Brenner, are all they realise of Alpine life in their passage ; and yet never in the whole year is that world of mountain and river, wood and snow, half so beautiful.

Ce joli mois de Mai! It brings sunshine and warmth and gladness in its hand, loosening the frozen streams, and sending them down with great leaps of gladness white from the glaciers that gave them birth, melting the snow-mantle that has kept the tender plants and roots warmly covered from the frost, and wakening them with smiles and promises of summer : so that bare hill-sides that looked grim and desolate with snow half melted in dirty brown patches, are covered in a few hours with a radiancy

of colour and bloom and sweetness, as the blossoms creep
out into the sunshine, and birds are singing and insects
humming their thanksgivings in a very jubilation of
honeyed delight. The world seems young again, fresh
and rested after its winter sleep, the roads have not grown
white with the accumulated dust of summer, and the
noonday heat which will bring headaches to weary August
travellers is still an unknown misery ; the days are long,
with bright sunrises and sunsets, and there is a frosty
feeling in the air which is wonderfully exhilarating; and
though the mountains be, many of them, only six or seven
thousand feet high, you believe in perpetual snow as you
see peak after peak gleaming sharply against the clear
blue of the sky, and forget measurements and theodolites
and any scientific assertions, taking it all on trust as unrivalled in grandeur and sublimity. The dark pine-woods
clothe the sides of the hills, and everywhere there is a
soft veil of greenery where larch and beech put out their
golden buds and light up the spaces between the fir-
shadows like veritable sunshine.

The still deep lakes of Tyrol, very small for the most
part, have wonderful colours in their depths—emerald and
ultramarine and gorgeous purple, as though Héré loved
them, and had made them beautiful with reflections from
peacocks' wings and breasts unseen by mortals ; or possibly
in later times, when German faërieland had supplanted
old Olympus, the gnomes had sunk shafts and mined out

galleries, piling stores of jewels and brilliant ore, and done a great business while shares were at a premium, till suddenly the world lost faith in them, treated them altogether as a myth, poor little elves, and so, finding the mine at a discount, they being not more than mortals, even a little less so in the matter of temper, let in the water and disappeared from the earth.

Writing of the spring as it ought to be in Tyrol, and as we found it during many happy weeks, it is only fair to state that, in the year of grace 1866, the seasons were a little behindhand, and somehow the frost held its own in an unconscionable manner; and there are disadvantages in travelling in a country where visitors only come in with the late vegetables, and no blankets are kept! We consoled ourselves with philosophy; but facts are stern things, and it is difficult to believe that 'whatever is is right' with the thermometer at 17°, and when you have to sleep in a German bed with one sheet and a *duvet* three feet square as your only defence against the cold. Certainly there are degrees of misery, and we were by no means at the lowest; but if the wind had not changed, and the frost had held, and we had journeyed far enough, we might have found ourselves in that outlying district where the cold was so intense that men's words froze as they were uttered, and conversation could only be resumed with the thaw in the spring!

We reached Berchtesgaden on the 22nd of May, in rather

a bad humour, after a long wet drive from Reichenhall, and found that pleasantest of summer haunts ostentatiously preparing for warm weather and the butterflies it was to bring, and ignoring any poor strangers who might be 'frozen out,' and needing warmth and comfort and shelter.

Our tired horses dragged us along the broad high-road past many pretty châlets with cool green jalousies and shady arbours, but all hermetically sealed and guiltless of smoke or human habitant, past König Max's villa, also shuttered and barred and silent, past plashing fountains, the very thought of which made one shiver with a dire foreboding that we might have made a terrible mistake, and that we were there *too soon*; on, with weary hoof splashing through the mud and sleepy driver nodding in the rain, till suddenly the *Kutscher* was smiling wide-eyed and wide-awake in a moment, and proving it by vigorous snappings of his whip. There was a quickening of the pace, a feeble demonstration of having done the last ten miles in an hour, and being a little blown in consequence, which imposed on nobody, and with a sudden jerk and rattle we drew up at the Hotel zum Watzmann, at the entrance of the little town. There was a big brown church opposite, a sound of sweet voices chaunting, and wreaths of greenery all over the inn-door, where people were standing in a state of suppressed excitement, and a little *Oberkellner*, like a puppet on wires—the sole marionnette of a theatre opened before its troupe had been made

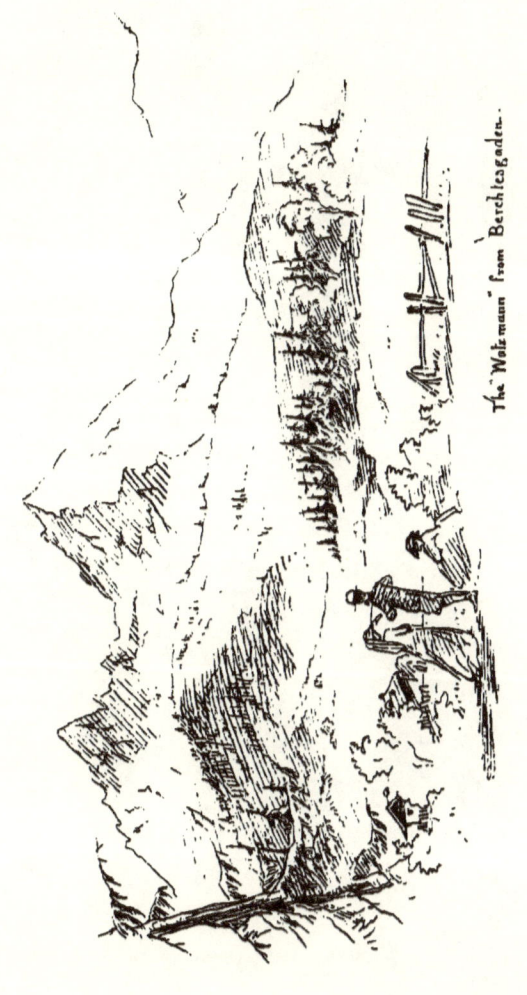

The "Watzmann" from Berchtesgaden.

ready, and with all the strings throughout the establishment attached to his small individuality,—who rushed to
open our carriage-door, precipitating himself upon a bundle
of cloaks with a vociferous welcome.

'Yes, the Herr had been there—the rooms were ready,
the Herr had himself selected them. We were fortunate
in our arrival—as, being the only guests, we could choose
what pleased us. Just now, it was true, there were people,
but that was only a wedding—one or two hundred of the
peasants who would sup there, and there would be a dance.
Could the Fräulein see them? Yes, surely—and dance
also—there would be music: they were singing now, they
were in the church over there, having already feasted.
Later they would drink again, and the Damen should see
the bride. There were the rooms: were the Damen satisfied?'

And so up the stairs and into the bright little chambers
he hurried us; keeping up a ceaseless flow of talk, with
much of hand-rubbing,—the cloaks being deposited,—
and little hasty runs through different doors, and busy directions to a quiet, slow, handsome *Kellnerin* who smiled
her welcome and hastened to make us comfortable. Such
fresh, clean, pretty rooms they were, gay with muslin
curtains and green jalousies, crimson cushions on the
window-sills, floors polished with much scrubbing, downy
pink-striped coverlets, a sofa and the little round table,
with its red cloth, to make believe we had a salon, and a

great white earthenware stove filling up a quarter of the room, and looking as though many hours and more faggots would be needed before any warmth could penetrate its icy smoothness. It was impossible to resist the friendly welcome, the promise of dinner at the moment, and a dance afterwards, the hesitating request that we would graciously eat in a small room adjoining, the *Speisesaal* being occupied by the bridal party. We thawed at once: fraternised with the waiter, with the chambermaid, with the whole establishment; threw ourselves heart and soul into the interests of the moment, and determined to enjoy the fun. It was freezing hard—about that there could be no mistake—and the little salon was two-thirds window and guiltless of a fireplace. We ate and shivered and listened to F.'s histories of his morning. He having preceded us on foot and arrived in time for the whole ceremony, and having witnessed sundry libations, was sceptical of the feasibility of our sharing even as spectators in the evening celebrations; but by this time the cold had become so intense, that his account of the big room with its warmth and light and many people, even with the tobacco-smoke, sounded welcome, and we ventured in, taking up a safe position near the door.

The scene was wonderfully picturesque and full of interest; the people enjoyed themselves so thoroughly, with such happy light-hearted merriment, with such earnest good-will, and the throng of glad faces, honest

hard-working men and women, strong and sturdy, was
a pleasant sight to see.   The men were tall, well-grown
fellows, with handsome sun-burnt faces, with gay-coloured
braces crossed over their white shirts—for there was hardly
a jacket to be seen in the crowd, the dancing was too
much in earnest for the carrying of any needless weight
—and wearing high-crowned hats, grey or black, some
with the broad green band of the Salzkammergut, all
with feathers—white *Lämmergeier*, black *Auerhahn,* glossy
and curled—a bunch of flowers, or a tassel, green or silver.
The women were in dark brown or black garments, hanging in heavy folds half-way below the knee, the bodice
relieved with dainty chemisette or gay-coloured kerchief
matching the brilliant apron, the hair glossy and braided,
the dancers in green wreaths.   One or two maidens who
might, perhaps, aspire to belong to a higher class than
the peasants around them, wore flowing white robes, with
trains that mournfully recalled Western civilisation.

Down one side of the room sat the men and matrons,—
house-fathers gossiping together over the weather and the
crops, and clinking beer-glasses ; the mothers, with mild
quiet faces and steadfast eyes shining out under the shade
of their broad hats, with kind glances at the younger life
around them, and pleasant smiles over the bright faces so
innocently happy, and whispered reminders of past days
and other *Brautfests*, and of their own old romances.
Good souls, they looked quiet and patient, as though

through somewhat of sorrow and hard work, and blessed
home joys and cares, they had kept their hearts fresh like
a deep still pool made bright by the reflections from
others' sunshine, and glad with little ripples of their own
content, sending out rivers to barren places, and fed by
streams from other lives, which, whether sweet or bitter,
mingled with their own and made them more complete.
There is something wonderfully touching in the faces of
these German mothers—they look so good and hard-
working and thrifty, though often so very poor, as though
they might tell you sad stories of Hans being a *Wildschütz*,
and Jacob far too much given to quarrels over the
Branntwein, and that they and the little cows had to do
all the work, yet the good God gave His blessing, and the
kleine had never wanted for bread.

But all this time the dancing was going on fast and
furious, till the great beams swung again, and the boards
rose and fell with the hurrying feet. A little old man, the
master of the ceremonies, worked himself almost into a fit
in his excitement and eagerness. Standing in the centre
of the room he shouted and stamped in time to the music,
despotically marshalling his dancers, giving his orders
right and left with vehement clappings, wiping his heated
brows at every pause, and swallowing beer from many
glasses hospitably held out for his acceptance.

We made our way through the throng to one corner
where the bride and bridegroom were seated solemnly

The Breakfast.

drinking. We had all to shake hands, with hearty good
wishes, and to pledge them in some very sour liquid, like
steel filings on edge, diluted with vinegar. They were of
the peasant farmer class, neither very young. The man
tall and ungainly, working off his awkwardness in offers
of beer, and looking uncomfortably conscious of his long-
tailed coat and heavy hat, which, as full dress, was *de
rigueur* on the occasion. The bride was by no means
pretty, but she spoke happily of their little cottage on the
hills, and tried to do her part by asking the gentlemen to
dance, and quietly accepting their apologies, thanking us
for coming to them, and then relapsing into that stolid
calm which nature and constant association with their
dumb beasts teaches them, and which civilisation has
improved into the apathy of perfect good-breeding !

The dancing was perfect, the men changing their
partners in the middle of a waltz without losing a step.
The fiddlers played faster and faster as the dancers flew
round the room. Some danced by themselves, not to lose
a moment, leaping into the air, snapping their fingers, and
jodeling in very gladness of heart. We had a store of
magnesium-wire and coloured lights, and our father flung
the bright blazing papers among them amidst bursts of
ecstatic wonder and delight. They all showed us the
greatest respect and hospitality, and one very ugly old
man, probably thinking our feelings might be hurt if
we were altogether passed over, suggested, 'Possibly the

Fräulein will dance?' and on our professing ignorance of
the figures, met the difficulty graciously with 'Perhaps,
then, a cotillon?'

At last, leaving them to their revels, we retreated to our
rooms, but not to sleep; the noise across the passage was
deafening. When the bridal pair left about midnight, the
band preceded them downstairs, and all the guests followed
two and two, cheering and jodeling as they drove off in
an *Einspänner* for their mountain châlet. And then came
more dancing and more noise; and if any one had been
so unreasonable as to keep awake and listen to heavy
bodies falling downstairs, and the other slight confusions
attending their departure, possibly their views of the piety
and thrift and simple habits of these poor *Bauern* might
have been modified, with a dreamy sense that the good
and the evil has drifted pretty equally over the world we
live in, and that men are not necessarily better because
they live nearer the heavens, and breathe rarefied air.

No words can describe the charm of this small Bavarian
settlement, as we saw it again in the warmth and brightness of the later spring. A little hamlet nestling under
the shelter of the hills, the houses springing up here and
there as though self-sown, and seeming to grow by nature
among orchard trees and flowers: far away, like a fair
ribbon flung upon the grass, the river flows, now soft
green, now palest blue, as it glimmers into shade or sunshine, an old church with a rude brown tower makes a

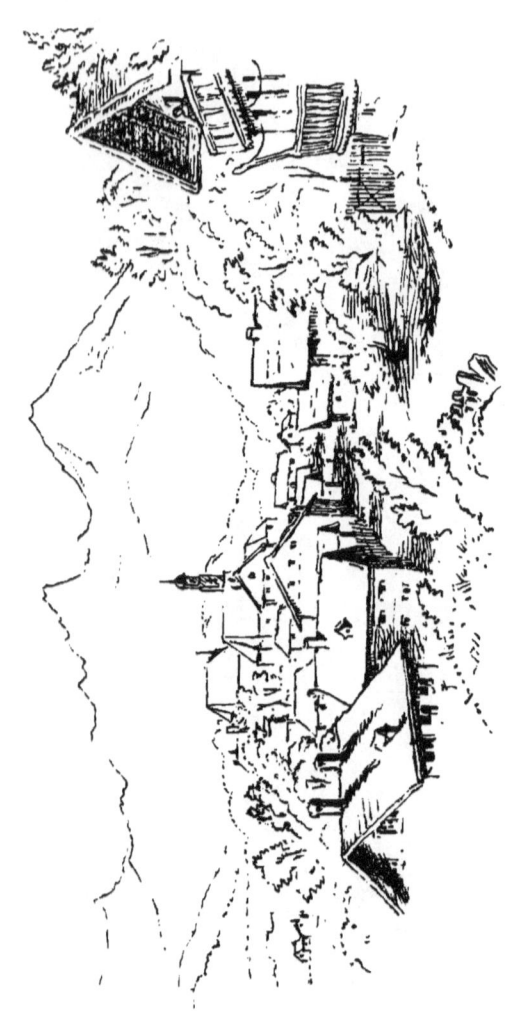

pleasant bit of warm colouring amongst the white homesteads and grey-roofed little cottages, and is apparently
well loved by the peasants, who congregate there and
chant their psalms and hymns with a strong goodwill and
earnestness of purpose that makes up somewhat for lack
of melody in the notes, leaving the stiff old *Dom Kirche*,
with its two iron-coloured extinguisher steeples, to the
slow work of renovation which scaffolding and bricks and
mortar show us is still going on within.   The ground rises
from the river on either side, here in soft undulations,
there in more abrupt slopes thickly wooded, and dotted
with a few boulders and great mossy mountain stones.
The fields of corn and barley wave in the wind, that is just
strong enough to rustle the stems and turn a fresh side of
the drooping ears to the sunshine, the meadows are all
ready for the harvest, waiting in the sweet Sunday quiet
for the morrow's dew, and the glad ring of the scythe
as the peasants gather to their work; now for one more
evening there is a glow of colour on the grass, where
purple *Campanulas* make a soft light like a pool of still
water, and Forget-me-not and golden *Bartsia* and deep
crimson Rose-Campion and dark-brown blossoms, great
white *Marguerites*, and flowers, yellow, and lilac, and
crimson, sweet-scented pansies, and pale fair lilies form a
lovely garden world, where Titania and all her fairies might
walk under the shelter of green leaves and drink their

G

draughts of dewy nectar, each from a freshly-coloured
cup, and sleep afterwards as intoxicated with the sweetness as the bees who hum their lazy bacchanals around
them.

The lower hills are clothed with woods to their summits,
and under the shade of the firs and beeches, winding paths
are tracked out in the moss and built up with branches
of pines. Climbing ever higher over the soft carpet of
twigs and fallen leaves, where the sunshine through the
branches above makes a chequered pattern, and picks out
little red lights in the tree-stems to delight your eyes, you
reach the open again, and far away rises the grand old
Watzmann, a giant with a solemn snow crown, who looks
down rather grimly on Titania and the flowers, and mere
humans, and the follies and littlenesses of the world
beneath him. His great rugged sides have wonderful
violet shadows in their depths, and a soft purple mist is
wound about him like a mantle: there is a divine smile
on his head where the parting sun touches it with its
radiance, a glow that deepens and lives there when the
world is cold and dark, wondrously beautiful, as though
when we had lost the light, the glory from the very
heaven shone upon and blessed it.

We spent a long quiet Sunday in that pleasant country
life, hastening down from the higher pastures to our
little inn as the shadows deepened under the dark pine
woods, giving them a new and silent charm.

'Nor moon, nor stars were out :
They did not dare to tread so soon about,
Though trembling, in the footsteps of the sun ;
The light was neither night's nor day's, but one
Which lifelike had a beauty in its doubt.'

Of all the pleasant excursions for which Berchtesgaden
is the best of headquarters, there is none more charming
than the hour's drive to the König-see, and a day spent
on its waters. Its great beauty consists in the grandeur
of the cliffs, which rise to a height of two or three
thousand feet, towering up abruptly from its margin, so
that only here and there a little shelving bank is to be
found on which a human foot can tread; the trees spring
out of the rocks wherever a root can cling, and cast dark
green shadows into the depths below. Very pleasantly
the hours pass as you sit in the high-prowed boat, rowed
by some sturdy damsel in gold-tasselled hat and velvet
bodice, and if you reach the head of the lake a walk
across a strip of barren ground will bring you to the
Obersee, a deep still pool lying in a cup of bare limestone
rock, and worth a visit for the sake of its weird loveliness.
Very early one morning we drove to the shore of the
König-see ; the world was just astir. The birds were
hunting for their breakfasts, and labourers hastening to
their work. In a little wood, we came suddenly upon a
group of men under the trees, standing with bare heads
reverently bowed, their tools lying on the ground beside
the trees they had felled the latest. We exclaimed,

astonished at the sight, 'Sie sind in Gebete begriffen.'
'Fräulein,' answered our *Kutscher*, 'it is Monday, and
they wait to ask a blessing on their work. It is the
custom,' he added, giving a little commenting shake to
the reins as our horses turned a corner.

The whole district is a little piece of Bavaria, ceded by
the Congress of Vienna as a hunting ground for its princes,
with whom it has always been a favourite resort. Old
King Lüdwig, who was a greater sportsman than his successors, spent many days in a queer château or *Jagdschloss*
on the borders of the König-see, and there is a gloomy old
palace built amongst the houses in Berchtesgaden, besides
the beautiful new Villa Max upon the hill, behind which
thick woods rise abruptly with country houses half hidden
in their shade, and wood walks cunningly devised with
openings cut out among the trees, and seats for weary
explorers, and here and there, at a sudden turn of the
path, the inevitable little châlet, with wood carvings for
sale, and other signs of the Philistines and predatory civilisation, only redeemed by the exceeding beauty of hill and
valley which bursts upon you as an ever fresh delight.
We rejoiced in the sense that we were there before the
arrival of the season and the *monde*, the hot weather
and gay dresses, when the shutters were hardly taken
down from the wood-carver's shops, when there were no
stalls of photographs in our path, and the blind beggars,
and the beggars with no arms, and the parents of large

In the dairy.

Buttercups and Daisies !

families of young beggars, who were taking kindly to the
ancestral business, had not yet established themselves in
their summer hunting grounds.

During our five or six days at Berchtesgaden we spent
many pleasant hours exploring the wood walks for fresh
views of the snow-covered mountain whose great jagged
peaks watched over the village below, or driving to the
beautiful König-see, where we rowed lazily over the water,
watching the long still shadows of the rocks, or landing to
visit some cascade hidden in their clefts; spending quiet
dreamy hours in the sunshine, sitting in a sheltered nook
in the higher meadows, with work and books and painting,
and a tinkling accompaniment of cow-bells, and far away
great snow-slopes growing into violet shadows as the sun
sank lower in the west; or discovering little out-of-the-
way homesteads, where we made friends with the kind
peasants, and heard their stories of good fortune or privation, admired the babies, and bought bowls full of
sweet new milk, for now the cold weather had come suddenly to an end, changing into the perfection of warm
noonday, with just a cheery thought of frost morning
and evening that kept the snow upon the hills.

   *   *   *   *   *   *

As the evening of a wet day in June was closing in, we
drew near the little village of Krimml. Having parted
from F. at Hallstadt, and seen him start with a country
guide and his trusty Almer for ten days in the mountains,

and taken leave of our father at Salzburg—where he left
us to return home—we four ladies, with the carriage and
horses which we had already employed in our drive from
Ischl, arranged to travel under Walther's* good care over
the Hirschbühl, rejoining F. at Krimml, and spending
a few days together in the Ziller-thal. For the last
twenty-four hours the weather had been the only drawback
to enjoyment; all the morning the rain had poured down
in chilly showers, which grew only colder and mistier as
the day wore on.

There was little traffic on the road, and few or no guests
at the inns at this early season, except, as ever, the crowd
of peasants in the *Stube*; and when we halted for a meal
we had much pleasant gossip with the honest-faced
Wirthins or sturdy *Kellnerins*, who watched us as we ate,
and were delighted to sit for their portraits, and receive
some little books from England, or a *Trinkgeld*, and a
compliment on their pretty faces and ready kindliness.
At Zell am Zee, where we halted for the night, we found
ourselves in the old familiar inn of German idyls: the
wainscoted walls and wooden tables and benches shining
with cleanliness and much rubbing; the rooms large and
low, with great beams supporting the ceiling, and broad
windows with tiny panes; crucifixes, little cups for holy
water, a faded wreath before some sacred picture deco-

* Bartholome Walther, of Pontresina, one of the best guides of the
Engadine.

rating the walls. But these touches of higher grace and art were generally reserved for the bedrooms—the grand apartments of the house, often of enormous size, two-thirds window, gay with roses and sweet-scented stocks, with a huge black stove filling up one corner, and beds, piled high with bright cotton *duvets* and wadded counterpanes, sheets of homespun linen, coarse and white, with broad-laced edgings to the towels and pillows, the orthodox stiff German sofa and inevitable cabinet, behind whose glass-doors reposed the heirlooms of the house—old china, quaint cups and mugs and vases, dear to the good *Wirthin's* heart, silver-handled knives and forks, glass and crockery of every kind; and on the higher shelves, a crowd of tinsel ornaments, bouquets, toys, wreaths for festivals, gold and silver pins—each relic, great or worthless, priceless no doubt to those good hearts, and rich in tender recollections: the bridal flowers of her happy wedding morning—dear soul, though stout and old, and seamed a little by the winters that had passed her by, there had been a spring too for her once, rich in all love and promise. There were the toys that little hands had played with—perhaps most precious because the eager fingers may have been folded once so quietly they never broke that stillness. There, too, the nosegay the young daughter had carried at her first communion, and many treasures, gay little pictures of saints, with flowers, and lace-paper, and legends, very like an ecclesiastical valentine, and with just the same tender

little meanings insinuating themselves under the angelic
wings, bought, as they may have been, at a country-fair
by some great shy Pinzgauer for that blue-eyed maiden
who waited on us below with the large silver spoon stuck
into her bodice, and her name, Marie, or Ursula, or Filomena, embroidered on her broad belt.

We had left Mittersill with many forebodings as to the
weather. The clouds were as low as they could well be to
be clouds at all, and they very soon changed into a drizzle,
and then came down in good earnest. So we pulled up at
the roadside, and Walther and the coachman built up a
close carriage carefully bit by bit, like a Chinese puzzle,
taking out doors and windows and cross-pieces from some
hidden receptacle in a truly marvellous and inexhaustible
manner. The puzzle, when finished, was not a perfect
fit; and we were glad to make cushions of our cloaks,
which comfortably imbibed the moisture, whilst we made
ourselves merry with riddles and stories and talk—the
country being unenlivening, a great extent of flat marshy
land and grass-fields where numbers of young horses were
feeding, with a few stray houses and one or two villages.
In many of the fields the poor people were kneeling in
rows in the wet corn or rye, busily weeding, and laying up
a store of rheumatic twinges for every half-dozen roots
they succeeded in extracting, to say nothing of the havoc
made among the green blades.

As the day wore on the clouds lifted, and in the sunlight

we saw the Gross Venediger crowned with snow. Gradually
the valley narrowed, and we drove into a kind of *cul-de-
sac*, the little village of Krimml lying before us, and a
glorious great waterfall, one thousand feet high, breaking
through a cleft in the rock.   The mountains looked very
unpromising, and the weather scarcely less so, as the
clouds again covered the hills, showing us here and
there through their rents black dismal rocks and deep
snow over which our path lay for the morrow.   The inn
was the roughest we had yet encountered.   A ladder-
like staircase led up from the darkness below to a vast
damp landing ; the boarded walls seemed exuding
moisture, and the rain and damp fog entered at will
through the great openings at either end : no woman
was to be seen, and no one, apparently, to make us
welcome, or at all prepared for the arrival of guests.   A
rough old landlord, begrimed with accumulated dirt of
the past winter, and smoked and seasoned by the fumes of
his own pipe, which was never out of his mouth, at last
came to our relief, and took us under his protection.
'The Herr had not arrived, but his portmanteau was
there, and no doubt he would appear shortly, and meanwhile we could see the rooms.'   On opening a door into a
spacious chamber matters began to look more promising.
We at once prepared to take possession and make things
comfortable, ordered everything eatable the house contained, lit the candles on the round table, and provided a

famous brew of tea to welcome F. and Almer when they should arrive, probably wet and weary.

While D. ran to the kitchen with the teapot, E. hunted out the salt, when a cry from Mrs. C. arrested them, as she stood gazing at them in blank despair, unable after the first scream to utter a word. Slowly they drew from her the direful truth,—the rain had penetrated her carpet-bag, and during the journey her precious possessions had been literally floating in soft water. As they extracted the moist masses, her companions suggested the evident wisdom of at once drying them; and making up a bundle of her garments, she hastened in search of a kitchen and a fire; but encountering the old *Wirth*, was hurried by him into the *Stube*, where a group of sympathetic and much interested peasants, busy with their pipes, offered to smoke the clothes for her! Indignantly rejecting their proposal, she was conducted to the kitchen, and propitiated by the sight of a good fire in the broad stove and the alacrity with which mine host assisted her to string her possessions on a long spit, which was afterwards suspended over the blaze, and turned till they were sufficiently done.

Calmness being restored, we settled down to our *Abendessen*, but with rather sad hearts, waiting hour after hour for F., who never came. E. and C. went to their room and vainly endeavoured to sleep. Ten, eleven o'clock, and no arrival! Sometimes they would be startled by a

Mrs C. dries her clothes on the spit.

Going downstairs in a Bergwagen.

footstep stamping up the stairs, as one of the herdsmen climbed to his nest amongst the rafters. E. always suffered from chronic anxiety during F.'s absences, and the attack became violent whenever he ceased to appear at the expected moment. C. declares that she was not the least uneasy till E. worked her up to a proper state of misery; but this fact E. doubts. It was dismal enough lying sleepless in the cold gaunt room, listening to the rain beating against the windows, and the wind howling round the lonely house, or eagerly looking at their watches by the dim light of a little candle, to see how many hours still lay between them and the possibly dread uncertainties of the morning.

Suddenly a shrill old bell gave a clang, and steps were heard and voices, and the anxious watching passed away into a happy dreamless sleep.

Very merry was the breakfast, making up for all the shortcomings of the night before. F. recounted his adventures, and we watched the gathering of men and horses below the window. Much could not be said for the weather; but if there were no distant views, there was a very picturesque foreground to clouds and mist as our little party wound up the steep wood-path and over the grassy hill-side above; we four ladies on horseback endeavouring, as far as we were able, to protect ourselves from the pitiless rain, and exchanging merry talk and jokes with F. and the guides, who made the poor beasts rest every three minutes, much to our discomfort, as their backs were nearly at an angle of forty-five degrees! A pause at an *Almhütte*, where some great bowls of delicious milk were brought to us, and then we pressed on, our steeds slipping and stumbling for the next hour along a track, in reality a succession of deep hollows between short wet turf, half black bog, half holes and large stones, so that we were glad to dismount and trudge through water and soaked grass till we reached a more level road; but any after attempt at riding made us so unpleasantly conscious of being wet through, at least as to our feet, that we were glad to run again to warm ourselves, and joyfully hailed the little inn at Gerlos, where we changed and dried our clothes over the kitchen-fire. The cloaks and rugs were hung across a beam over the great flat stove, *on* which a fire of wood was lit, a little tripod placed over it supporting a saucepan or fryingpan; the men held our boots in the bright flame, while the *Mädchen* fed the fire with dry chips of wood from a great pile stored in one corner; F. preparing a good portion of soup, with a cake of dried vegetables, a square *à la Julienne* being added to the stock.

Meanwhile, two *Bergwägen* were being got ready, and the baggage stowed away. They were the worst we had ever seen; the poor horses never went beyond a walk, the drivers tramping at their side for four long hours; and for these delightful vehicles the charge was sixteen

Gulden. D. and E. started in one, F. heading the procession on foot. Mrs. C. and C. were established side by side on the second seat of one cart, Walther and Almer on the one before them. The seats were merely boards, laid across a long narrow trough on wheels. It was exceedingly difficult for two people to sit anyhow without tumbling off sideways, and when the paths—for road there was often none—led over great stones or rocks, the sight was ludicrous of the unhappy victims swaying from side to side, half shaken out, and then violently thrown back upon the planks, steadying themselves by the exertion of every muscle in their bodies, or rowing themselves along with enormous fir poles, with which F. supplied them. Half the exertion expended would have carried us on our feet happily to the journey's end, but having elected to drive, we scorned to be turned from our purpose; Walther and Christian soon succumbed, and unable to endure such an amount of exercise, prepared to walk, though poor Almer was almost dead beat after his twenty-four hours' expedition of the previous day.

About a quarter of an hour after our start D. and E. came to grief, through the loss of the linch-pin or bolt of their chariot, which thereupon fell in two. A little *Wirthshaus* near by fortunately boasted another trough upon wheels, into which they and the bags were stowed—the appearance they presented forcibly reminding their companions of one of Mr. Leech's most vivid sketches of

L. of C.

the youthful and agricultural poor taking the air in a clothes'-truck. The victims consider their sufferings to have been indescribable.

The road was execrably bad, and often very steep, but full of beauty of woods and meadows in all the glory of spring. The path wound down the sides of a steep ravine, with a torrent far below breaking in white showers of foam over the stones and between the dark stems of the firs, and carrying away in its course branches freshly torn from the pines, red and odorous, with great jagged edges of brown bark, that came sweeping down, holding out their broken twigs like hands of drowning men, and sometimes getting caught out in quiet little eddies, where they may rest for years, and weld themselves into the rich marl of the banks, till the moss covers them lovingly and flowers grow out of their heart, or a bright-eyed water-rat builds its nest in a soft bit of fibre.

The sides of the wood were green with plants, luscious grasses, and golden lichens starred with flowers, and many streams crossed our path; some so small they only made a bubbling in the grass, some busy and important enough to turn a mill and needing a wooden bridge made in careless fashion of loose boards, over which we jolted, tossed helplessly into the air by the vibration. The woods rang with our laughter and moans; the stolid old driver giving no sign of sympathy, unless a chuckle of delight may be so regarded when a more fearful shock than usual

A Bergwagen!

elicited a cry of anguish.   A sort of stone staircase, which
announced itself as part of the high road, brought matters
to a climax.   D. and E. from the safer abasement of their
trough, looked back upon their companions.   The horses
took to the stairs as a matter of course, and the *Bergwägen*
came after,—bump! jolt! shriek! creak! stumble! cries
and laughter! bump! bump! bump!—the unhappy occu-
pants holding on to each other, to their great poles, to the
empty air, in an ecstasy of suffering and delight.

There had been a drizzle of rain all the morning, but as
the day advanced the clouds cleared off a little, and we
caught sight of the lovely Ziller-thal, to which we were
bound.   We were still journeying through a thick forest,
winding in and out on the edge of a steep slope, ending in
a ravine, through which the river ran; and opposite to us
rose another wooded mountain side, clothed to its summit
with soft green meadows, like little bits of sunshine cut out
of the trees, and dozens of brown châlets, the lower ones the
peasants' dwellings, the more distant, haysheds or *Almhütte*.
The cattle were all in their higher pastures, and very
sweet and Arcadian it all looked in the bright evening
light.   Gladly we hailed the emerald-green spire of the
village church far below us: the tired horses hastened
forward, and we reached Zell about seven, where we were
warmly welcomed by the very affable old *Wirthin*, and
while supper was preparing thankfully rested our worn
and weary bodies, listening later for an hour or two to

some pleasant *Volkslieder* and jodeling choruses, with a
musical accompaniment from *Zither* and guitar, and a
wonderful wooden instrument called *Holzgelächter*, which
at each touch of the little sticks gave out sweet clear
notes, indescribable, alas! except in the thought that an
angel in pattens was singing somewhere. And so, with
an interchange of friendly talk and conjuring and sketch-
books on our part, and singing from the peasants, our
day drew to a close; and while we slept, too soundly even
to dream of its misadventures or fatigues, we woke to
bright sunshine and glad plannings for another happy
day amongst the hills.

A late breakfast at the luxurious hour of eight, a quiet
drive through the pleasant country in a good carriage,—
blessed be the man who invented springs!—a soft air
scented with new-mown hay and crushed flowers drying
on the high crossed poles that made the fields look full
of great bears holding out embracing arms, or meek
Capuchins standing with bowed heads, brought us to
Mayrhofen, where we found a little room perched in the
balcony, very cool and airy, with lattice-work sides,
through which we looked down on an amusing little world
below: fat blue-eyed children toddling about with the
inevitable big baby, peasants resting with their cattle,
smoking and ruminant, an investigating cow endeavouring
to establish itself in a cosy stable, from which it was
driven by a young Tyroler with ironical hootings, to the

dismay of the fat children among whom it immediately plunged, an alarming guggle from the baby premonitory of a scream, bringing an anxious mother from a wash-house, whose sturdy arms speedily routed the enemy and restored peace. Our guides, who had followed us in an *Einspänner*, appeared, elevating an alpenstock on which hung, waving in the breeze, ' a banner with a strange device ' in the shape of F.'s knickerbockers—which, having been thoroughly washed during the night after his tramp down the mountain, had now to be dried *en route*.

That ride to the Karlsteg was one never to be forgotten. Great rocks piled one upon another in chaotic confusion made the path, marked by a long slide here and there on the smooth stone where a hoof had begun a *glissade*. If it had been up hill or all down, one might in time have become reconciled to the movement, but the hillocks were so small that each unfortunate beast formed an arc of a circle, and the still more unfortunate rider was first thrown forward almost on its head and then jerked over the tail. The path was in places so narrow that though a mule could pass, panniers, or anything so insignificant as the feet of the riders, had not been taken into account. After escaping being crushed between the rocks in a narrow defile, with a sudden lunge the animal would turn a corner and stand panting, its foreleg slipping on a loose stone edging the path, and your boots hanging over a precipice. A pleasant

H

position, truly, for those who cannot keep their seat at any
given angle of saddle or steed!

Lovely clematis with bright blue blossoms hung from
the rocks; the woods, as ever, were full of the sweet
spring fragrance; birds sung in the trees, and the torrent
roared with a mighty voice as the masses of water fell with
a great leap into the hissing cauldron below, and rocks
and hill-side showed out dimly through the whirl of spray.
It is only with an effort that the mind can so far triumph
over matter as properly to appreciate such a scene, when
the boots belonging to it are in the uncomfortable position
mentioned above.

'There is but a step from the sublime to the ridiculous,' and in the course of our travels how many bursts of
eloquence have not been cut short by a sudden slip or
stumble on the part of the most promising-looking steed
or most sure-footed of humans!

As the echo caught the roar of the water it sent it to
us mockingly, as though a hundred spirits of the stream
laughed back at us, and old Kuhleborn himself might
have grown out of the mist and steam and defied us, as
we passed on to find the still bed of the river higher up,
and eat and drink, and profane those quiet places by
mortal hunger and wonderment and laughter. Pleasantly
the old Folk-lore grows into its own surroundings, and we
have time to muse over it as we rest idly by the water,
sheltered from a sudden shower by the strong roof of the

old bridge, picturing to ourselves Undine's sweet white
face smiling out of the spray, or fading away, pathetically
mournful, as the wind sung her dirge through the pine-
boughs; and up through the gorge, as night falls and
clouds gather black and threatening, may still come, for
aught we know, the weird Erl König or the Wild Huntsman and his spectral hounds. The dark hollows of these
very rocks were full once of little gnomes and demons:
good little *gobbos*, some of them, who gave dowries to
pretty maidens, and wreaked fell judgment on prosperous
iniquity. We had read all these stories long ago, in those
sweet old days when everything was truth to us; and for
the sake of that happy time we spoke of the old myths
reverently, sighing because we were wiser and perhaps
somewhat sadder also.

Soundly we slept that night in the big rooms at Zell,
and loudly demonstrative was the good *Wirthin* at parting.
We gave her a packet of our English tea—so called in
contradistinction to the dried hay or carefully preserved
twigs with which we had been favoured at many good
hostelries. Her admiration of our teapot was boundless:
she evidently regarded it as a valuable piece of family
plate, as Mrs. C. always carried it in a chamois-leather
case and polished it carefully each morning; and E.'s
statement of its having cost less than three *Gulden* was
regarded as a vague anecdote totally destitute of truth, or
too intimately connected with the conjuring of the night

before, which had driven the good woman from the room with a cry of, ' Was für Hexerei!'

We had found an officer established in the little village, who had made our inn his head-quarters, and was hard at work drilling about a hundred and fifty volunteers, 'furlough men,' as *The Times* called them; and these young peasants made somewhat of a thoroughfare of our salon on their way to and from the officer's chamber. There was not much attempt at regular uniforms, but their costumes were sufficiently picturesque, and there was a great gathering of plumed hats and a vast display of belts and rifles. We watched them being put through their paces, the poor fellows looking very awkward, and very much ashamed of themselves and of these early attempts to learn discipline.

The distant war-thunder was growing nearer and more distinct every hour, but as yet no shot had been fired. The people everywhere seemed stolid and faithful, but totally without enthusiasm, and already suffering and privation were making themselves felt. In some of the higher mountain hamlets the peasants spoke to F. sadly of their future :—' All our able-bodied men are taken away; there is no one left to gather in the crops, and nothing before us but want and misery in the coming winter, however matters may go.' At Gmunden, a town of some three thousand inhabitants, they told us one hundred and forty of their young men had been taken by the conscrip-

tion, and the old *bürger* with whom we were discussing the
aspect of affairs and the war prospect, said, with a dismal
shrug, that as the youths had had to go, and they were
all forced to pay so much money, he thought for his part
their Emperor had better try a little fighting, peace could
not do them much good now. During all the time we
were in the country, both before and after war was declared,
the people were in a calm and utterly unexcited state,
sad enough truly, but knowing little and caring less for
anything but the one fact that all the strong-handed had
been draughted away, and that life was a hard struggle for
those who were left, with taxation weighing them down
heavily, and bread growing daily dearer, while the crops
were spoiling for want of labourers in the fields. At Innsbruck we saw regiment after regiment pass on to the front,
Jäger in heavy marching order travel-stained and weary,
the soldiers in their grey greatcoats and with their slow
tread, offering a great contrast to the little active wiry
men we had been accustomed to see among the Italian
sharpshooters. It was difficult to believe those good
placid faces could ever kindle into sudden fire and energy
when the need came; possibly a slow match is surer in
the end than one that spits out little flames and sparkles
and glistens before the train is ready to be lighted.

We saw nothing of the far-famed Austrian cavalry, but
at every little village there were gatherings of the people
round the inns, and drilling was going on throughout the

day by red-faced *Unterofficieren*, with much shouting and
gesticulation; and it was strange to meet suddenly, as we
did one day, a detachment of artillery in a quiet bye-lane,
kicking horses dragging a great cannon between hedges
green with their first spring freshness, and where the
wide-eyed peasant children stared dumb and awestruck,
half hidden in the dust from the heavy wheels.

There is a great deal of old German life and obsolete
custom lingering among the Tyrolers, and a quaintness in
costume and thought and word, that in other regions has
merged itself in the onward rush of more civilised life.
The peasants whom you meet greet you heartily with
'grüss Gott,' the ordinary salutation; or, 'Gott sei dank
für Jesus Christus;' and you answer, 'der für uns gestor-
ben ist. In Ewigkeit. Amen,' and the solemn words
never seemed to us irreverent, but to be a part of that
simple trustful life, though the 'grüss Gott' has grown
into so common an address that it has almost lost its
original significance, like the 'God be with you!' of our
'Good-bye!' These Tyrol peasants are very hospitable,
and seem heartily glad to see travellers, and even the
innkeepers absolutely avoid making them their prey.
The charges for the best food and accommodation the
inns could supply were often ludicrously small, and the
travelling is much cheaper than in Switzerland; strangely
enough, we found our Swiss guides spent more than they
would have done amongst their own mountains—and we

In the Zillerthal.—changing horses.

had to make them an extra allowance. The Tyroler does not seem to regard them as the institution they are looked upon as elsewhere, and they are not made welcome, as in their own country, for the sake of the travellers they bring. But for ordinary tourists who do not attempt the higher mountains, or require first-rate *Bergführer*, but are satisfied with the local guides, and who are themselves pedestrians, a few weeks in the Tyrol can be accomplished at considerably less cost than a tour of the same length in Switzerland, even allowing for the more expensive railway journey before they are on their ground. Of course posting or travelling *vetturino*, and first-class mountaineering must be pretty much the same everywhere—but the Tyrol innkeepers *have* consciences.

Christian recounted to us one day with great indignation an adventure that had befallen them on descending from the Gross Glockner, when footsore and weary, begrimed with dust, and their clothes none the better for hard work over rocks and snow and ice, and a tramp of many hours, he halted with F. at the little inn at Kals, where they rested on a bench in the open hall. In their hands were their ice-axes and a great coil of rope hung over their shoulders, and unwashed and unshaven, they were no doubt pitiable objects to behold, and so thought the good-hearted little Kellnerin, who, in her master's absence, ran to the oven, and drawing out a great loaf of bread, brought it to F. with a kindly greeting, while Almer, gazing at her in horror, exclaimed ' Wir sind keine Bettler; das ist ein Herr!' sending back the poor little Samaritan blushing to her stew-pans, after many explanatory ejaculations that, seeing the ropes and the dust on their boots, and how tired they were, she had believed they were wandering journey-men, rope makers (' Strichmacher') looking for work, to whom the good bread would be welcome. But while we gossiped over Tyrol customs, and watched the peasants from our windows at Zell, the horses were being har-nessed, and the men were impatient to be off.

Madame and the little *Kammermädchen* quite clung to us at parting, bringing us bouquets of sweet fresh flowers, and imploring us to return.

' Wollen Sie nicht gewiss zurückkommen, oder jeden-falls uns recommandiren; nicht wahr?' with a sudden eye to business and a tender pressure of our hands.

The bugles had sounded merrily, and the *Freiwillige* were ranged in order before the door as we drove away. Of those great brave awkward peasants, how many may not have fallen, silently gathered in by the grim Prussian death, before the grass they had been mowing that early spring morning had turned dry and golden under their old roofs at home!

The Tyroler in these mountain valleys are an honest people, strong in their simple beliefs and diligent in prayers. Often we heard them chaunting a solemn thanks-giving round the great table on which a mighty stew of

A mountain toilette!

' Wir sind keine Bettler !'

beans or polenta waited the onslaught of their wooden
spoons: masters and herdsmen and the women of the
house, each in their place, as in the good old Saxon times,
when churl and hind ate plum-porridge at a festival, sitting
below the salt.

Good faithful hearts, true to ' Gott und Kaiser,' fighting vainly for a broken cause and a fatal creed! God
grant that from that baptism of blood a new fatherland
may arise, strengthened and purified, and worthy of its
great destiny in the future!

A NIGHT

ON

THE SUMMIT OF MONTE VISO.

———◆———

'Being dight
In a thick caoutchouc yclept a bag,
That was well-lyned all, and yet was lighte,
And on his head the hood thereof he had,
From which the sweat, as he had chauffed been,
Did drop—the whilome snow his breath diswrought;
But meek-eyed Sleepe was frighted at the scene,
And his strange guise, and fled all vainly sought,
And he through weary hours to little joy was brought.'

After SPENSER.

A NIGHT ON THE SUMMIT OF MONTE VISO.

ON July 2, 1862, in company with my guides, Michel Auguste Croz of Chamouni and Peter Perrn of Zermatt, I left Turin for Pinerolo, proceeding the same afternoon as far as La Torre. On the following day we ascended the Val Pellice, engaging at Bobbio a good-natured, tough little fellow, Bartolommeo Peyrotte by name, as porter, for 2 francs 45 centimes and his food per diem, and reaching at 4 P.M. the summit of the Col de Seylières, where a glorious view of the Viso at once burst upon us.

We lingered there for an hour, and at five commenced the descent into the head of the valley of the Guil, which bears the name of the Vallon de Viso. Intersecting the route of the Col de Traversette, we skirted the slopes on the left, so as to avoid all unnecessary descent, and then, once more mounting, gained the summit of the Col de Vallante at 6.30. The weather was exquisite; and the sun, now getting low in the western sky, sent a blaze of golden glory on the rocky mass of the Viso, which towered up close at hand in the most majestic manner. The descent on the side of the Val Vallante is rapid, but presents no difficulty.   At the highest châlets we found inhabitants, but, either naturally churlish or suspecting our appearance, they positively declined either to take us in or sell us a draught of milk.   At the next lower group, which we reached about eight o'clock, we met with the utmost kindness and civility, the *berger* and his wife welcoming us heartily, apologising for the scantiness of their means of entertainment, and begging us to avail ourselves of them, such as they were, to the utmost.   The invitation was gladly accepted, a pot of milk and chocolate (the latter of course provided by us) was soon boiling merrily over the fire ; and refreshed by a hearty supper, yet sufficiently tired to make any bed welcome, we stretched ourselves upon some hay, and were soon in the land of dreams.

My sleeping-bag here came into requisition for the first time, and as I shall have occasion to refer to it again, I may perhaps be permitted a short description of its construction.   My friend, Mr. Galton, having kindly lent me a bag he has had constructed on the plan of those used by the French *préposés* in the Pyrenees, and described by him in the first series of ' Vacation Tourists,' my first attempt was little more than a copy of the model in question.   Composed externally of macintosh, it was lined with thick homespun Welsh cloth, and on the two or three occasions when I had an opportunity of testing its capa-

bilities in 1861, though answering the purpose of keeping
out the cold, its retention of the insensible perspiration
proved its weak point. To obviate this, my second attempt,
whilst covered with macintosh on its under side, and on
the upper surface, for a distance of about fifteen inches
from the foot, consisted simply of a bag of very stout and
dense scarlet blanketing (of the description known as
'swan-skin') opening like a shirt-front to admit the body,
and provided with two arm-holes for greater convenience
and facility of movement.   At the point where the upper
surface of macintosh terminated, a sort of bib or apron of
the same woollen material commenced, and could either be
thrown back over the feet if not required, or drawn up to
the chin and secured by a button to each shoulder if
greater warmth was desirable.   A hood or *capote*, also of
woollen, but uncovered with macintosh, to facilitate the
escape of perspiration and confined air, and constructed
after the fashion of Arctic head-gear, completed the
ordinary means of protection. 'Stuffiness,' however, though
a serious drawback, might be put up with in the event of
a night of rain or snow in preference to a state of more
or less complete saturation; and, therefore, in order to
provide against such a contingency, I added a loose sheet
of macintosh, with button-holes down each side, by which
it could be attached to a corresponding series of buttons
on the bag, and thus render the latter impervious to water.
As the material is exceedingly light, I had this sheet made

considerably wider than was necessary, and when not
required for the bag, it proved very useful as an addition
to the wraps of my guides, keeping out the wind admirably,
and lessening the one great objection to the use of sleeping
bags, the force of which I cannot wholly get over, viz. that
unless similar provision be made for the whole party, it
seems hardly fair to expose others to the hardships which
occasionally attend the practice of bivouacking. To conclude, the weight of the whole concern is about 8½ lbs.,
and as it is quite capable of doing duty as a knapsack, it
may for a time be made to take the place of that otherwise
almost indispensable article, either for clothes or provisions.
Indeed, I generally pack in it a small macintosh case,
which holds a spare pair of flannel trowsers, shirt, and
socks, as a change in the event of being overtaken by wet
before reaching the intended *gîte*. For I need hardly say
that however well protected when once inside one's dormi-
tory, it would be extremely unwise to risk a night, *sub
Jove frigido*, in rain-soaked garments. The wet clothes,
when taken off, may be stuffed into the case, which then
makes a by no means contemptible pillow. Thus much
premised, I will now proceed with my narrative, in the
course of which I hope to be able to show that my bed
fulfilled my most sanguine anticipations, and proved a
most valuable ally. It was made for me by Messrs. Heyes
& Co., waterproofers, of Bristol, at an expense of 1*l*. 12*s*.

for the bag, 12s. for the sheet, and 2s. 6d. for the clothes-case; I supplying the 'swan-skin,' which cost 1l. 2s.

As I proposed, weather permitting, to spend the night on the summit of the Viso, and it was clear that we had not a long day's work before us, we were in no hurry to quit the friendly shelter of the châlet; but at 8.15 on the morning of the 4th, after a hearty breakfast of bread and milk, we bade adieu to our hosts, and proceeded to climb the wooded slope immediately behind and to the E. of our quarters, which forms the southern prolongation of the Petit Viso, and the W. boundary of the Vallon delle Forciolline. After an ascent of about one hour's duration, we quitted the upper limits of the pine, and entered upon a region of grassy slopes, followed by débris, over which the remainder of our route almost uninterruptedly led. At 9.45 a short halt was called, and then, traversing a sort of shoulder or col, we found ourselves, at 10.30, on the bank of one of a chain of small lakes or tarns nestling in the bosom of the mountain, not far from the point at which the ascent to the Col delle Sagnette commences. These are formed by the melting of the snow-slopes above, and their surplus water is discharged through a rocky gorge into the Vallon delle Forciolline. The scenery is very striking, the huge and splintered crags around being reflected in the calm waters, ere they go dashing onwards to the valley below; and we lingered half an hour, under pretence of demolishing a second breakfast, in the shape

of a hard-boiled egg apiece.   Skirting the slopes of débris
which descend from the jagged ridge on the E., traversed
by the Col delle Sagnette, and avoiding the mistake of
our predecessors, Messrs. Mathews and Jacomb, which led
them to the summit of the Petit Viso, we reached, at 11.45,
the base of the steeper portion of the mountain.   As snow
had now to be ascended for a considerable distance, gaiters
were put on, though probably they would scarcely be
needed later in the season.   A steady, but leisurely progress for an hour and three-quarters, sometimes over rocks
and up couloirs, varied by occasional step-cutting, brought
us at 1.45 to the crest of the ridge descending from the
summit in a SSE. direction towards the Col delle Sagnette.

So far all had gone on smoothly, and time being less
than ever an object, it was decided to halt here for dinner,
rather than delay till the summit should be reached.
From the position we had now attained, the eye roamed
over the valleys of the Lenta and Po, and far away beyond
them to the boundless expanse of the great plain of
Piedmont, whilst above us the summit of the Viso towered
up in rugged grandeur.   The remainder of the ascent
gave us little trouble, except where the rocks were
covered with hard ice, rendering extra care and an occasional resort to the axe necessary.   An hour and a half
sufficed for the climb, and at 3.30 we stood on the summit,
just $7\frac{1}{4}$ hours ($1\frac{1}{2}$ of which must be deducted for halts)
after quitting the Châlets de Vallante.   The ridge

connecting the E. and W. peaks was, owing to the recent snow, in such a dangerous condition, and the advantage of attempting to reach the latter appeared so questionable, that we decided to rest satisfied with having attained the point which—thanks perhaps to its snowy cap—was, at the time of our visit, decidedly the loftiest. After an unsuccessful search for the minimum thermometer attached to the cairn erected by Messrs. Mathews and Jacomb, which was in good order and remarkably solid, I proceeded to instal my barometer, spread out my wet socks to dry, and examine the view, whilst the men busied themselves with small local explorations, pipes, and the conversion of very unpromising materials into a *gîte*. I shall not here dwell on the grandeur and beauty of a panorama, to which full justice has already been done by the first conqueror of this supposed inaccessible peak, but I may just remark that, after long and careful examination, I came to the conclusion that the Mediterranean was certainly not to be *distinguished* from the haze of the southern horizon. At the same time it results from a careful calculation of the effects of curvature and refraction that the Viso would be *visible* from the sea, at a distance of 148 miles, or 83 miles from the shore in the direction of the Col di Tenda, while this latter being 6,158 feet in height would vanish beneath the horizon at a distance of 103 miles, or 76 from the shore. Hence it follows that there is no obstacle to the sea being seen from the Viso,

I

or *vice versâ*, but the imperfection of the human vision or the haze of the atmosphere. It seemed to me just possible that some exceedingly distant high land seen almost over the Col di Tenda, and apparently separated from the range of the Maritime Alps by an expanse of *brouillard* such as would be produced by a large surface of water, might be the Monte Rotondo in the Island of Corsica. The height of this summit is 9,068 feet, but its distance is so great (200 miles) that the utmost I can claim for my supposition is that it is not physically impossible, the Viso being, as already stated, visible from the sea-level at 148 miles, whilst the Monte Rotondo is seen at 125.*

Though the mountains of Dauphiné are very well seen from the Viso, the position of the sun rendered their details extremely confused, and as their forms were comparative strangers to me, I could do nothing in the way of identification or determination of bearings with the theodolite. Reserving this for the morning, when the first condition would be reversed in my favour, and whilst the barometer was being allowed to settle, I deposited in the cairn one of Casella's new mercurial minimums and a Phillips' maximum by the same maker, to which I beg to call the attention of future comers.

At five, six, and seven o'clock I read off the barometer,

---

* I have since been informed by my friend Mr. Brown, of Genoa, that the Viso has been distinguished from at least one point on the Riviera di Levante.

and the mean resultant height deduced from comparisons
with Turin, Aosta, Geneva, and the Great St. Bernard,
comes out 3,860·1 metres (12,664 feet).   A fourth observation at 5·30 the following morning, similarly compared, gives the lower result of 3,840·3 metres (12,600
feet).   The former is within four feet of Mr. Mathews'
determination (12,668 feet), and the latter within one
foot of the trigonometrical measurement of the Sardinian
engineers (12,599 feet), so that the mean of both (12,632
feet) is highly satisfactory.   The boiling point at 6 P.M.
was 190° Fahrenheit or 87·78° centigrade, which, by M.
Regnault's table, corresponds with a pressure of 482·53
millimetres.   Now the barometer at the same hour stood
at 482·1 millimetres, and the difference, 0·43 millimetre,
is precisely the same as that found a week previously
on the summit of the Grivola.   Comparing the mean of
the readings of the barometer at five, six, and seven P.M.
(482·2 millimetres), with that of the aneroid (one of
Sécrétau's) for the same hours (477·2 millimetres), we
find a difference of 5 millimetres, an increase upon that
found on the Grivola, which was only 3·2 millimetres.
A similar comparison of the observation at 5·30 the
following morning, reduces the discrepancy to 4·3 millimetres, and the mean would therefore be 4·6 millimetres;
but as on the 2nd, at Turin, the error was already
precisely the same in amount, if this were used as a

I 2

correction, the two instruments would be absolutely accordant.

The sunset was magnificent, the huge pointed shadow of the mountain stretching away over the light veil of fleecy clouds which began to cover the surface of the Italian plain; but as at seven o'clock the temperature had already fallen to—2° C. (28·4° Fahrenheit), and the wind was beginning to rise, my position on the summit became rather exposed, and the question of shelter and a bivouac assumed increased importance. The sound of falling stones had for some time indicated considerable activity on the part of my companions, who had left me to attend to my '*machines*;' but on rejoining them, I found that their united efforts had made but little progress in the construction of a *gîte*. A small surface of ground at a point about forty feet below the summit had, indeed, been to some extent cleared of débris, and a sort of wall constructed of loose stones on the side of the precipice, but not a single jutting fragment offered even partial protection from radiation, and the creation of a tolerably level surface on a slope of 10° or 15° had proved an absolutely insoluble problem. The appearance of the weather, too, was by no means reassuring, and as fitful gusts of wind moaned amongst the crags, and the dull grey vapours came stealing up from the valleys, I confess I began to feel doubtful about the wisdom of the whole proceeding. There was no help for it now, however, as darkness was coming on apace; so,

Proofs of the activity of F's companions.

They arrange their costume for the night

whilst the final touches were being given to our nest, I
occupied myself with heating a bottle of wine in my boiling apparatus by way of night-cap. Peyrotte then got
into the sack in which he always used to carry his load,
Croz indued a comfortable knitted woollen head-piece, and
Perrn a seal-skin cap, with ample flaps to come over the
ears, which I had lent him.   Finally, covering themselves
with a *couverture* which we had borrowed at the châlets,
my companions drew my macintosh sheet over outside to
make all snug.   I meanwhile entered the bag, and, planting my feet firmly against a rock to prevent slipping, endeavoured to compose myself to rest, but the intensity of
the cold, aggravated by the wind, combined with an uneasy
position and the constant sense of being in motion downwards, proved too much for me; and, after long and per-
severing efforts, I calmly abandoned myself to a perpetual
condition of semi-conscious wriggling.   The time seemed
to pass very slowly, as usual under such circumstances;
but after what appeared to be hours of wakefulness I at
length dropped off, and did not rouse again, at least more
than partially, till about 2.30 A.M.   I had buried my face
so completely in the *capote*, and so closed every cranny
with a handkerchief, that at first it was difficult to ascertain the state of affairs, but an icy cold drop of water falling on my nose through some unguarded chink roused me
completely, and on peering out, I perceived to my surprise
that everything around was white, nearly an inch of snow

lay on my chest, and thick sleet mingled with fog was
falling. The prospect was anything but cheering, and my
feelings were so nearly akin to the painful, that I confess
the thought of having to hold out for some hours more
was peculiarly unwelcome. Still, though cold, I felt I
could yet bid defiance to the weather, and any grumblings
that tried to make themselves heard were silenced by the
sense of satisfaction at the manner in which my bag bore
the severe test to which it was exposed. A temperature of
—2·5° C. (27·5° Fahr.), as shown by a thermometer protected from radiation, snow, wind, and damp, the worst
possible combination in short, were all rendered endurable
by its means, and this in itself was worth finding out at
the expense of some little personal discomfort. Meanwhile, the guides were, I fear, in much more miserable
plight; for though tolerably protected, and having the
advantage of mutual warmth, they naturally were unsup-
ported by the same enthusiasm, and from poor Peyrotte's
sack especially dolorous groans would from time to time
issue. I ventured to cheer him by suggesting that the
honour of being the first subject of the king of Italy who
had reached the summit of the Viso, and passed a night
on it into the bargain, lasting for his life, and rendering
him famous to generations of Bobbioites yet unborn, would
amply atone for a few short hours of exposure. Besides,
it would recommend him to future travellers, who might
take him as guide on the strength of this performance. I
found, however, that all my eloquence was wasted, and

2 a.m. 28·4° Fahrenheit

3 a.m 27·5° Fahrenheit.

Caoutchouc versus Snow.

6. a m. they despair of taking observations.

that he would have sacrificed the brilliant future portrayed
had it been in his power to escape.   Thus time went on,
and sometimes we dozed, and sometimes we peered out
into the mist to see if there were any signs of its disappearing ; but at length, about 5.15, there being no appearance
of improvement, our little encampment was broken up, a
hasty breakfast taken, and the barometer observed and put
up in a very rusty condition from its long exposure to the
damp.   At six, despairing of any opportunity for using the
theodolite, which had been dragged up with considerable
trouble, we set out on our return.

As we descended the snow gradually diminished, then
ceased altogether, and at last we emerged from the cloud
which hung densely round the upper portion of the mountain and clung to it throughout the day.   The fresh-fallen
snow rendered caution necessary, and our progress was
slow, but at 7.45 we reached the foot of the steepest portion of the descent, about half an hour above the tarns
already described, and halting till 8.15 for breakfast,
arrived at the châlets in about two hours more, or at
10.15.   The time occupied in the ascent and descent was
therefore $7\frac{1}{4}$ and $4\frac{1}{4}$ hours respectively, including halts,
which amounted to an hour and a half in the first case,
and half an hour in the second.   At 2.30, we proceeded
down the Vallon di Vallante to Ponte Castello, whence a
pleasant walk of little more than an hour towards the head
of the Val Vraita brought us, at 4.45, to La Chianale, thus
terminating a most interesting expedition.

SKETCHES FROM PONTRESINA.

'Hills draw like Heaven,
And stronger sometimes, holding out their hands
To pull you from the vile flats up to them.'
E. B. BROWNING.

'Ah! bitter chill it was;
The owl, for all his feathers, was a-cold;
The hare limp'd trembling through the frozen grass,
And silent was the flock in woolly fold.'
KEATS.

———◦◦◦———

A HEAVY storm of wind and rain and snow had kept us prisoners all day, and we had nearly exhausted our resources. The stove in the little salon could not be lighted, on account of the smoke; and even with the piano (which is a very good one), the most ardent musician could not have supported life there for many hours if he were to be entirely dependent on the warmth of his feelings for any extra amount of caloric. The great *salle-à-manger* was still in process of preparation for the season, and damp with premonitory scrubbings. There remained the *stube* and the *café*. In the latter apartment we had spent many hours, and found them somewhat tedious. The clouds were low in the valley, and there was no view. We had read through the last pile of serials and papers from England. We had written our journals; had painted numberless small studies of wild-flowers, with mosses, leaves, and branches of wood and stones grey and golden with lichens, much to the astonishment of the *kellnerin*, who, when E. challenged her admiration for her handful of treasures, said, ' Ah, yes, she noticed that the foreigners

cared for sticks; as for her, she saw so many pieces of
wood, she was accustomed to them.'

We had the great hotel almost to ourselves, and had
taken vigorous exercise in the large unfurnished rooms,
and up and down the passages, and still the pitiless snow
fell, and the wind blew, rattled against the windows, and
shook the jalousies, making us humble and imploring as to
the matter of fuel, in which we considered ourselves somewhat stinted.   Half frozen, and sighing for real summer
and warmth, we appealed to Frau Gredig in the choicest
German, explaining our sufferings ;—that we, delicate
English, were not accustomed to reside in ice-houses, to
be frozen to the floors, to warm ourselves over the eggs at
breakfast; and live through the afternoons on the thought
of securing a little steam from the urn at tea.   'Feel our
hands, madame, and see how we suffer !'

Frau Gredig had not a bad heart.   For a moment, as
she took the suffering fingers into her maternal grasp, her
countenance relaxed, a gleam of compassion shone in her
eye, and a cry for more fuel trembled on her lips; but
second thoughts proved safest.   With a vigorous rub she
administered present consolation and a valuable moral
truth.

'It is not the fault of the climate that you suffer,
Fräulein.   *I* am not cold; my sister is not cold; and
why?   We run about from morning till night.   My head
and my hands are full.   We have to think and plan, and

do for you all, and—ach, mein Gott, sind wir nicht warm genug?'

Driven from all hope of external comfort, we evolved heat from our internal consciousness, and warmed ourselves by the brilliancy of our own imaginations. D. and C. had conceived a wonderful thought. We would utilize the snow. We would plan a day of delights to be realized from it, the very thought of which would cause every flake that fell to be hailed with jubilations. We would make a grand *schlitten partie* to the Bernina Pass. A messenger was sent to summon Walther, and we all eagerly discussed preliminaries.

Bartholome Walther, one of the pleasantest guides in Switzerland, and a capital one for ladies, had been with us as a sort of travelling-servant for some weeks past during our wanderings in Tyrol, and, though now off duty, was still considered as belonging, in a semi-attached fashion, to our party. He lived in one of the large houses forming the main street of the little Pontresina village, which, as it is a fair type of the homes of the people, may be worth a word or two of description. On the ground-floor was a small shop, a stable for cows and horses, a dairy well stocked, a large dark entrance-hall, roughly paved, with the usual arched wooden doors, a staircase leading to a hay-loft, where a *bergwagen* was stowed away, (how they got their carriages there I could never tell, but you invariably found them on the first floor,) and a pleasant little *stube* or living-room, wainscoted with wood, built like a nest into the great stone and plaster erection, the deep setting of the window, gay with flowering plants and shrubs, showing how great the cold must be in winter, and somewhere under the eaves no doubt a little colony of sleeping-rooms, into which we did not penetrate. It is a sort of *home farm*; everything is stored under the one roof, and when the long dark winter days set in, the women's work at least may be done under shelter. Madame Walther, a pleasant-faced, soft-voiced woman, always made us very welcome, and she and her little daughter were proud to show their pans of rich cream and stores of butter. 'Nine months of winter and three of bad weather,' say the Engadine peasants. They are wise, certainly, to gather all they can under their home eaves. The men, who during their short season are employed as guides by travellers, busy themselves when the strangers have departed in carrying on their wine-trade with the Valtelline. Early in the morning men and horses start for the summit of the Bernina Pass, floundering through the deep snow, the good clever beasts sometimes moving steadily forward on their knees, when unable to keep their footing, till they reach the shelter of the hut which marks the highest ground, and here they meet the people from the southern valleys with their casks of wine. Three or four times a week the journey is made, the Engadiners returning with well-laden sleighs to the village.

Walther entered with proper spirit into our plans and wishes, promised us great enjoyment for the morrow, fine weather, and plenty of snow; two *Bergwägen* were to be at the door at eight o'clock, and we went to sleep in a state of high contentment, to dream of wonderful adventures and successes. We were up early, and, breakfast over, started in full mountaineering costume, well prepared for whatever might befal us, with linsey or serge dresses arranged as riding-habits in case of need, boots stout and strong and rich in nails, our especial pride and boast, alpen-stocks, coloured spectacles, veils, and linen masks, the 'weisse Teufel' head-dresses now becoming well known to Swiss natives as another wonderful idiosyncrasy of the English. The men had provided two very small sledges, but we were as yet ignorant of how they could by any possibility be good at need. Walther had arranged for the regular post sledges to be ready for us when we reached the snow. The day was perfectly cloudless, the sky of the deepest blue, the marvellously beautiful range of the Bernina—Piz Palü, Piz Bernina, Piz Morteratsch, and other mighty mountains—rising up in almost dazzling whiteness against the clear background of colour. The sun was pleasantly warm, even at that early hour, and there was fortunately very little wind; we were in the highest possible spirits, and prepared to find amusement out of everything; the horses even seemed to share our enjoyment, as they trotted on, tossing their heads to the

merry music of their bells and the gay songs of the drivers.
As the way grew steeper we were glad to walk and to get
thoroughly warmed by exercise, before encountering a possible snow-bath higher up.   The road is a new one, made
about three years ago, but still liable to much injury from
the avalanches, which have been unusually frequent during this year.   In some places all the telegraph posts were
destroyed, and a sad desolation marked the course of the
snow—uprooted trees and masses of stone and broken
walls showing where it had passed.

We halted at the Bernina Wirthshaus, rather less than
two hours from Pontresina, to order dinner to be ready on
our return, and then climbed still higher; the snow lying
thickly all around us, not even a tree or rock to be seen,
nothing but a white wilderness, with soft blue shadows in
the hollows of the hills; and solemnly marking our way
like silent fingerposts of fate, the telegraph poles rose at
regular intervals, struggling up through the mass of snow,
sometimes scarcely showing a few feet above the ground,
though our road so far had been dug out and beaten hard,
and the travelling was by no means bad; but suddenly it
came to an end, winter reasserted itself, and the snow had
it all its own way. We dismounted, fastened on with
great care spectacles and masks, the men following our
example, and arranging their veils and glasses, and then
busying themselves in transferring the horses to the sledges,
which were lying by the side of the road, fastening the

seats from our *bergwagen* on to the slight wooden frame-
work of the runners. We watched, meanwhile, with much
amusement, a drove of small black pigs who were dis-
porting themselves on the snow, being ignominiously
captured by a leg or an ear, and tossed into a cart, where
they subsided into a most uncomfortable heap, with
shrieks guttural and expostulatory.

The sledges were soon prepared, and we mounted to our
places, D. and E., under Walther's care, heading the procession. They were very well off, the guide having
fastened the seat of his *bergwagen* bodily, by means of
cords, to the runners, so that they had something to cling
to besides each other. Mrs. C. and C. were not so
fortunate, they being enthroned on a long box, sitting
back to back, with a loose cross-board for the feet, and
nothing particular to lay hold of. A few yards brought us
to the place where a gang of labourers were at work
cutting out the roadway; unfortunately they had begun
laterally, and a great slice of hard snow was already gone,
leaving only a narrow ledge or shelf, not wide enough for
our carriages. But the peasants were good-natured, and
willing to put their shoulders to the wheel; that is to say
(having a strict regard to truth), they held up the runners
on one side to prevent our toppling over; and that
difficulty passed, we dashed on in famous style. The
workmen, with their veiled faces and goggle eyes, standing
silently in the dismal trenches, looked like a troop of weird

ghosts, who had somehow strayed from the Inferno, and were fated to dig their way down again into the darkness, while we mere earthly travellers passed on into higher air.

The horses rushed over the snow, and flung up the cold white masses into our faces, pelting us with snow-balls with their eager feet; a man stood behind each sledge balanced between the runners, and drove over our heads, with shout and song urging on the horses. Whenever we dared to turn our heads the sight was one never to be forgotten: C. and her companion, in an agony of terror and laughter, holding on by the strength of a fixed determination, and looking out despairingly for side jolts which might upset their equilibrium. A joyful shout reached us, and Mrs. C. announced that she had found a rope to hold by, and was very comfortable: a short-lived happiness, as the next moment she discovered she had been clinging to her own crinoline, from which no difficulties of the way had ever separated her.

We went on and on, the only moving things in that beautiful still snow world, except one little marmot, who raced away in the distance, uttering his shrill cry; a lake lay near us, but so covered over that only here and there a green glimmer of ice was to be seen. The mountains were entirely veiled, the great gallery on the Italian side was roofed with snow, which was piled up within and about it. Here our expedition ended, as we did mot wish to give our poor horses a toilsome ascent; so dismounting, we walked down the hill, and plunged into the soft bank beside the road, gaining the entrance to the first arches in order to see the immense icicles that fringed them, and then prepared to return in different order, D. being anxious to try her power of keeping her place on the wooden box. The pace was glorious, and it was the greatest possible fun to spin along through the snow—great hard masses balling under us, and throwing sledge, and seat, and travellers suddenly from side to side, as we dashed round corners, half blinded by the dazzling brightness; the cold and the speed at which we went taking away our breath with almost a terror of delight. Writing now in a warm quiet English home, such raptures sound too foolish to repeat, but our enjoyment was ecstatic while it lasted, our sensations so entirely new,—except in so far as old childish dreams came back of wonderful Siberian journeys, and tales of adventure with dogs and reindeer. And then it was our own escapade, and had not been ‘cut and dried,’ and arranged for us by the powers that be! There had not been such a season for thirty years, and there might never be another when such an expedition could be made in June. Of course, there could never be another; of that we felt quite sure, and we laughed in our content, like a rabid connoisseur who hugs himself in silent delight over the contemplation of a rare engraving, knowing that the plate has been destroyed.

K

Our day was unique,—a beautiful completeness, which could only live again in our memories.

And then there was the dinner. Other people may come to that little inn, and may dine there, but not with such appetites as ours. And again fortune favoured us; there had been a wedding on the Sunday, and the remains of the feast graced the board. In romantic descriptions of the highest class it is inadmissible to speak of a table simply as such; whatever may be the number of its legs, whether it be round or square or oblong, it invariably becomes a board and generally *groans*; and this practice probably originated the first idea of mahogany as a spiritual *habitat*; it may to many minds afford a triumphant refutation of the notions of idle cavillers who profess to regard the legends of Tintagel as vague myths, that the knights of King Arthur invariably met at a table; the use of that simple word conveying a sense of remote antiquity, and a quaint rudeness of expression, bearing, by all rules of criticism, a genuine stamp of truth that must be perfectly irresistible! Fancy an erection of spun sugar and a bouquet of roses in a little wainscoted salon, through the windows of which we looked out on nothing but the same dream of snow. That sugar temple and the flowers added the element of poetry to the adventure which was lacking in our prosaic and realistic minds. We grew sentimental with the good Wirthin over their festivities, and rested and talked and fraternised with the bright-

Our "schlitten partie"!

faced domestics, examined the kitchen, and saw that our men were well cared for ; and then, just as a lazy content was stealing over us, and even a somnolent tendency had manifested itself in Mrs. C., we were summoned by Walther and his companion, who carried the small sledges slung by ropes over their shoulders.   These are less than a yard long, and about eighteen inches in width, and are formed of small transverse pieces of wood, attached to iron runners, the rope being fastened to the front.

The men walked up a steep slope of snow, and we plodded after them, with many stumbles in the soft mass. At last, landed on a piece of stone which offered sure footing, we prepared to start.   Seating ourselves on the sledges, with our feet extended, we steered ourselves, and by a vigorous dig with our heels could come to a stop at pleasure.   At first, the men took the ropes and ran with us, but the sensation was horrible of being dragged into infinite space, with nothing earthly to hold to, but crumbling or melting snow.   When, however, we took the reins into our own hands the whole thing was different, and became an indescribable pleasure—a swift shooting through the air without sense of obstruction.   I began to realise what a fine time, if they were only sentient, the arrows would have belonging to an archery club, where the members were not clever enough to hit anything.   But that was the difficulty, the one flaw in the perfect enjoyment of our performance ; *there was an end to it.*

As a Frenchman once graphically remarked:—'Dans
une chute il y a deux moments terribles: le départ et
l'arrivée. Le voyage en lui-même n'est rien. On cite
même un maçon qui, tombant d'un cinquième étage,
adressait au ciel, pendant la traversée, cette fervente
prière : "Mon Dieu, pourvu que ça dure!"'

The sun had considerable power, and it was hard work
to struggle up to the starting-post, marked by an alpenstock, preparatory to each fresh glissade.   At last, fairly
exhausted, E. took refuge with Mrs. C., who had camped
out on a damp piece of grass, a wholesome dread of wet
feet having made all our descriptions of delight fall heed-
lessly on her ears.   For a few minutes longer D. and C.
ran races against each other, a sudden unlucky turn of the
foot bringing up now one, now the other, as a very bad
second, in a snow-drift, while the winner was often pre-
cipitated most ingloriously into the cold soft mass at the
bottom of the slope.

The hours had passed so pleasantly that we hardly
realised how rapidly the shadows were lengthening, till
the *Bergwägen* were announced to be ready, and it was
time to turn our face homewards.   Contented and weary,
we were glad to find ourselves once more rattling down
the road, and we reached our old quarters as a golden
glow passing over the tops of the fir-trees, and shining
through the tufts and branches of the great Arolla pines,
left the earth in a cold, frosty twilight, settled down for a

On the Glacier.

A Bergwagen.

moment like a veil of light over the higher mountains, and then faded slowly into the pale clear greenness of the evening sky.

*   *   *   *   *   *.   *

We spent more than ten days at Pontresina, the pleasantest possible headquarters for mountaineers or for ladies. The valley is at an elevation of nearly six thousand feet, and the air is deliciously fresh and bracing, even in July; and early as we were there, with sunshine and fine weather, the cold was very bearable and wonderfully invigorating. The history of each day would fill a long paper, and cannot be given here. A morning on the Morteratsch glacier was among our pleasantest expeditions; the ice was in good order, comfortably crumbly on the surface, and affording us plenty of foothold. You may walk for miles over this great sea of dirty ice, which is anything but beautiful, as there are none of the aiguilles which make the great charm of the Oberland glaciers, and very little colour. Here and there in a deep crevasse, one sees a tinge of soft sea-green, and the *moulins*, formed by little hidden streams forcing their way through the fissures, make an amusing variety in one's path; but as a whole, it is decidedly dull. At least, I can only write of it as we found it, and we may be told that 'as a whole' we did not see it, for truth obliges me to confess that wonderful descriptions of the beauty and grandeur of the ice-fall, 'combining the solemnity of cathedral architecture and the fantastic decorations of a Chinese pagoda, Druidical beards and dripping caves gleaming with diamonds in the sunlight,' have reached us from those who penetrated further than an inexorable fate allowed us to proceed. In our experience, the cracks in the ice were only a few inches apart, so there was nothing to jump over, and during our expedition it afforded such good foothold that there was no excuse for slipping. The amphitheatre of hills enclosing this great frozen sea has few rivals in grandeur, when, as we saw it, a great white mantle of snow sweeping from each summit, falls as in soft, noiseless folds, to meet the rugged mass of ice below. The little woods skirting the end of the glacier are full of beauty, and near by there is a waterfall that in any other place would alone be an object of pilgrimage. The water-meadows were like a brilliant flower-bed, gay with patches of gentians and forget-me-nots, masses of purple primulas, yellow pansies, and delicate little soldinella ; and clustering round the stones and rocks were sweet-scented daphnes and white crocuses, which sprout up on the barest-looking ground a few hours after the snow has melted from its surface.

These meadows, and the woods which skirt them, had a wonderful charm for us. A broad river flowed through the midst, often spreading itself over the valley when the warm sun melted the snows, and when the waters drew back again into their stony channel, grass, and moss, and flowers sprang up on the instant into vivid life; the trees cast their twisted roots about the soil to hold it fast, binding it with grey lichens and little fir twigs, and a soft carpet of dead leaves from last year's store; and before the hay was grown and there could be the sweet summer scent of mown grass drying in the wind, there was everywhere a garden of flowers, golden and violet, with soft pink blooms, and the blue gentians with their bright little eyes; the stones were encrusted with orange and scarlet lichens, and gray fringes hung in festoons from the old trees; the ice in great billows and ridges came down into the grass, turning it back in long furrows in its steady advance year by year, and down the rocks rivulets of cold snow-water trickled from among the stones, bubbled up under the moss, and turned into a sudden cloud of spray as they sprang from any jutting crag into the river at their feet; and far above, as solemn sentinels, the great snow mountains closed around the valley. Days among the Alps, though full of commonplace adventure and merriment, and the prose of ordinary life a little caricatured, are rich in deeper thoughts and feeling. There is a stronger spell than the mere love of exercising their muscles or the desire to conquer a new peak that takes men to the mountains, and he must have a poverty-stricken soul who does not return humbler indeed, but calmed and strengthened by a fresh revelation of the Divine power in which his life can rest.

The contrast of these mighty forces of nature,—ice and snow, torrent and avalanche, mist and cloud, and desolating power, and the tender beauty of the grass and flowers, and gentler life, held as in the hollow of a strong hand,—was very wonderful to see. This Morteratsch valley was a place that the old myths would have made beautiful and palpitating with life. Fair-faced Persephoné might have wandered through those meadows dimly conscious of a great dread where the cold darkness from the ice-caves fell across her path, as the mountain torrent spreading round her feet swept her away into the shadows. One dreams of a time when grand old Pan was strong and lusty, and could sing—

> " In my great veins—a music as of boughs
> When the cool aspen-fingers of the Rain
> Feel for the eyelids of the Earth in spring ; "

and Dryads made their home in the depths of the wood, where gnarled and twisted branches, gray-bearded and old, look like evil beings expiating their sins and cramped with rheumatism.

Evening after evening we watched the clouds draw away from the mountain tops, till they stood clear against the sky; the sunshine died from the earth, the fir-trees grew black, and a chill dimness crept over the soft gray meadows, and then suddenly a little flush spread over the crests of the mountains, and deepened into a rosy delight ;

one or two stray cloudlets caught the glory, that like a
great radiant smile touched them as it past, and then
slowly the light faded; a special beatitude vouchsafed to
the great mountains, emblems of purity and strength: a
host of Fra Angelico's gentle seraphs with their pink and
violet wings might have sung there their Gloria in Excelsis,
and sent their light upon the hills. And then came night,
and a frosty stillness and clear heaven studded with stars,
and a cold moonlight over silver snow.

In our wood walks up the Roseg Thal we often encountered droves of the long-eared sheep from the Italian
valleys, driven to the Alpine pastures by their Bergamesque
shepherds,—picturesque fellows, with dark, handsome
southern faces under the shadow of their broad hats,
roughly dressed in skins and leather leggings, tanned like
their faces by exposure to wind and weather.

A few miles away by the road and an hour distant from
Pontresina by a footpath through the wood, is the great
Bad-haus of St. Moritz, a ghastly water-cure establishment,
much frequented by true believers of all nations; where a
heterogeneous multitude are stowed away in hundreds of
little rooms, and live together in great cold salons, and
feed together, each after his own fashion in the matter of
forks or fingers, in an enormous *salle à manger*, and kill
time by drinking the waters, walking up and down the
passages, and watching for the diligence which has kindly
consented to go so far out of its way as to come round in

front of the great *établissement,* for the accommodation and amusement of the sufferers.

Beyond St. Moritz, there are little lakes, lying like gems set in a forest of pines, and more mountains, and wood, and waterfalls to be visited, all within easy reach of Herr Gredig's pleasant headquarters.

Our time at Pontresina was coming to an end, and we had been unable to accomplish the ascent of the Piz Languard,—an old friend we were anxious to revisit; but the quantity of snow, and its soft state, had hitherto made such an expedition impossible.   F. and his companion had joined us after a most successful ascent of the Piz Bernina by a new route, and entertained us with wonderful stories of their capture by the Austrians, as Italian spies; of a sudden attack made on them when peacefully reposing in a hay-loft; of a night-march with fixed bayonets down a horribly bad path; the completion of their broken slumbers in an Austrian fortress, the bayonets still on guard; and of a triumphant and apologetic acquittal from the gallant commandant in the morning.   In our state of excitement and suspense as to news from the army, which generally came to us first through the English papers, though there were Swiss troops at the time in the village, any one fresh from the frontier was doubly welcome, and our travellers joined us with somewhat of a halo of romance; and as to the guides, they were very great men indeed, and were duly glorified over wine and tobacco in

the *stube.* If the four were not patriots, they had been
considered a sufficiently good imitation, and vividly before
the imaginations of all hovered images of the horrors of an
Austrian dungeon !

Christian Almer, one of the heroes, looked as though he
had been kept on bread and water, and then dried and
smoked.   I never saw anything human so like an Egyptian
mummy or a red-herring ; but his miserable condition
was really due to the amount of work that had been
accomplished, and the great cold they had encountered.
Three passes and two new Spitze in twenty-four hours take
something out of a man, even the strongest, when you
have twenty-five degrees of frost at your lunching place.

The weather had broken up and looked very doubtful,
but with this accession to our numbers we were determined to make an attempt on the mountain.   Walther
and ten or twelve men went up on the Saturday to try to
make a little path through the snow by digging and
stamping it hard; and this they succeeded in doing in a
degree near the summit, where the snow lay less thickly
on the stones,—but anything like a tract was hopeless
lower down.   On Monday morning we were all called
soon after two ; the clouds looked threatening, but at that
early hour it was difficult to judge how the day would turn
out, and we hoped, at any rate, to make a good start.   It
is wonderful how the most glowing anticipations we may
have indulged in over night pale in the uncertain glimmer

of dawn. The only sensation E. admitted to being vividly conscious of, was a profound desire that some one would say it was raining hard, and there was nothing to be done but to go to sleep again. Of course this feeble expostulation of the flesh was crushed back instantly, and our spirits rising with the first plunge into cold water, we prepared to encounter hopefully the experiences of the coming day.

We had invited some English acquaintances to join our party—Major and Mrs. L., who were staying with us at the hotel, and Mr. N. and Lady L. N., from St. Moritz; and as we mustered our forces in the *salon* over an early breakfast, we rejoiced over the prospect of a successful ascent. It was very cold, and we were glad of warm dresses and plenty of wraps. C. was to remain behind; but a party of nine, exclusive of servants, started on horseback and on foot at three o'clock, with porters laden with provisions, three first-rate guides, and a following of boys or men belonging to the beasts. We rode for the first two hours in single file, with shouting comments on our steeds, on the weather, and on the comforts and discomforts of our saddles. These were wonderful constructions, on which you were mounted high above the horse's shoulder and very far forward; padded seats, on which it is difficult to keep your balance without pommel or stirrup, a flat board being substituted for the latter, which it is hopeless to try to grasp with your foot. Mrs. C. exhausted herself by her efforts to sustain nobly her equestrian reputation. One or two of the party were first-rate horsewomen; but the Engadine 'mounts' tried their mettle more than a five-barred gate or a stone-wall country with the hounds at home; and at every stumble of the animals during the slippery ascent a rider would fall forwards on the neck of the horse, or be jolted almost over its tail, with many outcries and much laughter. Poor Lady L. N. had provided herself with an English saddle, and set off in happy security, but her pony and the saddle would not fit; the pony was fat and the saddle was angular; and the mathematical problem how to make a round body fit into a square hole was proved to be insoluble, and the hopelessness of the attempt was illustrated by a sudden descent of the hapless rider, first on one side, then on the other, as the poor beast struggled up the winding path.

The track, such as it was, came to an end with the first snow, and here we dismissed our horses, and prepared for work. And now we discovered a flaw in the perfection of our mountaineering costume, which we had considered very perfect. Our riding-habits were looped well up over linsey petticoats, and the feminine mind exulted in the strong hobnailed boots, which looked as if they meant work; but unfortunately Mrs. I.—— alone had supplied herself with the leather leggings, which all travellers ought to know are essential to the comfort of any one intending to encounter a tramp through snow, and we thus found ourselves dependent on the charity of our companions. With great care and much expenditure of packthread, some leather or cloth gaiters, generously subscribed on the instant, were fastened over our boots ; but as the fit was by no means perfect, they soon became clogged with snow, and proved a very doubtful blessing. By this time clouds had gathered above us and round the higher mountains, and were rapidly rising below us, covering the valley and the little green lakes, and leaving stretched before us an uncomfortable mass of snow, with here and there a little oasis of stones, the only landmarks in its dreary uniformity.   It was very cold, a drizzling rain began to fall, and our spirits sank rapidly.   Light and sunshine would have made us go on our way rejoicing, but in the grey cold bleak dimness it was a dreary prospect to go up and up through deep snow into a cloud of snow-flakes, knowing all the time that we must come down again.   However, all being ready, we made our final plunge. F. put an ice-axe on his shoulder, and E. held firmly by the iron, keeping her alpenstock in the other hand ; and in single file we began the march. A few steps, and we were in a snowdrift, up to our knees, then to our waists, so firmly wedged into the soft mass that each step was a weary labour, and every muscle was strained and stretched before another yard could be gained.

For the first moment we felt thoroughly miserable and frightened, fancying the next we might go in over

our hats, or that we might start an avalanche on our own
account; but looking back at the slow procession of
figures showing dark against the white background, in
every attitude possible to struggling humanity, a sense of
the ludicrousness of the whole thing came to our help,
and amid peals of laughter we all agreed to consider our
difficulties infinitely amusing, and from that moment there
was no one so mean-spirited as even to ask under their
breath the reason of our encountering so much exertion,
and what we expected to see at the summit when we got
there?   The clouds rose up beneath us like the black roof
of a tent under which villagers and tourists might be tran-
quilly sleeping, the mist closed in damp and impenetrable,
wrapping us in a veil disagreeable and unexhilarating in
the highest degree. ' Ten minutes more of climbing and
everything was snow, and we were white all over, looking
like rash pillars of salt during the process of transforma-
tion, except where our breath melted out little blue and
black patches on our veils.   We stepped and stumbled on
bravely; every now and then a cry would pierce the
silence, and two or three men were needed to extricate
some unlucky pedestrian who had come upon a ' soft bit,'
and was half-stifled and unable to stir.

Mrs. C. presented a gallant appearance, and with the
large hood of her caoutchouc heavy with snow, and a dole-
ful dripping from the brim of her hat and nose and chin,
the black draperies of her waterproof only relieved by

voluminous drab gaiters, she looked like an image of
Father Christmas *thawing*, but cheery and brave even
under difficulties.

On we went, undeterred by the now certain knowledge
that there was nothing to be seen from the Spitze. We
had our provisions, and a luncheon party having been
planned for the summit of the Piz Languard, there we
would go, and eat our luncheon, and return with peaceful
consciences to Pontresina.

The latter part of the ascent was not really so difficult
as we had found it two years before, when the mass of
loose stones had added greatly to our fatigue; these were
now well carpeted, and the guides have built a sort of rude
staircase for the last ten minutes of the way, which has the
advantage of not rolling away beneath one's feet. At one
place we had had to cross a great plateau of snow, so soft
that progression was simply impossible to us. F. shouted,
' Gentlemen to the front,' and with hands and knees and
axes they literally pounded the snow hard. It was strange
to see how lightly guides and mountaineers walked over
the yielding surface, which seemed much less affected by
their greater weight than where ladies attempted to try
the same path; by long practice they have acquired a perfect balance, which is, I imagine, the real secret of walking
on snow successfully.

We reached the final plateau, which is about half-a-
dozen yards across, in a heavy snow-storm, and being by

Excelsior.!

In the snowdrift.

Lunching on the Spitze.

this time, spite of all precautions, thoroughly wet through, we dared not linger very long. To an outsider—say the Spirit of the Storm—we must have presented a ludicrously forlorn appearance, but that would only have been because the Spirit being German, or at least German Swiss, would be naturally phlegmatic, and unable to understand that sterling quality of the British character which delights in being jolly under difficulties, and enjoying life under an aspect totally differing from insular civilization. The champagne-bottles were opened, and we drank to the mountain and our own success, and ate chickens and potted meats and *compôte*, a ravenous hunger serving as *sauce piquante*; and then the guides joined in chorus, and the mountain echoes rang again to the wild wonderful jödels so full of unutterable joy and music to every Führer's and Bergsteiger's heart. We were dripping at our elbows and sitting in pools of water, while the great snow-flakes soaked our bread and settled in the salt, and came down so thoroughly in earnest that our hats and umbrellas were heavy with them, and we dared not linger lest we should suddenly stiffen. The descent looked a little formidable, a snow slope ending in blackness and mist, and with many inward tremblings a question was whispered as to how we were to get down. That soon settled itself. Franz Andermatten, one of the merriest, sturdiest of Valais guides, seized Lady L. N., and before she could utter one shriek of protestation they were flying down far below us. Her

L

husband quickly glissaded after her, and we all followed
according to our different fashions. Walther seated himself
on the snow, and bade E. sit behind him, and then with
a vigorous push—swish! they spun down, throwing up
snow-balls and a white spray about their faces, till, safely
landed at the first pile of stones, they could watch others descending.   F. had placed his plaid on the ground, and D.,
sitting on it, wound one end firmly round her, while he held
the other, intending to draw her luxuriously down the slope;
but the inclined plane being slightly uneven, D. swerved
aside, and came down in the end headforemost, rather like
a bundle of hay in a blanket, while Mrs. C.'s dignified and
successful glissade was in perfect keeping with her character.   Major L. and his wife were old mountaineers and in
capital training, and her walking powers cast the other
ladies entirely into the shade, though, judging by their own
accounts at a later date, the performances of each had
been unrivalled.   And thus with much laughter and enjoyment the ground was rapidly got over, and we found ourselves at about twelve o'clock once more standing on the
short scrubby grass, which later in the year would turn
this bare hill-side into pasture-land.   Here the gaiters were
unfastened, snow shaken off, and a few drops of wine
taken before we started for the final trudge home.

The mind of Pontresina, agricultural and commercial,
is slow and conservative, and difficult to convince, and it
was in vain we pleaded for the aid of the horses on our

"How we came down!"

return march. The owners resisted with dogged persistency
our most pathetic appeals; our ancestors, if ever they had
ascended the Piz Languard, had walked down again, and
so must we.   There was no more to be said, and we were
not long in descending through the little wood and the
meadows above the village; but we must have looked a
very motley company to any fresh eyes that encountered
us, judging by the amusement on C.'s face when she met
us.   One of our party who had fared the worst, her lighter
dress not having been prepared for such rough work, was
clothed in garments which by this time had assumed the
colour and consistency of tea-leaves, while her boots were
literally cut to pieces.   We were warmly welcomed by
Herr Gredig at the Krone, that worthy landlord killing a
fatted calf in the gladness of his heart (at least this is our
only way of accounting for the fact that veal formed the
chief ingredient of all dishes served on that and subsequent
occasions), and absolutely submitting even with cheerfulness
to the choice on our part of the hour for dinner.   To those
by whom he is known, this fact will speak volumes. Herr
Gredig has a great soul, but it moves in a narrow groove,
and he is a man who believes implicitly in precedent. The
law of the Gredigs of Pontresina, which altereth not, is
carved on the door-post, and engraved on the ductile but
abject minds of his followers.   It afforded us exquisite
gratification during our say to infringe the regulations
in every possible manner; and such was the ascendancy

that we acquired, that we were recognised as despots, and were graciously permitted on all occasions to eat our *Abendessen* when we were hungry, and not when the inmates of the Gasthaus zur Krone thought we ought to be.

Our St. Moritz companions hurried off to seek dry clothes and shelter, while the rest of our party adjourned in the afternoon to Flury's studio, eliciting deep-drawn sighs from that conscientious artist by desiring to be photographed *en masse* (with a background of snow, and a grand moraine built up of loose stones), in perpetual remembrance of our very successful ascent of the Piz Languard.

A NIGHT ADVENTURE IN THE SULDENTHAL.

—— ✦ ——

'In these distracted times, when each man dreads
The bloody stratagem of busy heads.'
                                        OTWAY.

'For what obscured light the heavens did grant,
Did but convey into our fearful minds
A doubtful warrant of immediate death.'
                                Comedy of Errors.

A NIGHT ADVENTURE IN THE SULDENTHAL.

JUNE 18, 1866.

—+—

CONSCIOUS of our own rectitude of intention, and confirmed in it by the assurances of the police in the
Val di Sole, that 'der Krieg' was, as the Germans finely
say, 'noch nicht los,' and that, if duly provided with
properly viséd passports, we might cross the frontier
without fear of molestation, my friend B. and I, with
our respective guides, Christian Almer and Franz Andermatten, proceeded quietly to carry out our plan of campaign in the Orteler group, by first effecting (on June 16)
a new pass from Cogolo and Pejo, in Val di Sole, to Sta.
Catarina.   An account of this expedition, as well as of the
subsequent and very successful one from the last-named
place to the Suldenthal, will be found in the September
number of the Alpine Journal, 1866, and I will not weary
the reader with topographical details which he may find
elsewhere.   Suffice it to say that, having despatched most
of our baggage direct to Bormio, we had left Sta. Catarina
at 1 A.M. on June 18, intending to sleep at Gampenhöfe
in the Suldenthal, and make our way thence to the Val-

telline on the following day, by a pass between the
Orteler Spitz and Klein-Zebru. Before 3 P.M. the first
half of the programme had been accomplished in what we
flattered ourselves might be considered a brilliant manner,
for in little more than ten hours' actual walking we had
ascended two hitherto unclimbed summits,—La Fornaccia
and the S.W. or highest peak of the Cevedale,—amongst
the finest of the group, and discovered three first-class
new passes, from 11,400 to 12,200 feet in height (the
last being, I believe, the loftiest in the Austrian Alps),
besides traversing a fourth, the beautiful Janiger Scharte,
first crossed last year by my friend Herr Mojsisovics, the
Secretary of the Austrian Alpen-Verein. Our reception
at Gampenhöfe was most friendly; the weather was
charming, and promised well for the morrow; and as we
lay stretched at our ease upon the soft turf, quaffing
bowls of creamy milk, in full view of the Orteler and
Königsspitz, recalling pleasant memories of past triumphs,
and anticipating fresh victories, we might be pardoned if
our reflections were at times of an exultant order, as we
rested in happy unconsciousness of what a few hours were
to bring forth.

Travellers in the Suldenthal usually avail themselves
of the hospitality of the worthy Geistlicher at St. Gertrud
(or Sulden), about half-an-hour lower down the valley,
but Gampenhöfe itself, being inhabited throughout the
year, furnishes better quarters than are usually to be met

Conjuring in the Stube.

'Sie schlafen.'

with at so considerable an elevation (6,165 feet), and
within a quarter of an hour of the foot of the glacier;
half-an-hour, too, is worth saving in a long day's work, so
we decided to let well alone, and contented ourselves
with sending Christian and Franz down in the course of
the afternoon for fresh supplies of cheese, bread, and wine,
with which they returned in time for the evening meal.
One by one the various members of the household dropped
in, and as soon as the table was cleared, a little entertainment was improvised for our worthy hosts and their
family, in the shape of sundry simple conjuring tricks,
winding up with a display of 'drawing-room lightning'
and magnesium wire, a small store of which portable
articles can highly be recommended to mountaineers, as
an unfailing means of making themselves agreeable to
the simple Alpine folk. Amidst shouts of 'Was für
Kunst!' 'Das ist Hexerei!' and peals of merry laughter,
an hour passed away, and just as we began to hint at bed,
the arrival of a small outlying Geisbube, whose duties as
a sort of pastoral long-stop had detained him late afield,
thus causing him to miss the fun, was hailed by all as an
excuse for a repetition of the special wonders, till we were
obliged to insist on the absolute necessity of betaking
ourselves to rest. The supply of hay being small, it was
allotted to the guides, who retired to a neighbouring
grange, whilst our hospitable hostess made up a comfortable bed for B. and me on the floor of the cozy Stube,

on which we stretched ourselves about 8·30, after giving instructions to be called a little after midnight.

All had been quiet for about an hour, and B. and I were buried deep in our first sleep, when we were both startled and roused by a loud noise, and in a moment the room was half filled with a noisy gesticulating crowd of armed men. At first, between sleeping and waking, we half imagined them to be robbers, and I almost mechanically sat up in bed with a vague idea of seizing one of our ice-axes, which lay under a bench near at hand. A moment, however, sufficed to show that they were regular soldiers, two or three of whom advanced upon us with fixed bayonets pointed at our breasts, whilst those in the rear proceeded to load their rifles in the most business-like and unpleasantly suggestive manner. They shouted to us in Italian and German to lie down and not stir, or they would shoot us, and on our complying, with the remark that we wished nothing better and should like to know why we were thus disturbed and what they wanted, proceeded to put to us a string of enquiries as to whether we were Italians, whether we could speak Italian, how we came there, &c., without giving us time to reply. It is not easy to answer violent interrogatories as you lie flat on your back, and I again attempted to sit up in bed, but was immediately treated to a vigorous pantomime executed with bayonets, which unmistakably suggested an 'as you were' movement. It was all very well for B. to

laugh, being himself inside and protected as to his
flank by me on one side and a table on the other, and
with an all but bomb-proof *duvet* over all, so that he
would have ample time to parley whilst our assailants
were engaged, as John Bunyan says, in 'drilling a hole
in my carnal kettle past mending.' Possibly, however,
my thinness and the length of our assailants' bayonets
suggested the idea that he too might be spitted simul-
taneously ; but, at any rate, when some of the men
again addressed us in Italian, he gave them a condensed
statement of facts, interspersed with bits of his mind,
in that language of which he is a master. Feeling
stronger in Teutonic tongues myself, and cunningly reflecting that, as it was clear they took us to be Italians,
it would be best to avoid all appearance of such evil
tendencies, I still stuck manfully to German, and discharged it vigorously at an angle of 90° from my recum-
bent position. The sudden waking, the semi-darkness,
and the general noise and tumult, coupled with the
strangely excited demeanour of our visitors, their use of
Italian, and our own confused impressions, at first suggested the theory that they too might have crossed the
frontier ; but as soon as we were fairly awake, we at
once perceived that we had fallen into the hands of an
Austrian patrol. After a short time the sub-officer in
command, and a police official who accompanied him,
came forward, whilst a party was detached to secure

our companions in the hayloft, who presently made
their appearance, looking rather solemn and evidently
a good deal ruffled, but keeping their tempers admirably and offering no resistance, though they had been
stirred up in their nest with as little ceremony as ourselves.   We were now told that we might rise and put on
our coats, in the absence of which we had no documentary
proof of our nationality.   We answered all their questions,
assured them that they had made a mistake and found a
mare's nest, exhibited our passports, the correctness of
which they could not dispute, and, when informed that we
must submit to be searched, gave up the contents of our
pockets without hesitation.   I must say it went to my
heart to surrender my note-book with numerous sketches
and all my memoranda of the journey, as well as sundry
maps, both printed and manuscript; but I was almost
consoled by the terror of the officer when he felt from the
outside the pipe which I carried in my right coat-pocket,
and made a convulsive grab at it, exclaiming, 'Sie haben
da eine Pistole! Geben Sie's mir!' The truth is, that
in a spirit of mischief I had just before asked him
whether he had secured our arms, and on his asking,
with a most comical expression of consternation at this
confirmation of his worst suspicions, where they were, had
referred him to the bench beneath which our axes were
still peacefully reposing.   These were entrusted to four
soldiers, but the mention of weapons suggested further

'Bleiben Sie ruhig!'

'Das ist eine Pistole!'

The women all side with the prisoners!

The frontier looks a little dangerous!

investigation, and involved my pipe in undeserved suspicion. 'Fürchten Sie nicht; es ist nicht geladen,' said I, and with an essentially German sympathy for a 'Raucher' it was at once returned to me. Our purses, watches, and small articles of value, such as pencil-cases, were left in our possession, and the articles seized were carefully packed in a copy of the *Evening Mail*, which found itself in the same predicament. The search being now completed, we were informed that we must proceed under escort to Gomagoi, on the Stelvio road between Prad and Trafoi, and nearly opposite the opening of the Suldenthal, there to have our fate decided in the morning by the officer in command of the Fort. We protested that our passports were all right, that our statements were thus fully and satisfactorily confirmed, and that they were making a fuss about nothing; but they replied with a military sense of duty, 'It might be so, or it might not; the decision did not rest with them; they had positive orders to bring us down forthwith, and go we must.' On this we, of course, gave way with a good grace, thinking it impolitic to aggravate them, as they were doubtless only acting up to their instructions, and knowing that anything like resistance was not to be thought of. So at ten, or a little after, we bade good-bye to the group of trembling peasants who had gathered around, and, preceded by an individual in plain clothes bearing a lantern, whom I strongly suspect to have been the cause of our

arrest, we issued forth into the darkness. The inspection
of the passports had evidently not been without effect on
the official mind, and we were, accordingly, allowed to
march in any order we pleased, but, by way of precaution,
were not indulged with the possession of our axes. The
path, more particularly below St. Gertrud, was bad, and
in places either carried away by, or at least buried
beneath avalanches, over which it was not easy to pick
one's way in the dark without an occasional slip, and in
more than one place, if we had chosen to make a rush
altogether, a majority might probably have given our
captors the slip, at least for the moment. Larking with
armed men who have a duty to carry out is, however,
neither wise nor safe, and we conducted ourselves literally in a guarded manner. The men were civil, and
stood a little gentle chaff after their pipes were once well
alight,—at last even admitting that the affair might possibly turn out to be after all a 'dumme Geschichte ;' and
we enjoyed the variety, novelty, and spice of excitement
of our situation, though vexed at the disturbance of our
sleep, the overturning of the plans for the next day, and
the possible risk of the loss of our possessions if the
Commandant at Gomagoi should prove to be a martinet
or red-tapist, and, choosing to ignore the existence of
such a pursuit as mountaineering, interpret notes and
sketches as being of evil tendency.

It was between 1 and 2 A.M. when we pulled up on the

familiar Stelvio road a little below the Fort, and, on the return of a messenger sent forward for instructions as to our disposal, were marched into the inn at Gomagoi, and shown into an upstairs room with two beds, in one of which the guides, and in the other B. and I, were directed to bestow ourselves. A sentinel, with fixed bayonet, was stationed inside the door, whilst a couple more, I believe, occupied the landing, and as we settled ourselves into a sound and refreshing sleep, I was really sorry to have been the means of giving so much trouble to our luckless captors, who were far worse off than ourselves.

We rose soon after five, invigorated by three hours' rest, and were informed that we must be ready to proceed at six to the frontier station of Der Schmelz, a little above Prad, where our guard seemed to imagine that our case would finally be disposed of. Water was supplied for washing, and little acts of civility were performed, which led us to believe that they were conscious of having made a mistake and performed their duty in the night with needless severity, though from first to last there had really been little to complain of, the preliminary threats of personal violence having evidently resulted from the belief that, being spies, we must of course be armed, and if suffered to rise, might show fight and give trouble.

During our walk I had enquired the name of the Commandant at the Fort, but our captors either could not or would not enlighten me, and I was naturally anxious to

know what sort of man we should have to deal with, as
the fate of our note-books, sketches, &c., as well as the
length of our detention, might a good deal depend on his
disposition and sympathies.   On announcing that we were
ready to start, we were requested first to step into an
adjoining room, where we found the Commandant—Ober-
Lieutenant Gustav Tomek—standing by a table on which
were placed our passports and other possessions.   I commenced the conversation with an expression of regret at
having been the cause of so much needless trouble, and a
hint that the Herr Commandant was doubtless by this time
aware that an unfortunate mistake had been made.   He
at once replied that he had, of course, no idea till he saw
our passports in the morning who or what we were, as the
hour of our arrival had prevented his being at once com-
municated with.   'And now,' he added, turning to me, 'if
you are Herr T., permit me to say that, whilst regretting the
circumstances under which we meet, I have much pleasure
in making your personal acquaintance.   For you are, in
fact, already well known to me through our mutual friend
Mojsisovics, who spent four or five days with me here last
year.   If you see him, pray give him my very kind
regards, and say that I am very sorry to have caused
annoyance to any friends of his.'   'You know, however,'
he added, 'that these are critical times, especially on this
frontier ; and as a report was brought to me yesterday by a
peasant, that four strangers had reached the head of the

Suldenthal from the Italian side, and were making enquiries as to the number of troops at Gomagoi, &c., I
was bound to send up a patrol to enquire into the matter.'
I need hardly say that the story about our enquiries was a
pure invention of the messenger, as B. and I had carefully
abstained from opening our lips on the subject, and the
guides, who we at first conjectured might have said something on the subject when they went down to St. Gertrud,
did not, it appeared, know enough of the geography to be
aware even of the existence of such a place as Gomagoi.
I subsequently heard that about a fortnight previously
two strangers, said to be suspicious in appearance, had been
seen somewhere in the Suldenthal by a woman, who at
first said nothing about it to anyone, and had been a good
deal blamed in consequence. When we appeared, it was
resolved that the blunder should not this time be repeated;
hence no time was lost in informing the authorities. Had
we reached Gampenhöfe three or four hours later, we
should probably have effected a start for Bormio before
the patrol could have arrived, and in our light marching
order and fine training, aided by superior local knowledge,
should doubtless have easily given them the slip.

Reassured by the Commandant's friendly tone, I enquired whether we might resume possession of our pro-
perty and consider ourselves released from arrest, and at
liberty to proceed. He at once assented, remarking, as he
glanced at the outlines and maps, 'These are doubtless

topographical sketches for mountaineering purposes. No further explanation is necessary; take them by all means. And now you must present yourselves at Der Schmelz, just to get your passports viséd for departure from Austrian territory, after which, if you desire to return to the Suldenthal, which I think can be arranged, and you have time to give me a call, I shall be happy to see you. This road being now closed, the police may not understand how you come to be descending the pass, so I will send some one with you to make all needful explanation, and as you must be hungry, and a much better breakfast is to be had at Prad than here, I advise you to start at once, and will wish you a very good morning and a pleasant journey whatever route you may take.' Shaking hands very heartily with our kind and gentlemanly friend and the pleasant young officer who accompanied him, as well as with the leader of the patrol, we set forth down the valley, congratulating ourselves on our good fortune in getting out of the scrape with such flying colours, and heartily blessing, I need hardly say, the name of Mojsisovics.

At Der Schmelz there was unfortunately only a subordinate official, who informed us that he had received positive instructions to allow no one to cross into Italy by that frontier, and did not see the force of our suggestion that the prohibition of course referred to the Stelvio Pass, and not to a passage over the glaciers from the Suldenthal to Val Zebru. He was civil but firm, and we did not

contest the point, especially as our companion intimated
that he thought he could suggest a way of getting over
the difficulty; so our passports were duly made good for
an 'Ausgang,' and adjourning to the inn with our friend,
we discussed over breakfast the idea at which he had
hinted. This was to proceed to Glurns, see the 'Bezirk-
Vorsteher,' who was the *chef* of him of Der Schmelz, and
obtain his special authorisation to carry out our original
object. In the event of his refusal, we could enter Switzerland by Val Mustair, and either reach the Engadine by
the Ofen Pass, or make for Sta. Maria on the W. side of
the Stelvio, *viâ* the Wormser Joch. Wishing him good-
bye, we set out for Glurns, saw the superior official, and
laid our case before him. He was very polite, said that
his instructions would hardly have warranted him in
granting our request, but that our being friends of the
Commandant of course altered the case materially; and if
we could obtain that gentleman's written permission, he
had not the slightest objection to endorse it. We thanked
him, but considering that this would involve another
double journey to and fro between Glurns and Gomagoi,
as well as entail a somewhat unreasonable responsibility
on Ober-Lieutenant Tomek; that the weather did not
look likely to continue fine the next day; and that we
might even meet from the Italians at Bormio with a repetition of our recent adventure, we decided to adopt the
safer course, give no further trouble, and, leaving well

M

alone, slip over the frontier into Switzerland. I was confirmed in this determination by the consideration that, after all, we might bag the Klein-Zebru next day from Sta. Maria by crossing the Madatsch Joch and skirting the slopes on the N. side of Val Zebru beneath the Trafoier and Thurwieser Spitzen, and then 'descend the valley to Bormio in the evening.

We started accordingly in a carriage for Sta. Maria, in the Münsterthal (Val Mustair), and then strolled up by the Wormser Joch—the lower portion of which is very beautiful—to the fourth or highest cantoniera on the Stelvio, around which the snow still lay deep. The Swiss portion of the Münsterthal was in a ferment, as an entire battalion of Federal troops was expected the next day, and every available sleeping-place had been engaged for officers or men. At the cantoniera there were no soldiers, and only a couple of custom-house officials, who declined even to look at our passports when tendered for their inspection.

We soon turned into bed, not having had a superabundance of sleep for two nights previously, and gave instructions to be called between two and three. The people of the house, however, failed to awake, and though we roused about three and the guides still earlier, we were unable for a long time to stir up anybody, the consequence of which was that it was five o'clock before we got under way.

We proceeded first to the top of the Stelvio to inspect the Italian frontier-post, which we found, to our surprise, to consist of only about a dozen national guards and a couple of douaniers, who looked cold and miserable, as if uncomfortably conscious that they were utterly incapable of offering a moment's resistance to the Austrian force, about tenfold more numerous, which crowned the crest of the ridge just above them, within easy musket range. Looking up, we could see the line of heads and glittering barrels peering over the rocky *arête* which runs in a northerly direction from the summit of the pass, and so completely dominates the small building usually tenanted by a couple of frontier guards, that it seemed as though the occupiers might be compelled to beat a retreat by five minutes' vigorous pelting with stones.

We mentioned our intention of crossing into Val Zebru by the glaciers, but the Italians assured us that Austrian vedettes were stationed along the frontier for a considerable distance to the south of the Stelvio Pass, in the direction of the Video-Spitz, and that, though anyone attempting to cross by the regular road would probably be merely turned back, they would not hesitate to fire if the frontier were passed at a higher, or unusual and therefore suspicious point. Under these circumstances they recommended us at any rate to keep well away to the right on the Italian side; so, thanking them for their advice and information, and wishing them well out of their unpleasant position, which

M 2

they were allowed to hold undisturbed for only three days longer, we started off up the slopes to the S.W. for a depression which looked as though it might give access to the mass of snow and ice radiating from the Nagler-Spitz.

The snow was in bad order, it was by this time nearly six o'clock, the weather looked threatening, and when the supposed col was gained, it was found to lead nowhere in particular, except into a snow-filled hollow terminating opposite the third cantoniera. We must either have descended nearly 1,000 feet and then worked laboriously up steep slopes of soft snow on the left, or at once have proceeded in the latter direction in full view of the Austrian post, and with the probability of being compelled after all to cross the frontier within range. A council of war was held, and we at length decided that, if we persisted and got into a scrape, we should have nobody but ourselves to blame, and might expect small sympathy from anyone else; that the weather was not such as to offer any particular temptation to run a known and definite risk; and that, all things considered, the most sensible course was to make straight tracks for the high road, and proceed down it to Bormio and Sondrio. Christian and Franz were, I believe, heartily glad when this determination was arrived at, for though perfectly ready to do their best to carry out our plans, whatever they might be, they had no desire again to fall into the clutches of the Austrians under suspicious circumstances; and as the day remained cloudy, the feeling of

disappointment gradually wore off from our own minds. At
Bormio, and indeed throughout the Valtelline, no soldiers
were to be seen, and we sympathised with the unfortunate
manager of the Bagni, whose only expected guests were the
company of the Kaiser-Jäger regiment we had seen in the
morning, and whose downward swoop was in truth not long
delayed.

I cannot conclude without bearing my willing and
grateful testimony to the almost universal civility, honesty,
and forbearance of Austrian officials, at any rate on German ground; and if anything I may have said in the foregoing pages should lead to a contrary inference, I can
only regret that I should have so far failed to present the
circumstances of the case in their true light. Boisterous
and denunciatory language, impatience of contradiction
or restraint, and an unlimited belief in the free-and-
independent-Briton theory, combined with a fair amount
of ignorance of the language, more often than is supposed
underlie the difficulties in which our countrymen get involved from time to time on the Continent; and without
pretending to be immaculate in these respects, I may
perhaps be allowed to urge the desirability of a little more
patience with *employés*, whose duty it is to carry out their
instructions, whatever they may be.

ISCHL AND ITS SURROUNDINGS.

———

'But yet there is a time
   Before the Vesper chime
From nestling birds, and odorous leaves ascending,
   When in the west, the sun,
   His day's work almost done,
O'er purple clouds is for his farewell bending;
   Then every icy crest,
   And every marble breast,
With sudden life doth seem to heave and glow;
   Touch'd by those ardent beams,
   A golden glory streams
O'er adamantine heights and caves of snow,
   And, blushing rosy red
   With joy, each radiant head
In ether springs to meet the parting kiss—
   Then every snow-white brow
   Doth humbly seem to bow,
And sink to rest in quiet thankfulness.'

                         Poems by S. H. F.

ISCHL AND ITS SURROUNDINGS.

OUR first visit to Ischl was in May, 1866. The unusually late season had changed for the moment the
face of Europe, a prolonged shiver ran through the country,
the sun, when it did shine, was wonderfully feeble and
helpless, the trees gave up budding as a hopeless matter
till better times came, and grass and flowers kept themselves as warm as they were able under the snow, which
still had its own way in everything, making hills and
fir-branches beautiful as a dream, seen through a fretwork
of tiny frost sprays which decorated the windows of our
little mountain-inn every morning. The water in the
village fountains was frozen, and there were icicles on the
rocks beside the roads. We travelled through the country
under a mass of cloaks and shawls, and within the shelter
of a big *Stellwagen*; and our first care at each day's halting-
place was to see that the largest possible fires were lit in
the cavernous stoves, and that all the windows were firmly
closed, and everything eatable made as hot as possible.

We had reached Salzburg on the 23rd of May, and

listened to mournful tales of the weather and the injury
to the crops and the people's fears for the future, and
going to sleep under the weight of these prognostications,
woke to some pleasant sunshine and a general brightening
of the outside world.

It would take many weeks to exhaust the interests of
the whole district surrounding Salzburg. The landlord of
the Nelbök, a first-rate house, tried to persuade us to make
it our head-quarters, the old city is full of interest with its
grand castle crowning the hill which rises abruptly from
the midst of walls and houses, a splendid bit of old mediæ-
val power—full of memories of proud ecclesiastics, princes
of the empire, who, when danger threatened, carried their
archiepiscopal croziers up to the higher battlements, and
defied peasants and *Kaiser* alike. Murray says, 'Salzburg
by common consent is allowed to be the most beautiful
spot in Germany.' With all due deference for such an
authority it must be admitted that the common consent
assumes that in speaking of the city you include the
district that surrounds it, and for ordinary tourists Ischl,
Gmunden, and Berchtesgaden are pleasanter points of
departure—to those, at least, who prefer a foreground of
woods and hills to mere streets and houses, even though
their foundations date back to the Romans and are rich
in legendary lore. Mozart was born in a dwelling still
standing near the University Church, and his statue by
Schwanthaler may be seen in the centre of the Michael's

Platz, within sound of the chimes from the Palace Tower hard by, where the bells ring out softly, ' Es klingelt so herrlich, es klingelt so schön ' and the tones of his own beautiful Zauberflöte float round the image of the great dead master.

Salzburg is almost encircled by a chain of Alps through which the Salza passes to join the Danube, and the plain is rich with fields and meadows, luxuriant trees, villas and homesteads, a *riant* landscape pleasantly contrasting with its more rugged surroundings.

We started in two large carriages, which throughout the Salzkammergut and Bavaria are invariably good and cheap, and drove away towards Ischl. But suddenly, as we were trotting merrily along the high road, carriage number two came to grief; a young horse shied violently, tumbling its companion over into a deep ditch, with a general upsetting of people and vehicle that was anything but pleasant. Matters, however, were soon set right, the sufferers were picked up, condoled with, brushed, shaken, congratulated, and put back into their places; the ill-behaved horse secured a day's holiday, and was sent home to its stable, apparently unabashed by the disgrace; a second appeared in a mysterious manner from a barn hard by, and the travellers resumed their journey. Long files of soldiers, many of them composed of young recruits, passed us on their way to Salzburg, where each day large detachments arrived, bivouacked on hay in the great riding-school, and then marched southward to their various depôts.

The scene was very lovely in the morning light, and as we came into a more sheltered country, it was wonderful to see what spring had done with the help of a few days of brighter weather; the snow had melted from the dark green of the firs and pines, the beeches shone between them with their soft powdering of golden green buds, some newly-cut hay scented the air, and was drying on high poles, but as yet the fields were undisturbed for the most part, to our great content, and brilliant with flowers. Often they seemed covered with a crimson or lilac or purple haze of colour, where some especial plant had made its home; a delicate rainbow, sparkling through the dew, might have fallen on the grass, and been held captive by the swift-spun webs of the busy little gossamers. Filling up every distant view, a fair snow-peak shone in its winter drapery, white and glistening, looking a great deal higher than it really was through the magic aid of its adornment, and pleasantly imposing on our senses, though one of the travellers, who was scientific and learned in theodolites, always endeavoured to anchor us to facts and the stern truth of things.

We were deluded into stopping at St. Gilgen to dine— a mistake which in later journeys we have been careful to avoid. There is a charming lake, the *Wolfgang See* and the *Wirthshaus* is an old-established halting-place,

Ischl.

and roomy enough to supply the needs of many passing
travellers; but the host was dead, and the *Wirthin* was
given to strong liquors, and the management generally
seemed to have devolved on a rather dilapidated *Kellnerin*,
who had an unappetising way of wiping the forks in the
dinner-napkins between the courses, which were repetitions
of ham and eggs under various disguisements more or less
successful, but inclining to the latter. There was a great
dog who came to be petted, and who apologised in his
dumb way for the deficiencies of the inn, and was quite the
best thing belonging to it.

From St. Gilgen an easy ascent of three hours brings
you to the summit of the Schafberg, nearly 6,000 feet
high, from whence a fine view may be obtained of the
whole district of woods and lakes, a perfect *vue en ballon*
for those who like to get their ideas of a country systemati-
cally aranged. There is a good hotel on the summit, where
all the delights of sunrise on a cold morning, the usual attack
on the blankets of the establishment, and other remini-
scences of the Righi Kulm may be revived, pleasantly or
otherwise, according to the state of wind and weather.

We reached Ischl by a rapid descent, the road winding
amongst clustering trees and pretty houses nestling in the
shelter of the hills. The little town is simply a collection
of pleasure-houses, the oldest of which only date back for
forty years or so, dwellings and gardens, boulevard and
Kurhaus, that have grown up when and how they liked

around the Emperor's beautiful little villa, and the saline springs that are the nominal excuse for the gay world who later in the year find their pleasure in this sheltered valley amongst the hills. The place must be warm in August, as these same hills are thickly clothed with trees, and the town is shut in by them on all sides, save where the busy river goes splashing and foaming over the stones towards the south, doing a great amount of business on its way, as it has to float down the thousands of logs which are lying ready stored along its banks. Everywhere one sees saw-mills busily at work and shallows where the water is kept back by a dam, and the wood is collected. The logs are left in a gigantic circle, packed tightly together, and bound effectually by narrow pieces of wood which form a cordon round it, till at a convenient season they are let loose from the *Klause*, and set off for an independent race that used to afford us endless amusement. As we drove beside the river, we delighted in watching the more adventurous pieces of wood, becoming interested in them individually, backing our favourites, and noticing with keen anxiety when they approached a shallow and were in danger of being stranded, or of being caught in the whirl of a rapid. Some weeks later, we came upon a fresh store of wood floating down the Inn in a deep gorge below Nauders, and we looked sympathisingly at the logs that were dancing about in the rush and swirl of the river— *kaiserliches königliches Holz,* with strong Austrian pro-

clivities, going helplessly into the very grasp of its
southern foes; for just then the frontier was well guarded
by Italian sharpshooters, and the German logs, if they
ever went too near the shore, might be made into watch-
fires and condemned to warm their enemies, though at the
worst they would have the satisfaction of being too damp
to do much more than smoke!

But meanwhile war was only a thunder-cloud in the
distance, and above Ischl at least the sky was clear, and
there was warmth and sunshine to gladden us. We took
up our quarters in the best of hotels, the Goldenes Kreuz,
where the kind people did their utmost to make us comfortable. We had rooms à *discrétion*, as there was no one
else there but one solitary Hungarian on the other side of
the house. The old landlord and his wife are thrifty good-
hearted Germans; Madame a capital *Hausfrau*, reigning
over a pleasant little kingdom, a beautiful mountain farm,
from which large supplies of fresh milk came down in
barrels, and turned into cream and cheese and butter
under her skilful hands and those of her bright-faced
Mädchen. The 'son of the house' is a clever well-edu-
cated man, who does his utmost to make the hotel comfortable, and with whom our father enjoyed many long
talks over fishing tackle and sport, visiting with Herr
Sarsteiner his trout-nurseries, and discussing the promise of the coming season. He rents all the rights of
fishing about Ischl, and is a keen sportsman; and as he

speaks English well, anyone anxious for triumphs over
Forellen or *Reh* or *Gemse* could not do better than place
themselves in his hands. The hotel is unpretending-
looking, but thoroughly comfortable, the horses and carriages are good, and the rooms cool and pleasant. The
windows look down upon a tributary stream, or branch of
the main river, which is divided up in every imaginable
way to suit the fancy of the *Salinenwerke* and saw-mills,
and across it to the Imperial villa and its gay gardens,
which climb up the slope and lose themselves in shady
wood-walks. The royal house is quite small, a toy-palace
with verandahs and creeping flowers and pretty little devices of spiral iron staircases hidden away under clematis
blossoms. It multiplies itself in numbers of tiny erections,
each smaller than the rest, like a Chinese box of houses,
in which all can fit one into the other. There is a kitchen
with a covered arcade, and one is puzzled to know how
the Imperial dishes can come all that long way, even under
bowers of roses, without becoming prosaically chilled.
The hall of the villa is ornamented with the heads and
horns of game in Tyrol fashion, and there is a pretty
fanciful *Lusthaus* halfway up the garden slope, with a
tiny library, and a drawing-room, and more light verandahs and clematis and Virginian creeper, which must be
in all the glory of its colouring when the sweet young
Empress comes there for some idle hours with her little
children in the pleasant country quietness. Higher still

ISCHL AND ITS SURROUNDINGS.   189

there is another summer-house, a size smaller, and open
on all sides to the breezes, which must be much needed
here, and then there comes the wood, full of shady places
and seats arranged so as to command lovely distant peeps
through the trees, and coffee may be served here sometimes and fresh milk to the fair court ladies who, wearying of state dignity, and even of the Kiosk and the
Pagoda, seek 'Nature at her source,' which means sitting
on the grass when it is rather damp, listening enraptured
to the songs of the birds and the hum of the insects,
being stung by the midges, and finding an earwig in your
ripest peach ! We grew very fond of that garden, which is
generously thrown open to the public during the spring
months, and spent many long hours wandering about its
walks.

Our first morning at Ischl dawned in a glow of sudden
heat. Summer seemed to have come in a moment, and we
spent our Sunday in the woods, choosing a sunny spot to
bask in; and there, in the sweet country quietness, with
little bright-eyed lizards as our only companions, except a
stray peasant strolling home from mass, and the water far
below making a pleasant music over the stones, we read
the lessons and psalms to that tinkling accompaniment,
and a sermon, which was fortunately a short one, as we
were nearly frizzled before the end, having in our delight
at welcoming the sun again, ventured to camp out too
directly in his way, and we were glad to seek the deep

shade of the pine wood, where the wild strawberry blossoms, which were as large as our cultivated ones in England, made fair white stars amidst the moss and leaves.

We hunted out a wood-stream which sprang out of the ground from a shelving bank of brown earth and leaves matted together with ivy and ferns and creeping plants, and here we lay down and dipped our heads into the water, drinking and bathing at once, and, as we rested on the grass, dreamed that it was all untrue that 'Pan was dead,' and traced the little footmarks on the crumpled leaves, where sweet sandalled feet had passed before us, and as the sunlight flickered through the greenness and ran in and out amongst the stems of the trees, to our half-shut eyes came a vision of tawny Dryads, brown-eyed and laughing, circling in a mazy dance around their magic spring. I do not think many people have ever found it out: for two years we have sat beside it, and drank the clear water and dreamed our pleasant dreams. But amongst those who visit Ischl some may long to find our *Quelle*, some may chance upon it unawares. There are few landmarks to remember, and another's words can give them better than mine :—

> ' Oh, the sweet valley of deep grass,
> Where through the summer stream doth pass,
> In chain of shallow, and still pool,
> From misty morn to evening cool;
> Where the black ivy creeps and twines
> O'er the dark-armed, red-trunked pines,

Ischl & Imperial Villa .

In the meadows . Ischl .

Whence chattering the pigeon flits,
Or, brooding o'er her thin eggs, sits,
And every hollow of the hills
With echoing song the mavis fills.'*

We wandered home through the woods having a good 'paper hunt.' Our father had preceded us, declining to join in our Pan-heroics on the ground of a general dampness, which he had the hardihood to say detracted from the merits of our *Quelle*, leaving sundry pieces of the *Allgemeine Zeitung* on the branches to guide our steps. We had a grand scramble, getting suddenly caught in boggy places the sun had not had time to dry, losing ourselves in by-paths that led nowhere, and coming upon bits of the river as usual shut up for *Klausen* and full of logs, and at last emerging on to the high road and the covered bridge leading into Ischl.

The baths and medicinal springs are of various kinds; beginning with the ordinary hot and cold baths common to all peoples and countries where water can be obtained and be persuaded to boil, the favourite ones are those supplied by the liquor (*Soolenbäder*) drawn off from the salt-pans after a portion of salt has been extracted from the brine. This contains a strong solution of chloride of sodium, and is let down with water from the river or from a sulphurous spring in the neighbourhood, according to the needs or fancies of doctors and patients. There are

* Morris.

N

also vapour baths, little cupboards considerately constructed in the roof of the evaporating house, which thus
combines business and pleasure, visitors being enabled to
sit in the steam as it ascends from the boiling brine which
is being converted into cakes of salt below.

There are people of wonderful constitutions to be found
who can live through almost any amount of medical
cures; but ours being less hardy, we found three minutes'
breathing of the salt vapour as much as body and mind
could bear without evaporating altogether.

There are two mud-baths, or Schlammbäder, made from
the refuse slime of the salt-mine reservoirs, but these were
depths into which we declined to penetrate.

The woods round Ischl have been laid out with much
care, with good level roads, or winding paths, and there
are seats and summer resting-places at all the best points
of view.   The favourite drive and promenade is through
the wood at the side of the river, where are several *Quellen*
and tokens of Imperial favour in the form of ornamental
stonework, statues, inscriptions, &c.   Through this wood
you pass to Laufen on your road to Hallstadt or Gmunden; but many may prefer a journey altogether by water,
and the pleasant excitement of encountering a succession of
rapids larger or smaller in a little boat, or on one of the
great salt-barges that are constantly floated down the
stream.   It is a wonderful sight to watch these great unwieldy vessels shooting the rapids at Gmunden, where the

Traun, flowing through the lake, rushes down a precipitous slope between narrowing banks on its way to the falls
below.   The shouts of the men, the promise of prompt
action in case of danger, and their utter powerlessness
against the tremendous force which they are seeking to
utilize, the roar and dash of the water, and the sight of
the heavily-laden barge, floating like a log at the sport of
the waves, running apparently to instant destruction, and
cleverly steered by the men between the threatening
rocks, make a picture whose force and energy is not soon
to be forgotten.

An easy drive of from one to two hours brought us to
the shores of the Hallstadt See, from whence some sturdy
maidens rowed us, in one of the great flat-bottomed high-
prowed boats, to the little town, which lies on the very edge
of the water, or rather clings to the rocks above.   Road
there is none, the houses grow on to the stones like lim-
pets, and are brown and shining as though the wood had
been freshly soaked, with black timbers here and there,
and some are built out upon piles, amongst which the
green water moves with a pleasant lapping sound, catching
fresh ripples of colour as the sunlight plays upon the
wooden sides, or bright-faced children lean out to throw a
stone below, and send a reflex of dimples and rosy cheeks
or a little scarlet bodice into the circle of quivering light
to which the water steadies back after the splash.

N 2

As we were moved along by the slow steady sweeps of the oars, the scene was exquisitely beautiful, the lake still and clear, with trees and banks and towering hills mirrored so faithfully that one began to grow giddy in the uncertainty as to who or which was upside down !

> ' Inverted in the tide
>   Stand the gray rocks, and trembling shadows throw ;
>   And the fair trees look over, side by side,
>   And see themselves below.'

We landed at a little garden pier belonging to the inn, where was a very small steamer already high and dry in the middle of the flowers, under the hands of some very idle workmen. A jodel greeted us from a stone terrace high over head, some of the party having preceded us, and we were soon installed in a little balcony-salon over the water, where we dined and fished vainly for trout or *Salbling*, and then wandered through the meadows, seeing F. and his guides on their way towards the Dachstein, a snow-giant who was to be comfortably conquered before they rejoined us at Krimml, in preparation for which they had arranged to sleep at some châlets higher up, and make an early start next day by moonlight.

Hallstadt, like many of the Italian towns on the Corniche, seems part of the ground against which it has grown ; the hill might have been honeycombed by many diligent workers, so embedded are the houses in the rock. You mount from one to another by stone stairs or wooden

Ein See Fahrt.

Hallstadt.

Hallstadt

balconies flung out suddenly at abrupt angles, or the path
tunnels under buildings and descends into queer cellar-
like places, from which you emerge under the green
shade of a vine carefully trained over arches, or encounter
a wooden watercourse crossing your path from a perpendicular height above.   One might make short cuts up
the winding path through upper windows, and come
suddenly upon little gardens and a goat or two, and a
stable in the middle of the roofs!   A Protestant and
a Roman Catholic church share nearly equally between
them the inhabitants of the little town.   We passed the
Lutheran building at the moment when a peasant's wedding was going on within.   It was a small party, rather
a shy and awkward one ; the marriage had just been completed, and the clerk, a very busy official, arranged his
company with great expenditure of breath and gesticulation in two rows, men in front, while we all listened to
some very sweet singing, and then the procession moved
out of the church and wound up the steep hill-side, the
bride only to be distinguished by her green wreath from
her companions, who wore white flowers in their hair.
The men's hats were elaborately decorated with great
bunches of flowers and huge satin rosettes ; they looked
very stolid, and as though, if they held their hats long
enough in their hands, they might probably eat the
decorations from shyness or utter absence of mind—a
state which is, I fear, somewhat chronic.

Spite of the intense heat, we managed to walk to the salt-works, and watched with great interest the evaporating process going on. The sun shone down on us with such power that S. declared she found it refreshingly cool, in comparison, to be shut into a sort of cupboard on the rim of the tank full of boiling brine and steam, the fumes of which would have suffocated her if she had tested their strength much longer. The salt is entirely a government monopoly, and they showed us great store-houses filled with the large blocks waiting for the barges, and much decorated with spread eagles, and *königliche kaiserliche* black-lettered inscriptions.

The heat prevented our visiting the Rudolph Thurm, a building perched on a projecting rock 1,000 feet above the lake, built by the Emperor Albert in 1299, to defend the royal possessions, when he and the Prince Archbishop were quarrelling over the salt. In these more prosaic days, it is devoted to a collection of fossils, antediluvian and otherwise, Celtic antiquities, and the manager of the mines. You go up a staircase, or at least may do so if you have sufficient energy to ascend steps for half an hour, and having reached the tower, a trifling addition of 500 feet brings you to the entrance of a salt-mine.

At Aussee the brine is conducted in wooden pipes along the sides of the hills and over bridges from the mine, which is about four miles off. It looks like an early and very clumsy system of telegraphic wires, which may have been 'isolated' by wooden casings, from the effects of a damp climate. Some of the party drove to Aussee from Ischl, having altogether rather an uncomfortable experience.

The road as it approaches the lake becomes very precipitous and execrably bad, and the drivers of the small country carriages seem to take an exquisite pleasure in the sufferings of their employers. Mrs. C. gave a piteous description of her sufferings, and D., who was a lighter weight, was flung so recklessly from one side to the other, that fears were entertained that she might arrive at their destination in several pieces. This was an inn, *die Sonne*, as to which our hopes had been raised by the glowing descriptions of our Ischl landlord, and grievous was the disappointment on the arrival of the party. The *Kellnerin* was a repetition of the brilliant domestic of Hindelang, and the travellers were shown into one big gaunt room which was supposed to be sufficient for their accommodation. A remonstrance procured for them a slightly preferable arrangement, in the form of two chambers, very cold and draughty, divided by a movable paper screen fitted into a groove in the floor. With this they were obliged to be satisfied, and to make the best of the *Abendessen*, which was anything but a success; but strengthening themselves with the philosophy of contentment, which was always admirably sustained by the calm courage of Mrs. C., and never permanently shaken by any joltings of the way, or *contretemps* of food, weather, and lodgings, they finished everything eatable that was to be obtained, and retired to rest, placid if rather stiff and aching. There is some good to be got out of everything, and the sufferings of the moment, however severe, when related to the rest of the party at Hallstadt, where our forces were again united, added zest to our enjoyment at the little Hotel Seeauer, though the latest arrivals, who had slept peacefully at Ischl, and dined well, were cruel enough to laugh over the history.

There is great truth in good old Jeremy Taylor's apothegm, 'He that threw a stone at a dog, and hit his cruel step-mother, said, that although he intended it otherwise, yet the stone was not quite lost; and if we fail in the first design, if we bring it home to another equally to content us, or more to profit us, then we have put our conditions past the power of chance.'

Aussee is beautifully situated at the junction of three streams, which flow from the lake of Aussee and Grundl, and by their union form the river Traun.   The fishing, as on all these lakes and streams, is very good.

In the spring of this year, when we again visited Ischl, we reversed our route in degree.   Leaving the Danube at Linz, we journeyed by rail to Lambach, visiting the Traunfalls and Gmunden, and driving from thence to Ischl. The scenes through which we passed were described at the time in one of our home letters, part of which I may be allowed to quote here, as a history written on the spot, however slight, is generally, like an artist's sketch, very little improved by any touches added afterwards.

Gmunden, May 28th.—How strangely our impressions of a place are affected by the circumstances under which we see it, and how quietly our praise or blame is meted out according to our own sensations, the beauty or charm of a particular place being sadly dependent on the fact that we have found a good hotel, or have dined, or that the weather is too hot and everything is dirty. Last year we thought Gmunden rather tiresome, and never wished to see it again, because we approached it from the water, from which it is not seen in its most picturesque aspect, landed from a hot grimy steamboat on a dirty pier, and spent our time between a large gloomy cavernous hotel and a high mound, up which we climbed for the sake of the view from the summit, and whose sole interest consisted in a dreary chapel and the orthodox number of *stations* leading up to it. This evening the little town looked perfectly lovely and picturesque with its houses smiling out from the trees; mountains and lake lay before us transfigured in all the glories of sunset light, a deep red glow lighting up the snow peaks as though they were touched with fiery fingers. We are in a pleasant new hotel, the *Bellevue,* facing the lake, and our room has a glass-covered balcony, from which I have been trying vainly to paint the colours before they faded away. We found

capital quarters at Linz, breakfasted at the demoralised
hour of nine, and then all started to walk up to the
Jägermeyer. It had rained very early, and the country
looked pleasantly fresh. Our path lay by the side of the
Danube, which rolled in a grand stream of deep green
water between steep rocks richly clothed to their summits
and lower banks covered with houses, the town spreading
itself out along both sides of the river. We ascended by
a steep wood walk between the stems of the firs and hazel
and beech trees, the air was scented with wild flowers and
new-mown hay, a pleasant breeze tempered the hot sun,
and the shady woods looked wonderfully inviting with
numberless tempting little paths losing themselves in their
depths. The distant view over the broad plain of Austria
with a blue range of Styrian Alps beyond, was infinitely
lovely. We wandered back by the market-place and
through many streets, admiring the old German houses and
the shops gay with Paris goods. An hour's rest in the hotel,
and some ices, and diligent sketching of a few of our wild
flowers, and we set out for the station. An hour and a
half's travel brought us to Lambach, where we had tele-
graphed for a carriage to meet us.

We have had a perfectly beautiful day, full of delights,
a pleasant drive of less than two hours through a Tyrol
wood, a level road for the most part and very badly kept,
over which our carriage stumbled and jolted at a tolerable
pace, till the near horse cast a shoe, after which we limped

S: Bartholomä im Königssee.

Traunfall.

on till three old men and a hammer came to our rescue, and knocked the iron somehow on to the unfortunate beast. A very steep road led down to the falls of the Traun and a small country inn, where we dined on trout and potatoes, with a dessert of cheese. The resources of the place are not great, and I fancy the usual demand for supplies is limited to coffee or an afternoon cup of milk and strawberries, when the Austrian ladies drive over from Gmunden or excursionize from the more distant Ischl with provident picnic baskets in the rumble of the carriage :— this fact by the way for those who may come after us.

No words of mine can describe that mad whirl of waters, the side stream rushing over its artificial floor like a broad flat shoot, at the rate apparently of a hundred miles an hour, the great river at its side from a height of nearly fifty feet plunging in a cascade of white foam on to the rocks, splitting them asunder in its fury, working its way through them—till you see a stone bridge spanning the waves—in its persistent flow, falling in one broad sheet of translucent green like melted glass, or flinging a veil of sparkling spray over the dark trees on the shore. The river wanders on in a succession of *side* falls all wonderfully beautiful. Where the artificial aqueduct ceases below, it is curious to see how the water, which has been pent up for more than 1,000 feet, unable to stop itself quickly enough to mingle at once with the main stream where the waters unite, dashes *under* it for a hundred yards or

more, while the Traun flings itself in a tempest of spray
and foam against the sudden rush. An unpleasant moment
that 'meeting of the waters' must be to human weakness
in a boat. There were no barges of any description on
the spot, nor would there be for many hours, so reluctantly
we gave up our hopes of experiencing the delights of an
entirely new sensation.

At 5.30 we climbed the hill again to the high level
along which our road lay, and then drove for nearly two
hours through woods and fields, and a country too beautiful almost for reality. Far below us the green river wound
between the trees, dashing itself in a white fury here and
there against the rocks that came in its way, and foaming
over the rapids ; beyond were wooded hills, and still farther
away, cutting clear and sharp against the sky, ran range
upon range of mountains streaked and powdered with
silver snow, and violet in the evening light. On the
thick mass of trees close to our road the sun, now low in
the West, shone with side rays, transforming them as by
the touch of an enchanter; flowers of the most brilliant
colours grew beside them, the air was full of their sweetness, and the vespers of the little birds who were too tame
or too innocent to take the trouble to fly away from us;
a partridge ran out from a copse, and a squirrel darted
away into the shelter of the tree. The shade deepened
under the firs and grew into purple blackness with soft red
lights where the sun shone on the carpet of dried twigs

and brown mosses.   The sunbeams, like the very spirits of
mischief, wrote their names in great sprawling characters
on the stems of the pines, with delicate tracery, figures
and emblems and wonderful devices, legible no doubt to
sympathetic spirits, but as far above our human and finite
understandings as the *patois* of our honest-hearted and su-
perlatively stupid *Kutscher*. Far above our heads, wherever
the twisted branches of the pines were shaken naked and
bare against the blue sky, they brought a glory of crimson
and orange light, and clothed them in it like a veil. Slowly
the violet shadows deepened in the farther hills, slowly the
snow peaks glimmered and lightened and flushed with a
tender pink as the green radiance lifted itself from the
yellow beeches and the sombre woods, and the great wall
of rock stood bathed in mist as if poised between earth and
heaven, in a divine beauty that one remembers as in a
dream.

Wednesday, 29*th.*—We were roused this morning at seven
by the sound of a solemn chant of many voices singing
out of time and to no particular tune, and, hurrying to
our windows, we watched a long procession of priests and
banners, men, women, and boys following, and all joining
with a great fervency of heart and voice in this propitiatory
act, which is, they hope, to insure a good and plentiful
harvest. The scene before us was indescribably lovely,
the lake calm as a mirror, with mountains brown and
grey and soft blue, and distant snow edges reflected on

its surface, and the *Kloster* and church, rising from a narrow strip of flat land just above the water, sending long white quivering pictures almost across the narrow *See*. Instead of the clearly defined peaks and jutting crags and glory of last evening, or the cold brightness of the night, there was a glow of warmth and colour, a blue light like heat made visible, a hum of insects in the air, and a sweet scent of morning and fresh spring beauty.

This would be a charming place to spend a summer in. It is very popular with the Viennese, and no wonder, as it makes capital head-quarters for excursionists ; there is plenty of sport, good fishing and shooting in the neighbourhood, well-made roads, and easy carriages for invalids, and both here and at Ischl many a long day might be spent in pleasant rides through the woods, which are well adapted for equestrians, who can penetrate where the ways are too narrow for anything larger than a *Bergwagen*, and often too boggy for explorers on foot.   This hotel is new and very good ; our bedroom is like a spacious *salon*, with four large windows draped with white ; facing the lake is a covered balcony like a small orangery or ' chamber on the wall,' into which one of them opens ; the furniture is all good and handsome, a new grand piano of shining satinwood fills up one corner ; the landlord, who speaks English, is most attentive, and the *cuisine* excellent ; families may board here at a charge of seven shillings a day per head, supposing they occupy the best apartments, but of

course the rate of payment varies with the rooms selected. . . .

We found the drive to Ischl an infinitely more charming 'means to an end' than our journey by water of
the former year, and in the intense sunshine Nature
looked at her best and brightest, all the dust having
been washed off by the rain and snow of the past week.
We passed through a perpetual garden, beautiful villas
half hidden among the trees, Italian, Swiss, German
houses, every style and fantastic form which architecture
assumes when it indulges itself in the pleasures of holiday
life, and, like its employers, renounces for the nonce the
rules and necessities of sterner existence. Above villas
and cottages rose wooded hills promising good cover for
game; close at our side lay the blue lake, and beyond
it the great warm grey hills. The fields were studded
with flowers, large purple *Campanulas* growing in such
masses that at a little distance they looked like pools of
water reflecting the sky, and it was only on nearing them
that we discovered the reality.

We came suddenly upon a peasant gathering, men and
women resting under the shade of some trees, while the
priests offered their prayers at a little wayside shrine; the
poor earnest devout faces were bowed in a reverent stillness, over which the shadows of the leaves

> ' Dropt and lifted, dropt and lifted,
> In the sunlight greenly sifted,'

went and came, throwing flickering lights upon their
heads; the resonant chant swelled solemnly through the
utter silence which we shrank from breaking by noise of
hoofs and wheels. That rough altar built up in the midst
of the hay-fields with the earnest group of worshippers,
seemed to us a wonderfully beautiful sight which clearer-
eyed Protestants might be none the worse for studying.

At Ebensee we parted from the lake and our old friend
the Traunstein, and drove for the next two hours by the
river, watching the logs from Ischl as they met us floating
down the stream. We stopped at a road-side inn to water
the horses and have some bread and wine, and enjoyed
a half-hour's rest in a cool little wooden arbour overgrown
with creepers, where big and little dogs came to be petted
and fed; one very fat three-weeks-old Newfoundland
puppy would thrust investigating paws and nose into
everything, so we painted the latter with vermillion as a
warning to the others, and watched it waddle off thus
decorated to express its disgust at the world in general
by various sneezings and contortions of its very stumpy
little tail. The great river rushed past us, carrying away
broken reflections of homesteads and farmhouses and
overshadowing fruit trees, of wooded hills and one snowy
mountain top, the only rapidly moving force in that still
life where everything seemed so peaceful and so very dull,
from the old *Wirth*, who came to sit by us on the bench,
and his stout helpmeet—who stood with arms akimbo,

"At Ischl. a study!

as we drank her white wine, beaming a delighted sense
of what our enjoyment must be, 'Das ist gut, nicht wahr?
Ah!'—to the sleepy mother of the busy little puppy, who
lay in the sunshine blinking sleepily at her son, as if to
say, 'It is all very well, but you will soon learn to take
life as easily as the rest of us.'

The hotels at Ischl are all good; the new Hotel Bauer,
built on the summit of a little hill, commands a fine view
of the town, and is a large and somewhat imposing edifice.
Herr Bauer, the present manager, was earnest in his
endeavours to persuade our father to remain at Ischl over
the Sunday. We had strolled up to the house and were
admiring his new *salon*.

'Ah,' cried the good man, 'if you would only stay till
Sunday, my Reverend is coming from England, and it is
so much to be regretted that you should be going. Can
I not tempt you to remain and listen to my Reverend!'

There was a strange procession which we encountered
one day returning from the church, a funeral of a woman;
the coffin, carried on men's shoulders, was covered with a
shabby pall, and decorated with tin crowns wreathed with
paper flowers, and with paste-board figures of saints
like children's toys tottering on the top. Behind there
followed a promiscuous assemblage, all the men, women,
and boys who had been at the afternoon service, hundreds
of people walking two and two, chanting with more or
less of fervour. Never had we seen such a collection

o

of faces and figures, deformed goitred old women, young
ones unutterably ugly, idiotic-looking men; the women
in their stiff black dresses and kerchiefs bound across the
forehead, and sanctimonious faces, reminded one of queer
old wood-cuts of puritan saints, giving thanks meekly that
chastisement had fallen upon an erring brother. This
walk in the heat after the shaking coffin was a work of
supererogation, a fact which spread a mild and virtuous
satisfaction over the bland faces.

Judging from the people one sees, Ischl, beautiful as it
is, must be anything but healthy as a dwelling place;
the inhabitants who throng the streets are an utterly
different race from the strong sturdy peasants of Bavaria
or Tyrol. At the *Fête Dieu* we saw a very different
assemblage; this great church festival filled the town
with people from the whole country side, dwellers on
the hills, or in the plains. For days beforehand, young
men and maidens had been busy planting forests of
beech boughs, or forming arcades of green branches
before the principal houses, framing sacred pictures in a
bower of leaves, and hanging gay draperies from the
windows; wreaths of flowers and tasteful bouquets decorated the walls and covered the temporary altars erected
in the streets. As we walked down towards the *Kurhaus*
we met hundreds of peasants in gala attire, streaming in
from the neighbouring villages, bright-faced sturdy girls in
groups of twos and threes, tramping along the road with

A golden headdress

Guards from the Saltworks.

From the Saline.

An official at the
Fête Dieu.

Ischl.

bare feet thrust into roughly-made clogs, while the clean
black shoes and white stockings were carefully carried
in the hand to heighten the effect of the *toilette* at
the last moment. The little children were beaming over
with happiness, and even the small babies were in white
muslin and green and flowery wreaths, with their hair
beautifully dressed; at Gmunden, which we had visited
the day before, the whole of the younger portion of the
female population were in anticipatory curl-papers! The
boys were resplendent in green stockings and plumed
hats, the men lounged about in picturesque groups,
grey coated and with stockings and hats of Tyrol green,
the latter decorated with *Lämmergeier* feathers or plumes
from the *Auerhann*. There were two bands belonging to the
königl. kaiserl. Salzsolenwerk, manufactory or distillery,
or royal monopoly of something *salinen* or otherwise, the
men all well turned out, and others appeared from the
same works carrying rifles, a sort of guard of honour to the
Heilige Jungfrau or any saint of distinction. Very curious
it was to see these men dressed in a strange livery, the
black blouse of the miner, and a plume of green feathers
in their dark soldier-like caps. Some of the men from
the Bavarian salt works, whom we saw a few days later
at Berchtesgaden, carried hatchets that glistened in the
sun as they stood on guard round a little temporary altar,
while the officiating priest elevated the Host and performed
mass for the people. It was a pleasant sight, spite of the

superstition and the little follies that grouped themselves
round the religious rites, from the devout feelings of the
worshippers, and the keen delight of each unit in that
great mass in the general festiveness of the day; there
were old grandames so proud and happy over the little
ones and their pretty dresses, the children so innocently
glad, the men with quiet reverent faces, holding lighted
candles wreathed with flowers which did nothing but
gutter or go out, and chanting vigorously to an accompaniment of drums and trumpets, and a great clanging
bell that of course always came in out of time, and in
the midst of the banners and candles, singing priests,
and devout worshippers, with the sunshine covering
it with a halo like a glory, was the great picture of the
festival, the Christ showing his wounds to the Father,
the *Christus Salvator* of the *Frohnleichnam's Tag*.

There were endless decorations and ornamentations,
the churches had turned out all their treasures of relics
and upholstery to enrich the procession, a sermon or
Evangelium, which unfortunately we could not stay to
hear, was to be preached in the open air, the people
disposing themselves to listen, and camping out on
steps and balconies.   One little group was especially
to be remembered; on a flight of steps, a green bower
of fresh beech boughs, sat a sweet-faced young mother,
her sober colouring forming a perfect foil for two little
bits of living sunshine, beaming golden hair and starry

Returning from the Fest.

Im Schatten.

eyes, rosiest cheeks and lips and dimples, two cherub
children, flower-crowned and dressed in white : one of the
dear fat beauties was lifted towards us in the arms of
a proud old grandmother, and gave us a soft little round
hand through the beech leaves with a burst of happy
laughter.

But our carriages were ready and it was time to depart,
and reluctantly turning away from this pleasant spot
and all that day's gladness, we drove up the steep hill
and left the happy valley far behind. A very pleasant
drive was ours to Salzburg : we had by no means said
good-bye to the festival, every little village was gay
with flags and greenery, every wayside chapel bright with
wreaths, and the roads swarmed with peasants, men and
girls, like great nosegays as we saw them through the
trees, so brilliant were the colours of their dresses ; one
of the peculiarities of the Tyrol costumes is the absence
of patterns or *fusings* of tints, they shine out bright
and distinct like the field flowers.

Our party was a very merry one; we amused ourselves by jumping out of the carriages, unknown to our
worthy drivers who plodded up the hills beside their
horses unwitting of lighter or heavier loads, hunting for
treasures in the hedges, collecting ferns, stopping to
drink at wayside springs, and exchanging greetings with
the peasants, and when once installed again in our places,
filling the seats with small maidens whose sturdy little

legs seemed very weary even with the delights of that
day's gladness, and setting them down at the cottage
doors as we passed, where busy *Hausmutters* were preparing the simple supper.

At St. Gilgen the lake instead of 'sleeping in the
sunshine' was all astir, the wind rippling it into real
waves almost white-tipped in their energy. We bought
stores of white *Lämmergeier* feathers at a quaint little
shop, and then after an hour or more of progress halted
at a way-side inn to rest and water the horses; the men
joined a little group under the trees, where a good *curé*
and some peasants were drinking coffee; our father sat
in the carriage with our last 'Saturday,' and we lay on
a bank in very happy 'idlesse' watching the water trickle
from a spout and three ducks come and drink it.   There
was a stream near, but the ducks returned with much
expenditure of strength and breath from time to time,
drank with infinite satisfaction, waddling back comforted
to the ditch below.   Were they Ischl birds, we wondered,
who had learnt the practice from much watching in their
youth of autumn visitors to the baths and *Quellen*, studying
the amount of exercise prescribed between each swallow?
To us it seemed a very common pump, old and somewhat
leaky even, but the ducks thought otherwise.   There was
a big grey fellow with one black feather in its tail, and
its head held a little on one side, who was evidently
a deep thinker; the pump was doubtless good for some

At the Pump!

The natives see the last of us !

symptoms, weak nerves or dyspepsia, and the bird knew it! Bladud was a real live prince, according to historical legends, though like a poor prodigal he was turned out amongst the swine, but it was a learned pig that taught him the virtues of the Bath waters, and here before our eyes was doubtless a fresh proof of the marvellous instinct of beasts and birds: what an interesting study for the psychologist! In an affable voice we addressed the duck on the instant in all the appropriate euphemisms of the German language:—

'Gnädiger duck, hast thou, like the much-belauded doctors of Austrian and Bavarian Spas, discovered a specific for human ills? Art thou, too, a general benefactor, if only to thy companion ducks? Art thou a —— ?'

'Quack!' said the duck, so suddenly and solemnly, that startled by the unexpected response we gazed helplessly at the pump and then at each other, and all laughed till the ducks being offended retired into the ditch.

Among the learned physicians whose fame draws the travelling public, when more or less invalided, to drink and bathe and study peripatetic philosophy, combining Aristotle and a water diet in due proportion, there are many more especially sought after by the English. Our visits to these medicinal springs have almost always been out of the season; we have found the establishments alto-

gether closed, or have been ushered through large halls of
a general and unpleasant dampness, declined the draught of
water kindly offered to us by a mouldy-looking attendant,
and satisfied our curiosity by a study of the frescoes and
other decorations of the walls, and the inevitable bronze
or marble bust amongst the shrubs outside, with its lau-
datory inscription to the special providence in the form of
a *medico* who first made the spot famous.

Many of our friends have been more fortunate ; they
have drunk at the well, bathed in the hot and cold waters,
and been visited with solicitous care by the attendant
minister.   One case I remember in which there was a
slight uncertainty as to treatment, owing to the want of a
perfect understanding of the form of words employed.
The patient was described by a brother, whose English
was of that pure Saxon obtaining at Eton and Rugby, as
' not much amiss.'

' A little down in the mouth, you know.'

' Ah !' said the doctor, ' that symptom is strange to
me,' and out came the note-book.   ' A leetle down in the
mouth, did you say ?   Ah ! Um !' and the troubled
physician paused, meditating over this new and difficult
diagnosis.

Travellers, as a rule, are not wonderful as linguists, and
we have all in our time made great blunders ourselves,
and listened to ludicrous mistakes from others.

F., when sitting one day in a *restauration*, heard an

English traveller ordering his dinner in spasmodic but apparently fluent German; and leaning forward, when the *Kellner* had disappeared, said in a deprecating voice, as dreading to interfere between any man and the *menu* he had selected :

'I am afraid, sir, you hardly know what you have ordered.   Can I be of any help as an interpreter ? '

' Oh ! thank you ; but what's the matter ? I want some fish and potatoes. Isn't it all right ?' cried the poor victim.

'Possibly,' answered F., 'only I thought I heard you asking for *péchés* and *pantoufles*, and I am afraid you may find " sins " and " slippers " a little indigestible.'

We English have curiously little talent as linguists, though we may have a superficial knowledge of two or three languages, and may succeed in making ourselves understood more or less as we travel, whereas a Russian or an Austrian speaks five or six with the most perfect mastery of their difficulties, and delicate appreciation of their idiomatic correctness and beauty. We complimented a young Viennese girl on her beautiful English ; she answered quite simply :—

' I am glad you think I speak it well ; we all like English, and it is taught everywhere in our nurseries.   The Austrians are fond of the study of languages, and learn easily; my little brother, who is only four years old, speaks three languages, one of which is *Hongarisch*, as his nurse is an Hungarian.'

We were astonished to find such familiar knowledge of some of our latest authors amongst the people we met during our journey. One of our acquaintances, an Hungarian lawyer, eagerly discussed with us the works of J. S. Mill, Buckle, &c., and it is strange to see how much better known such books are in Germany than similar ones would be with us; modern German thought failing to penetrate in England beyond a purely intellectual or critical circle.

But we must return to our halting-place on the road to Salzburg, where by this time the horses were rested; one of the drivers came up to us with a huge bumper of some dark liquid in his hand, of which he pressed us to partake. We just touched the glass with our lips, not to hurt his feelings, and pronounced it to be decidedly '*süs.*' It was very abominable, quite sweet and dark, meant to be coffee, I believe, but was a sort of black *eau sucré*, made of coarse burnt sugar. The *curé* and the old *Wirthin* said '*Guten Abend,*' the peasants nodded over their beer in friendly recognition, and a young girl we had brought with us from St. Gilgen came to wish us good-bye, and kiss our hands; the grey duck looked at us disparagingly, as anti-hydropathists, and we drove away gaily from the little *Gasthaus* to our good quarters in the Nelbök at Salzburg as the shadows were beginning to lengthen, and a pleasant and cool air came to temper the heat of that bright summer's day.

EXCURSIONS AMONG THE ORTLER AND LOMBARD ALPS.

———+——

' Blue, and baseless, and beautiful,
Did the boundless mountains bear
Their folded shadows into the golden air.'
                                            RUSKIN.

' Der Ortler, aus Granit geworben,
Zur Gränzenhut emporgehoben,
  Ragt glorreich allen Nachbarn vor,
Und trägt aus frommen Hirtenthale
Des Dankes volle Opferschale
  Zu deinem Thron, o Gott! empor.'
                                            BEDA WEBER.

EXCURSIONS AMONG THE ORTELER AND LOMBARD ALPS.

—◦◦—

IT is by no means one of the least of the benefits conferred on the geographer and the mountaineer by the
publication of Mr. Ball's admirable ' Guide to the Central
Alps,' that in directing attention to the topography and
high attractions of the Orteler and Lombard Alps, it has
thrown much new light on a district which has hitherto
received a very inadequate share of notice. The construction of the great Stelvio road, indeed, familiarised the
public with a portion of the country in question, whilst
the valuable work of Schaubach (' Die Deutschen Alpen,
B. iv. Handbuch für mittlere und südliche Tyrol ': Jena,
1850) afforded much useful information; but curiosity
seems to have been limited to the immediate scenery of
the pass, and though the summit of the Orteler Spitze
itself has during the last sixty years been several times
attained, few have cared to push their explorations farther,
or to investigate the numerous other peaks which, whilst
rivalling it in height, perhaps surpass in beauty the
monarch of the group.

Stimulated alike by the charms of novelty and by the

glimpses which a passage of the Stelvio the year before had given me of some of the grandest features of the district, I resolved at the earliest opportunity to devote a few days at least to the more thorough exploration of its recesses ; and finding that my inclination was shared by my friends E. N. and H. E. B., whom I had arranged to meet at Pontresina about the end of July, a combined scheme of operations was agreed upon, the results of which I now propose to lay before the reader.

In pursuance of our compact, the various members of our band collected on the 25th of July 1864 at Samaden, whence on the following morning we sallied forth a merry company of ten (five of whom were ladies), to establish ourselves for a week at that pleasantest of headquarters, the Krone at Pontresina. Here, amongst other Alpine friends, we found Messrs. Tyndall and Hinchliff, and learnt from the former that Mr. Ball was actually at Santa Catarina in the Val Furva, whither he was himself bound, and that they had designs of a similar character to ours. The chance of obtaining such an accession to our forces at once decided us to cut short our stay in the Engadine ; and accordingly, after devoting a couple of days to some new excursions in the Bernina, which previous expeditions had suggested, we reassembled at the comfortable establishment of Le Prese, and thence journeyed on the 29th to Tirano and Bormio. Arrived at the latter place, and hearing discouraging accounts of the chances of accom-

modation at Santa Catarina, it was thought most prudent
for some one to proceed thither at once, and ascertain the
actual state of affairs.   Accordingly, after despatching a
hasty dinner, H. and I started at 9.25, in a char, for
the Val Furva, whose torrent, the Frodolfo, joins the
Adda at Bormio.   The night was dark, and as we generally proceeded at a foot-pace, it was past midnight
when we drove up before a large plain-looking stone building, from whose goodly array of windows, however, many
a bright gleam of light shone forth upon the silent valley,
and sparkled in the swift waters of the Frodolfo.   It was
a comfort to find a waiter still astir, and to learn that,
though the entire building was packed to the roof with a
dense mass of humanity, something in the shape of beds
might and should be improvised for us in the billiard-
room.   The result was very superior to anything we had a
right to calculate upon under the circumstances, whilst we
had afterwards the satisfaction of being undeservedly pitied
by the other members of our party, amongst whom a
legend long gained credit that the billiard-table itself had
constituted our couch.

The next morning was everything that could be desired
for a preliminary investigation, and having sent a message
to our friends at Bormio and discovered Mr. Ball, a
consultation was held as to the first point of attack.
He so strongly recommended us to begin with the ascent
of the Monte Confinale, and the position of that mountain

was so obviously calculated to give us a general insight
into the topography of the Orteler chain, that we resolved
to assault it at once without awaiting the arrival of the
main body. Some provisions were therefore hastily collected, and at nine o'clock we set out amidst suppressed
excitement on the part of the inmates of the establishment.

I must here premise that the Confinale is the loftiest
point of a spur from the main ridge which, quitting the
latter at the S. foot of the Königsspitze, and running
for a short distance nearly due S., bends round more and
more till it gradually assumes a westerly direction, thus
dividing the Val Forno and the middle portion of the
Val Furva from the Val del Zebru, of which latter it
constitutes the E. and S. boundary. Though the actual
summit is invisible from Santa Catarina itself it dominates
the whole neighbourhood, and being equalled in height
only by the peaks of the main chain, which sweep round
it in a semicircle from the Cristallo to the Corno dei tre
Signori, it will be seen at once that no better point could
be selected for a general survey.

We crossed the Frodolfo by a bridge close to the
Stabilimento delle Acque, passed through the little village, and struck up the mountain-side by a path on the
left bank of a torrent which comes leaping down in a
series of cascades, and is derived from the snows of the

Confinale. Traversing a little pinewood we soon came
out upon beautiful grassy slopes, commanding views of
constantly increasing beauty and extent of the head of the
Val Furva and its S. arm leading up to the Gavia Pass,
guarded by the noble peaks of the Tresero and Corno
dei tre Signori. Comforted by sundry draughts of milk,
which the burning heat rendered most acceptable, we
held on our way towards a line of cliffs which form the
E. boundary of a small elevated valley running right
up into the heart of the mountain. Here our course
became more level, but our progress was slow, as we had
to traverse a succession of slopes of débris descending to
the level of the stream, whose right or W. bank would
have afforded better walking. Gradually the cliffs circled
round in front of us, but were broken by gullies, through
one of which we scrambled up, amidst a perfect chaos of
fragments of huge size and fantastic arrangement, to the
level of the snowfields above. The actual summit was
now seen for the first time, separated from us by the névé
of a small glacier which descended to the left of our
station in a southwesterly direction. Half an hour's steady
but by no means rapid ascent across the snowfield, and
then parallel with the SE. ridge of the mountain, brought
us to the foot of the final rocks. These were free from
difficulty, and in five minutes more we stood upon the
summit at 1.45, just four hours and three quarters after

quitting Santa Catarina. Our progress had been leisurely,
and our various halts having amounted altogether to one
hour and a quarter, it will be seen that the ascent may
be easily accomplished in three-and-a-half hours' walking.
The height of the peak is 11,076 English feet, according
to Von Welden, and that of Santa Catarina being about
5,000, the difference of elevation is upwards of 1,000 feet
greater than that between Pontresina and Piz Languard,
with which it may be most conveniently compared. It
seems difficult to suppose that so excellent a station
should not have been made use of by the officers charged
with the survey of the great military map of the Lom-
bardo-Venetian Provinces; but we could discover no trace
of any erection, and flattered ourselves with the idea of
being the first to discover the great attractions, easy
access, and admirable view which characterise the
mountain.

Whilst my companion set vigorously to work at the
construction of a cairn, in which to deposit a record of
our visit, I occupied myself for the next hour or two in
transferring to my notebook an outline of the glorious
succession of peaks, snowfields, and glaciers which
stretched in an unbroken line around us through a
horizon of something like 200°, and included nearly all
the highest summits of the Orteler and Lombard Alps.

After a stay of rather more than three hours we started
at 4.45, quitted the snow at 5.5, and at 7.15, after a

quarter of an hour's halt, reached Santa Catarina—thus effecting the descent in two-and-a-quarter hours' walking. Here we heard that our companions had come up from Bormio in the morning; but finding the available accommodation less satisfactory than could be desired, some of them had returned to secure beds at the Bagni di Bormio, whilst the remainder had kindly waited for us. Our second detachment started in a carriage at 8.30, and, after a pleasant drive in the cool of the evening down the romantic Val Furva, rejoined the first at 10.45. Unfortunately, in the dark, both my barometers somehow contrived to fall from the carriage and get broken, so that during the remainder of our journey we were limited to an aneroid by Browning, belonging to E., which proved, however, to be a first-rate instrument.

The following day (July 31st) being Sunday, we spent the morning quietly between our capital quarters and the shade of a somewhat meagre pine-wood, and a little before five took our departure for the third cantoniera on the Stelvio road, which we proposed to make our starting-point for further explorations on the morrow. It was arranged that all the ladies, under the charge of Michel Payot and the two remaining gentlemen of our party, should proceed to Santa Catarina on Monday, and establish themselves there as comfortably as circumstances, modified by the kind exertions of Mr. Ball, would permit; whilst E. and H. and myself, accompanied by our

P

respective guides—Franz Biener of Zermatt, and the gallant old Christian Michel of Grindelwald—devoted one or, perhaps, two days to clear up the mystery of the Cristallo, and investigate the Vitelli Glacier and Val del Zebru.

Two-and-a-half hours' easy walking brought us to the third refuge or cantoniera, situated between the steep ascent known as the Spondalunga and the higher station of Santa Maria. The landlord is a decent fellow, disposed to do his best, but the accommodation is of the most limited character, and appeared only to have reference to the wants of passing travellers. One bed was all that could be provided, but a mattrass on the floor answered equally well, and after a good supper on our own provisions, we laid ourselves down to rest.

It was just 3.15 on the morning of the 1st August when we issued forth upon the noble Stelvio road, and proceeded down it at a rapid pace till just before reaching the cantonnier's house standing at the commencement of the zigzags by which the descent of the Spondalunga is effected. Here we turned off sharp to the left, and traversing slopes of débris by a path which in the faint light was barely distinguishable, found ourselves at 4.15 at the right or north bank of the Vitelli Glacier, not far from its extremity. The main body of the ice appeared to descend right in front from between a somewhat uniform ridge on our left and a fine snowy mass on the right, which we rightly conjectured to be the western termination of the spur described by Mr. Ball ('Guide to the Central Alps,' p. 415 b), as 'including two principal summits, of which the eastern peak in form somewhat resembles the Lyskamm.' Further to the right a succession of inferior elevations sweep round till they terminate in the rocks which over-hang the second cantoniera, and give rise in their intervals to two or three glaciers of secondary importance, the most easterly of which constitutes the western affluent of the Vitelli. With these we had nothing to do, our course clearly lying up the main arm beneath, and to the north of, the conspicuous snowy mass already referred to, which formed the centre of the picture. E. had indulged in the unusual luxury of a stereoscopic camera, which after doing good service in the Bernina was now again made useful, and after a short halt we stepped upon the ice at 4.40. The glacier, which is beautifully pure, presented no diffi-culty, and keeping straight up the centre we reached the foot of the ice-fall immediately to the north of the western extremity of the Vitelli ridge at 5.30. Here the rope was put in requisition, and at 5.40 we commenced the ascent. Keeping close under the south boundary of the glacier, our progress was facilitated by the slopes of snow which obliterated the crevasses on this side of the ice-fall, and though the huge masses of overhanging séracs, towering high into the air on our right, were suggestive of ava-lanches, the *débris* of which we frequently traversed, this course would probably be at all times the best.

At 6.30 the level of the upper plateau was gained, and a glorious expanse of snow was descried sloping gently upwards towards a broad col, and bounded by two great ramparts of considerable uniformity of outline, but whose exquisite purity as they glittered in the bright clear morning light rendered them strikingly beautiful objects. Scarce a rock was to be seen, and it was at first very difficult to determine the relative altitude of the principal prominences, or the scale of the scenery as a whole. As we progressed, however, it became more and more evident that of the two ridges, both of which attained their greatest elevation towards their eastern extremities, that on our left, which we afterwards ascertained to be the Video Spitze (11,361 feet), or second highest point of the Cristallo, was the loftier, whilst the conviction was momentarily strengthened that neither could rival for a moment either the Orteler Spitze, or many other peaks of the group. The ridges in question are indeed but little more than great snowy hummocks, of exquisite beauty it is true, but scarcely attaining to the dignity of mountains.

Twenty minutes' steady walking at a rapid pace up the level floor of this noble corridor brought us at 6.50 to the depression at its head already mentioned, and all doubt as to our further course was at once set at rest by the discovery that we were looking down from a height of some 10,700 feet into the centre and lower portion of the Val del Zebru, from which, however, we were cut off by apparently impracticable precipices of enormous depth. Feeling anxious to investigate the other side of the Cristallo ridge, and not knowing how large might be the demands on our time and strength before night, we did not attempt to test the chance of effecting a descent by *force majeure*; but retracing our steps for a few hundred yards and then gradually bearing away to the north, we made for the ridge at a point between the Video (11,361 feet) and Nagler Spitze (10,687 feet). Turning round the north-west shoulder of the former peak, we found ourselves at 7.15 standing on the west side of the upper névé of the Madatsch Glacier, and separated by it from the series of summits terminating on the north in the Madatsch Spitze proper, over which towered the grand mass of the Orteler Spitze itself. Farther to the right a depression was visible, and beyond it a dome-like summit. Next to this came a sharpish cone through whose snowy mantle a few rocks cropped out here and there. Again the eye was puzzled to say whether this summit or its neighbour, the nearer Video Spitze, was the loftier; but on the whole the betting was in its favour, and the event justified our estimate, as it proved to be the highest of the series of eminences to which the name of Cristallo has been collectively applied.

A glance sufficed to show that our course would lie over

the depression between the cone and the most westerly of
the upper peaks of the Madatsch ridge, as from it the
ascent of the former (which on the side of the Vitelli
Glacier was impracticable) appeared easy of accomplish-
ment, and it seemed besides to offer the greatest chance
of effecting our intended subsequent descent into the Val
del Zebru. Again the camera was called into requisition,
and operations were on the point of commencing, when
the box containing the plates was suddenly seen to glide
from its moorings, and set off on a voyage of discovery
towards the névé beneath. Franz started in pursuit, for-
getful that he constituted a link in a chain, and came to
grief and the length of his tether at the same instant.
Whilst he was detaching himself the rash adventurer slid
merrily onwards, and laughter was mingled with vexation
as we saw Franz wildly plunging downwards and, though
gaining ground at every step, arriving at the upper edge
of a crevasse just in time to see the object of his pursuit
topple merrily over into the dark depths which he dared
not approach more closely. We all rushed to the rescue,
and after a short hunt Christian appeared holding the
truant aloft in triumph. Another attempt to photograph
was more successful, and after sketching and indulging in
a second breakfast we quitted our station at 8.45, and at
nine reached the level surface of the Madatsch névé, over
some steep slopes intersected by numerous crevasses.

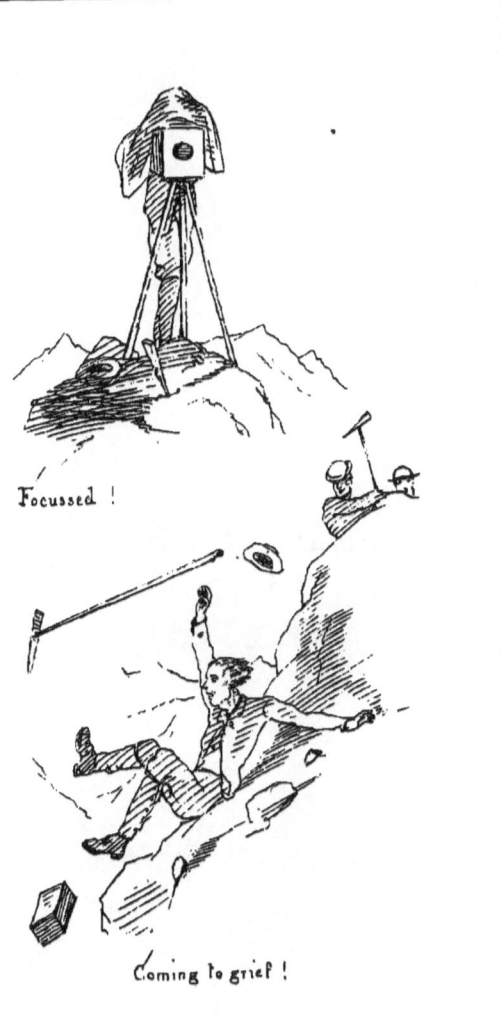

Focussed !

Coming to grief !

Fifteen minutes' steady walking brought us to the foot of the steep wall leading up to the col. Here step-cutting became necessary, the slope being very rapid : our progress was slow, and it was 9.40 before we stood on the summit. The view on the other side was at once mag-nificent and satisfactory—magnificent because it included the massive Orteler and glorious Königsspitze with the Klein Zebru and other intervening peaks, and satisfactory because the hope of being able to descend to the level of the Val del Zebru was on the whole strengthened. For the third time the camera was set up, and two slides, forming a panorama of the chain from the Orteler Spitze to the Königsspitze, were rapidly secured by E., whilst I worked away more slowly at my outline.

Depositing our various traps on the col, we struck off at 10.30 to our right, climbed a steepish ridge broken in its lower part by rocks, and then keeping a little to the left found ourselves at eleven on the conical summit already alluded to. The Video Spitze appeared to the eye to be but little less elevated than that on which we stood ; but the superiority of our position would have been in-disputable even without the authority of the Kataster Survey, which assigns to the two points the respective heights of 11,370 and 11,361 feet. On the south we looked down into the Val del Zebru, from which we were cut off by enormous precipices, but could see nothing of the Vitelli ridge, even the highest point of it being entirely concealed by the intervening Video Spitze, which must therefore be the more elevated of the two. We spent a most enjoyable hour on the summit, though our view was cut short in the direction of the Königsspitze by clouds sweeping up from the south.

Starting again at twelve, we regained the col, which we propose to call the Madatsch Joch, at 12.30. Its height, as determined by an observation of E.'s aneroid compared with Aosta and Turin, comes out 10,838 feet; but as the reading of the same instrument on the summit of the peak gives a height for the latter of 11,576 feet, or 206 in excess of the Kataster determination, these figures must be looked upon as probably too high by at least 100 feet, if not more.

Collecting our baggage we quitted the col at 12.35, and proceeded down the gently-inclined slopes of a glacier which, as it descends from the Cristallo and the ridge connecting its different peaks with the Schnee Glocke and Trafoier Spitze, I have ventured to name the Cristallo Glacier. Its termination towards the Val del Zebru is for the most part pretty uniform, but at the corner farthest from the Cristallo it thrusts forward a long narrow tongue of ice, forked at the end, which is well seen from the Confinale. Whether the valley may be reached at this point we did not attempt to ascertain, for our ultimate object being to cross into the Val Forno by the ridge separating it from that of Zebru, it was obviously desirable to strike

the latter as near its head as possible. We therefore
kept well to the left, beneath the terminal cliffs of the
Schnee Glocke and Trafoier Spitze, and at 1.15 halted on
the summit of a ridge, part snow and part rock, dividing
the Cristallo Glacier from another further to the east
descending from the Thurwieser Spitze. This last is in its
turn separated by a similar barrier from a larger mass of
the Zebru Glacier which has its source in the eastern slope
of the Thurwieser Spitze, the southern side of the Klein
Zebru, and the south-western shoulder of the Königsspitze.
An attack was now made on the provisions, and at 2.10
we again got under way.

The reconnaissance from the Confinale had satisfied us
that it would be better to quit the ice by the lower edge of
this small intermediate glacier, on whose W. boundary we
were now standing, so we worked down diagonally to our
right, and at 2.30 got on to the slopes of _débris_ below
without the slightest difficulty. Here began the most
troublesome and fatiguing work of the day. We had to
traverse a seemingly interminable waste of unstable stones,
inclined at a high angle and treacherous in the extreme.
Our progress was thus slow, but at three o'clock we reached
the singular and highly-attenuated tongue of the Zebru
Glacier (like that of some gigantic ant-eater), traversed it
without difficulty in five minutes, and at 3.15 gained some
turf slopes. Round these we now wound at a tolerably

uniform level, from time to time coming upon extensive patches of the detested *clapier*, till 4.15, when, wearied of this scrambling mode of progression, which had now lasted nearly two hours, we reached to our delight the mass of ice occupying the head of the valley and formed by the union of a glacier descending on the NE. from the Königsspitze with two others from the Confinale spur on the E. and S. The first was crossed in a few minutes, and then scrambling up the slopes on the left bank of the second or most easterly, and taking to the ice at 4.45, we gained the depression at its head at 5.30. We here stood upon the ridge separating the Val del Zebru from the head of the Val Forno or Val di Cedeh, and connecting the principal peaks of the Confinale spur with the main chain at the S. foot of the Königsspitze. For some distance to the N. the barrier maintains a pretty uniform elevation, and its passage might doubtless be effected at almost any point over a distance of half a mile or more. We kept as much to the right as the SW. boundary of the glacier permitted, in order to reach Santa Catarina with the least possible delay, for the day was already well advanced and we had no time to lose. On the Austrian maps a pass is indicated near the point selected by us for crossing, but as no name is given we proposed to adopt that of Zebru Pass. The height calculated from an aneroid reading by comparison with Aosta and Turin comes out 9,908 feet, but judging by the error in the case of the Monte Cristallo observation, it would probably be safer to adopt 9,700 as the more probable figure.

The beauty of the view over the upper portion of the valleys on either hand as well as of the glorious peaks which form their respective boundaries, induced us to linger till 5.40, when we proceeded down the short and easy glacier on the E. slope and quitted it at 6.15. At 6.30, finding an excellent stream and remarkably sharp appetites, we disposed of the remainder of our provisions; but time was precious, and at 6.45 we once more set forth. We now kept more to the S. and pushed down the Val Forno at a rapid pace over lovely slopes of pasture and along the grass-grown summit of a beautifully-developed ancient lateral moraine, till we dropped at length into a well-defined path. This led us at 7.30 to a little village perched high on the mountain-side, whence a very steep track zigzagging downwards on the left over broken ground and amidst rocks and trees brought us at 7.45 to the main path, which is still, however, carried along the W. side of the valley at a considerable height above the stream.

By this time it was getting dark, and of the remainder of our tramp we saw but little more than enough to convince us that the lower part of the Val Forno possessed charms of the highest order. Stumping along over an unfamiliar road in that peculiar half-light which is almost more confusing than perfect obscurity is a process that soon becomes wearisome and monotonous, especially if one has

been already seventeen hours on foot; and it was therefore with feelings of lively satisfaction that, after traversing
some meadows and turning a corner, we descried the lights
of the Stabilimento delle Acque at Santa Catarina, and
finally reached its hospitable door at 8.40, after a most
interesting, but somewhat fatiguing day.

Having as yet seen but little of the immediate neighbourhood of Santa Catarina, it was resolved to devote the
following morning to the congenial occupation of lounging
about, picnicking in the woods, &c. As the sunny hours
sped rapidly by, the charms of scenery gaining new zest
from those of the social circle which our goodly company
of ten might fairly claim to constitute, one felt that it is
good sometimes to be idle and go with the stream; but
the lingering flavour of recent adventures, the consciousness that much yet remained to be accomplished in the
very limited time still at our disposal, and above all the
sight of the glorious mountains themselves encircling our
little Capua, recalled us to a sense of duty, and reminded
us that we must not allow ourselves to be more than
temporarily demoralised in a climbing sense. In the evening we saw the ladies under the good escort of the same
faithful squires drive off down the valley for the Baths of
Bormio, with the intention of passing the Stelvio on the
morrow, whilst we remained behind to explore more
thoroughly the head of the Val Forno, and, if possible,
cross over to meet them at Trafoi *via* the Suldenthal.

Building a cairn.

A lazy day at Santa Catarina.

The Val Forno, from Santa Catarina

Anticipating a long day's work, we retired to rest soon after eight o'clock, and rising again at 11.30, breakfasted sharp at midnight—an arrangement which, whilst convenient for us, prevented the establishment from being unnecessarily disturbed, as the guests did not, and the waiters could not, get to bed till a late hour.

At 12.45 A.M. on the 3rd we quitted the house, led by a man with a lantern, who was to accompany us up the lower portion of the Val Forno, and return as soon as there was sufficient light to distinguish the track. We retraced our previous course, and passing the point where the small path already referred to led steeply up to the pastures on our left, we found ourselves opposite the foot of the Forno Glacier at 2.30. This is a noble stream of ice which deserves careful exploration, and might be investigated in conjunction with attempts to effect passes into the Val della Mare on both sides of the Viozzi Spitze, or with ascents of the latter peak and the beautiful pyramid of the Pizzo della Mare. Whether the summit of the Tresero could be gained from this side is, I think, uncertain, but there is little doubt of its accessibility from the direction of the Gavia Pass, or even by the glacier which descends between its W. and SW. arêtes. Which of its two peaks is the higher I am unable to state positively: my own impression and that of Mr. Ball is, that the one visible from Santa Catarina is the lower, but it would certainly best repay the labour of an ascent, as everything

may be seen from it which would be visible from its more
easterly neighbour, besides much which it conceals from
the latter.*

For some distance beyond the Forno Glacier we stumbled
uncomfortably onwards over slopes of turf, occasionally
diversified with patches of *débris* and torrent-beds, till the
increasing light rendered the use of the lantern no longer
necessary, and enabled us to dismiss our attendant and
improve our pace.   It was just 4.30 when we reached the
left-hand or most westerly glacier at the head of the valley,
descending partly from the SE. slope of the Königsspitze,
and partly from the adjacent portion of the ridge connecting that peak with the Sulden Spitze and Monte
Cevedale.

We felt some doubt about the identification of the
Sulden Spitze, which is apparently a mere knob or pro-
jection, as may be inferred from the fact that its height is
only 11,109 feet; whilst that of the lowest point of the
ridge, where we supposed the Cevedale Pass to be situated,
can scarcely be less than 10,700 feet.   Time would not
admit of my securing a careful outline of the amphitheatre
of snow summits from the Königsspitze to the Monte
Cevedale, enclosing the head of the valley, which I the
more regret, as the scenery is very fine.

* For further details as to the typography of the Orteler group, clearing
up various points which were doubtful when this paper was written, see
the 'Alpine Journal,' No. XI. (pp. 143–147) and No. XV. (pp. 353–358).

The ice proved extremely slippery, and the snow (which covered the glacier in patches) rather treacherous in places, so we halted for a quarter of an hour to put on gaiters. Keeping straight up the glacier—which was very slightly crevassed, of great width, and probably inconsiderable depth—we found ourselves about six o'clock at the foot of the steep slopes leading to the ridge near where it unites with the colossal mass of the Königsspitze. Up these we worked, bearing away slightly to the left so as to gain the ridge as near its origin as possible, and at 6.30 stood in a depression just beneath the peak. The view over into the Suldenthal and away beyond to the mountains of the great Oetz Thal Group, the Vorarlberg, Lower Engadine, &c., as well as looking back towards the regions we had quitted, was most beautiful; and as we had the day before us, and were here tolerably sheltered from the high wind which was raving about the more exposed and lofty crests, we determined to enjoy it at our leisure whilst discussing a second breakfast, already almost too long postponed.

The height we had now attained appeared, by a rough observation with a level, to be about the same as that of the Tresero, or in round numbers 11,600 feet; and as that of the Königsspitze is 12,648, according to the Kataster, there still remained 1,000 feet to climb. At 7.15 we addressed ourselves to the final tug, which proved steep, though presenting no serious difficulty. A snow slope at a high angle, occasionally assuming the character of névé,

and intersected here and there with incipient bergschrunds
which were easily crossed or turned, led straight up to the
summit, and is perhaps the best mode by which the latter
can be attained, though on this point there may exist
some difference of opinion; and I will not therefore insist
on this view, which an ascent direct from the W. portion
of the head of the Sulden Glacier by one of the glaciers
between the Königsspitze and Klein Zebru may possibly
prove to be erroneous. At any rate, the result justified
our selection; and though, with snow in less excellent
order or replaced by ice, the rate of progress might be
very different, I think future travellers will do well to
follow our example—as was done by my friends Messrs.
Freshfield, Walker, and Beechcroft, who repeated the
ascent a few weeks later.

It was 8.20 when we reached the highest point. The
wind was here so furious and the cold so intense that it
was impossible to remain still for many minutes without
risk of frostbite. I managed with infinite difficulty to
secure an outline sketch, which gave some idea of the
majestic aspect which the Orteler here assumes as it towers
grandly aloft on the other side of the W. head of the
Sulden Glacier. In form it strikingly resembles the Piz
Bernina as seen from the Piz Zupo, though more precipitous and apparently less accessible than the former peak.
The view was of the grandest description, and, though
perhaps equalled by that from the Monte Cevedale, is

surpassed by none in the whole district, from the mere fact that whilst the Königsspitze is second only to the Orteler itself in height, its situation on the axis of the chain gives it a far more commanding position than the latter peak, which only cuts off a small and comparatively uninteresting portion of the panorama in the direction of the Lower Engadine. To the N., S., and SE. the summit, which is narrow but drawn out from ESE. to WNW. into a flattened arête, sinks away in precipices of wonderful height and steepness, on which snow only rests in places. To the E. the slope, as already stated, is more gentle, whilst to the NW. the ridge falls rapidly to the depression on the further side of which is seen the fine peak of the Klein Zebru. In this direction it might be practicable to creep down a few hundred feet, and then, turning to the right, effect a descent to the Sulden Glacier by a steeply-inclined and much-crevassed mass of ice between the Königsspitze and Klein Zebru. Christian and Franz, however, both protested against any such attempt being made, and so, after exploring for a short distance without ascertaining anything very definite, we returned to the summit, and starting again at 9.10 regained our breakfast-place at 9.40. A descent to the Sulden Glacier at this spot appeared difficult, if not impracticable, so we proceeded to a point further to the E. and several hundred feet lower, which seemed to offer a better chance, and was reached at ten o'clock.

Q

The exact locality, which we proposed to call the Königs Joch, is distinctly marked by a conspicuous pointed rock like a gigantic cairn, which rises immediately to the E. of it to a height of twenty or thirty feet. The rocks here show indications of copper, and glowed with purple tints in the bright sunshine. Below us to the N., a very steep slope led down to the glacier, but the snow which covered it was soft and unstable, and moreover rested on hard ice at a slight depth below the surface. Here were all the conditions requisite for the dislodgment of an avalanche and the production of an accident, so we turned as an alternative to a ridge of broken rocks on the left which promised more secure footing for a portion of the descent, and till an involuntary glissade in company with a mass of snow would no longer be dangerous. After reading off the aneroid—which gave, by comparison with Aosta and Turin, a height of 11,063 feet (probably some-what in excess of the truth)—we stept over the edge at 10.10, and soon found that we had got our work cut out for us.

The rocks were very steep, but this we should not have minded if they had been trustworthy, or our number had been smaller; but the fact was that a more utterly disintegrated, rotten, and untrustworthy collection of stones professing to be rocks I never saw. Not even the never-to-be-forgotten ridges of Monte Viso present such a complicated scheme of treachery and deception, and doubt and distrust were the garment of our minds. This state of

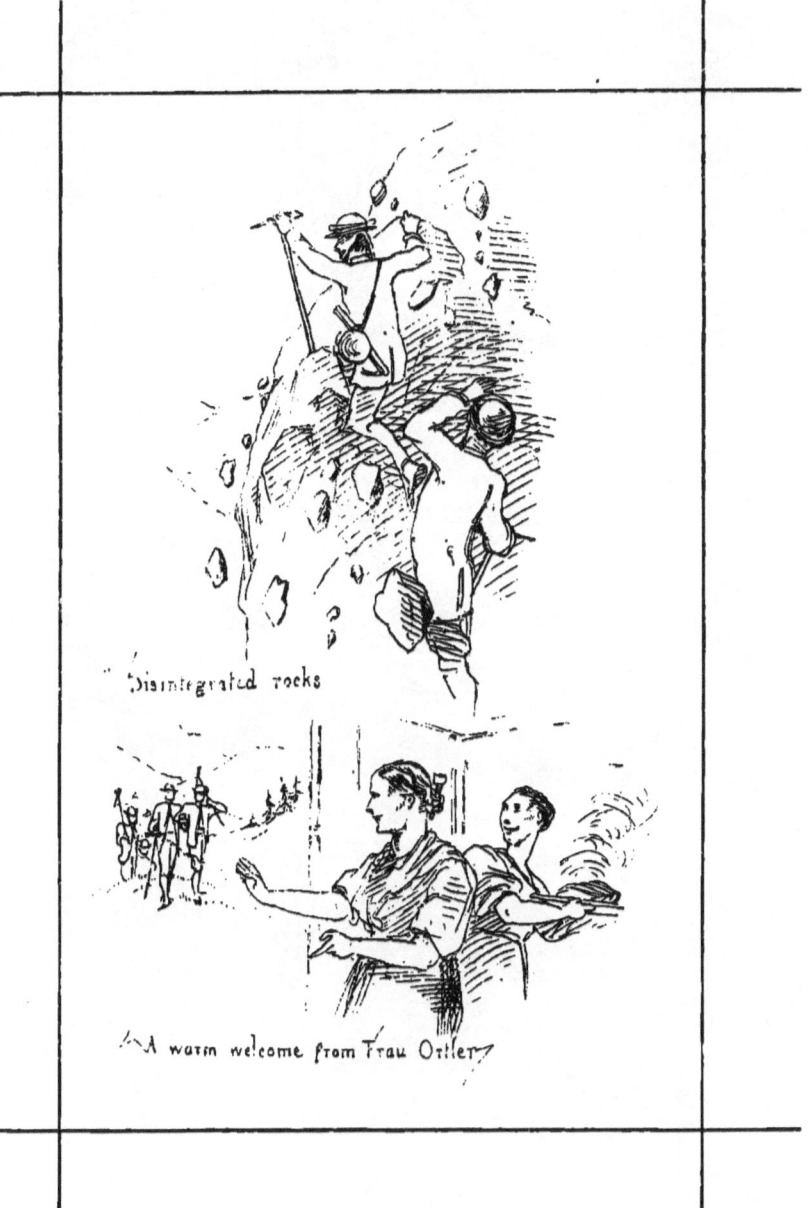

Disintegrated rocks

A warm welcome from Frau Ortler?

things was all due to the circumstance that the ridge in question is composed of a very pure variety of dolomite, which I believe had not previously been observed in this portion of the chain, but of the character of which there can be no doubt, as, through the kindness of Mr. Ball, a small specimen has been analysed at the Museum in Jermyn Street. We crept slowly downwards, those behind in constant fear of dislodging fragments upon those in front, and it was not till 11.15 that we stood on the more gently-inclined surface of the névé of the great Sulden Glacier.

An hour's halt was here called for lunch, and at 12.15 we again set forth, keeping rather to the left beneath the rocks of the Königsspitze, whose glacier-covered summits, however, forbade a too near approach. An hour's walk, varied by about the average amount of glacier difficulties in the shape of crevasses and other obstacles, took us to the central portion of the glacier amidst scenery of the highest order. The apparent height of the Orteler Spitze is, indeed, slightly diminished by the convex form of the back of the glacier descending from it, which conceals the lower portion of the mountain; but in close proximity the huge mass of the Königsspitze, followed by the Klein Zebru, was seen from base to crown, and formed a most imposing feature in the view.

Whilst I halted to complete a drawing, my companions, who were anxious to reach Trafoi with as little delay as possible, pushed on down the glacier, leaving me to follow

at my leisure with Christian and Franz. Three-quarters
of an hour thus passed away very pleasantly, and at two
o'clock I started in pursuit. The glacier is of large
dimensions but gentle inclination, and is fed, in addition
to the two affluents from the Orteler Spitze and Königs
Joch, by a third, which descends from the angle between
the Sulden Spitze and the southern portion of the ridge
dividing the heads of the Sulden and Martell Thal, across
which further to the N. lies the Suldner Joch.

Following the right medial moraine for half an hour,
we quitted the ice at 2.30 for the right bank, and at three
o'clock reached Gampenhöfe, the highest hamlet of the
Sulden Thal just after passing the entrance of the Rosim
Thal on our right. The Sulden Thal in its upper and
central portions is a pastoral valley of considerable width,
flanked on the W. by the magnificent snow-capped cliffs
of the Orteler, and on the E. by a series of minor summits
which separate it from the Valleys of Martell and Laas.
Fine pinewoods clothe the lower slopes ; and these, with
the broad expanse of bright-green grass that covers its
nearly level floor, contrast most beautifully with the
rugged grandeur of the higher regions. It is a striking
scene of quiet peaceful beauty, enhanced by the charms of
its setting amidst features of the highest order of grandeur.
The peasants were all actively engaged in cutting or
securing their hay-crop, and for miles the busy groups
enlivened the solitude of this rarely-visited spot.

I lingered for half an hour at Gampenhöfe to indulge
in some milk, and at 3.30 set off once more, halting
for thirty-five minutes a little lower down to sketch.
At 4.25, just after crossing the torrent to its W. bank,
St. Gertrud was passed on the left.   The path still
traverses the meadows for some distance nearly on a level,
and then descending more rapidly, as the gradually con-
tracting valley assumes more and more of a ravine-like
character, again returns to the right bank, and continues
along it as far as Gomagoi, which we reached at 6.10.
Here we turned sharp to the left up the Stelvio road
towards Trafoi, where I arrived at 7.15, shortly after my
companions.

The rest of our party had arrived from the Baths of
Bormio some hours previously, and thus our forces were
once more reunited.   The little inn at Trafoi and its
excellent hostess, Frau Barbara Ortler, did their best
to make us comfortable, and it was voted unanimously
that we could not think of hurrying away, but would take
up our quarters there for two nights at least; that the
next day should be devoted to the quiet digestion of the
beauties of the neighbourhood, and the following one to
an ascent of the Orteler Spitze, with which we proposed
to close our investigations for this season at least.

The next morning after breakfast there was a fresh
arrival, whose appearance and equipment at once showed
him to be a mountaineer.   Entering into conversation I

found, to my delight, that the stranger was no other than Herr E. von Mojsisovics, the well-known secretary of the Vienna Alpenverein. This was indeed a fortunate meeting; for though his arrangements compelled him to be at Santa Maria on the 5th, and he could not therefore accept our invitation to unite with us in the projected ascent of the Orteler, I obtained from his travelling library, as well as from himself, much very interesting and valuable information, which might otherwise have never come to my knowledge.

After several delightful hours spent in Herr von Mojsisovics' company I followed the rest of the party, who had started after breakfast for a stroll to the Heiligen drei Brunnen, and found them encamped in a fir-wood—the ladies busily engaged in sketching, and the gentlemen intent on abandoning themselves to the luxury of laziness. By-and-by we were joined by the Herr Secretär, who remained with us till it was time to return to the inn. The walk from Trafoi to the Heiligen drei Brunnen, being described in all the guide-books, scarcely comes within the scope of this paper; but the scenery is so indescribably grand, and the union of grass slopes, rock, and wood, which occupy the foreground of the picture in ever-varying combinations at each fresh turn of the path, is so exquisitely lovely, that I cannot refrain from urging others whose special object may be merely to cross the Stelvio, to halt at Trafoi for at least a couple of hours, and devote them to a stroll up the valley.

The slopes bounding the valley on the E. are merely the lower portion of the ridge which, descending from the summit of the Orteler in a nearly northerly direction, separates the Trafoi from the Sulden Thal, and call for no special remark here. Next to the right, and separated from them by a hollow or groove (called by Schaubach the Dobretta Thal) running up to the crest of the northern spur, is the mass of the Orteler, which presents the same majestic appearance characteristic of it when seen from every other point of view. The actual summit is invisible, but a portion at least of the extensive névé which caps the shoulders of the monarch is clearly distinguishable, whilst the ' Pleis,' a steep tongue of ice or névé occupying a broad couloir by which the ascent is usually effected, is very conspicuous from the neighbourhood of Trafoi. On the W. the mountain sinks rapidly down in a series of step-like crags to the level of the Unter Trafoier Glacier (the lower Orteler Glacier of Schaubach and other writers), as I have ventured to designate the eastern of the two ice-streams which descend into the head of the valley from the main ridge, of which the Orteler itself and the Madatsch Spitze, on the E. and W., are only gigantic spurs. Further to the right the eye rests on a rocky ridge separating the Unter from the Ober Trafoier Glacier, and then on the various peaks of the Madatsch ridge seen in perspective, till all further view is cut off by a projecting buttress on the N. side of the valley

round which the Stelvio road winds. In the angle between
the foot of the Unter Trafoier Glacier and the Tabaretta
Thal is a steep slope intersected by lines of cliff which
stretch across it, and clothed with a mingled growth of
pine and *legföhren* to a height of 1,000 feet above the
valley. Up and across this lies the track usually taken in
ascents of the Orteler. After attaining the summit of the
wood, the foot of the ' Pleis' is reached over masses of
débris which have fallen from the cliffs in front. This
' Pleis' constitutes the main difficulty of the ascent, from
its great rapidity and the frequent occurrence of falling
stones and hard ice requiring caution and step-cutting;
but when once its head is gained, there seems to be no
difficulty in getting on to the upper plateau of névé; and
to reach the highest point of the Orteler over this is
simply a question of time and endurance, as no obstacles
of a serious character are met with.

Herr Mojsisovics had engaged Josef Schöpf to accompany him in his various excursions during the next week
or two, and on his arrival we all strolled up the road to
reconnoitre the Orteler and decide on the route to be
adopted on the morrow. A careful examination of the
' Pleis' with the telescope showed that almost its entire
surface consisted of *glatt-eis* which would necessitate an
enormous amount of step-cutting unless, as Christian suggested and affirmed, the rocks on its left bank could be
climbed. We had previously almost determined to cut
out a new route for ourselves by way of the Tabaretta

Watching for the mountaineers.

They skirmish for provisions. Trafoi.

Thal, and this idea became a fixed resolve ere we returned to the inn.

Some of our party had already started for Mals, and the remainder were to follow in the morning and then proceed over the Ofen Pass to Zernetz and Pontresina, whilst we rejoined them by way of Mals, Nauders, and the Engadine. At 9.30 we retired for a few hours' sleep, after bidding adieu to the ladies and Herr Mojsisovics.

We rose at 12.30 on the morning of the 5th of August, and at 1.45, headed by a lantern-bearer, proceeded along the now familiar path to the Heiligen drei Brunnen, which we reached at 2.30. Striking up into the wood above, we now commenced an ascent over the miseries of which it were perhaps better to draw a veil. Of course the guide contrived at an early stage of the proceedings to miss the way. Equally of course, the lantern was always glaring in one's eyes when it was not required and blinding one for the next few minutes, or mysteriously disappearing just when farther progress seemed impossible without its aid. Sometimes we tripped over the rotting stumps or fallen trunks of firs, or were brought up dead against miniature cliffs, or fell headlong over the long prostrate snake-like branches of the abominable legföhren (*Pinus Mughus*), which excited our especial antipathy, as the annoyance they caused us was infinitely varied in character. Their favourite trick was to curve round as each of us in turn would force his way through their interlaced

foliage, and then execute vengeance on the next in the
file, against whose undefended face their heavy tufts of
needles would sweep back with stinging effect.   How
hot we became, how cross we were, and how our unlucky leader fared at our hands need not here be told.
Suffice it to say that at four o'clock we found ourselves
clear of the wood and standing on the edge of the great
débris-covered hollow leading upwards, in a southerly and
easterly direction respectively, to the 'Pleis' and Tabaretta Spitze.   Schaubach refers to this as the Dobretta
Thal, but as the Austrian map of Tyrol calls the peak at
its head the Tabaretta Spitze, I think we may fairly adopt
that form of spelling.

The porter was now dismissed, and descending for a
short distance, and leaving the route to the 'Pleis' on our
right, we proceeded to traverse the slopes of débris diagonally in the direction of the rocks rising above the right
bank of the glacier in front which fills the head of the valley.
The ascent was by no means excessively steep, and several
masses of well-consolidated snow (probably the remains of
avalanches from the cliffs of the Orteler) facilitated our
progress, and proved an agreeable exchange for the small
rolling stones.   At 4.50 the ice was reached, and a halt
called till five, when we again proceeded rapidly upwards,
keeping as near as possible to the rocks till forced by the
dislocated state of the glacier to diverge a little to the
right.   This course was not altogether free from risk, as

for some distance the surface was strewn with fragments
of ice, which had evidently been recently detached from
the overhanging masses of névé crowning the cliffs of the
Orteler. There was, indeed, no fear of being caught unawares, as the source and direction of the danger were
evident; and though the fall of avalanches is perhaps due
as much to the state of the weather as to the direct action
of the sun, yet as a general rule they are least likely to be
encountered during the early morning hours, whilst in the
descent the space exposed to them may be traversed so
rapidly as practically to prevent any risk. Since our expedition, however, this source of danger in the new route
has been entirely avoided by the selection of the next
valley to the N. of the Tabaretta Thal as the line of
ascent, and as this is doubtless the more direct course
from Trafoi it will probably be adopted in future. My
friend Mr. Ormsby, who himself reached the summit of
the rocks forming the N. boundary of the upper part
of the Tabaretta Thal, but was prevented by stormy
weather from getting farther, informs me that this variation of our new route was for the first time struck out
this autumn by the local guides, and Mr. Headlam, of
University College, Oxford, who made an ascent of the
Orteler shortly after us. Having thus reached the head of
the Tabaretta Thal, they followed our track to the summit,
and, in proof of their and our success, found the bottle
containing our names, attached to a small fir-tree which

we had planted on the highest point.   But this is anticipating.

The névé of the glacier we had been ascending was
nearly level, and occupied a well-defined hollow between
the rocky spur from the Tabaretta Spitze on the N. and
the steep slopes of snow and ice descending from the
upper portion of the Orteler on the S., which here take
the place of the cliffs passed farther to the W.   In front
a low but precipitous and much-weathered ridge of rocks
formed the eastern boundary of the névé of what I may
perhaps term the Tabaretta Glacier, and cut off all view
in the direction of the Sulden Thal.   At 5.55, just before
reaching this, we struck off sharp to the right, and addressed ourselves steadily to the real work of the day.
The inclination was considerable but by no means excessive, and as the ice and snow were very hard at this early
hour some step-cutting was necessary. Soon a bergschrund
was encountered and crossed without the slightest difficulty, and at 6.40, after a steady and stiffish pull, we halted
for breakfast at the edge of a crevasse where the surface
was tolerably level.

The weather was, as usual, everything that could be
desired, and the view had by this time become most magnificent, including range after range of peaks away to the
east, as our present position enabled us to look over on the
side of the Sulden Thal.

At 7.20 we resumed our march, and winding steadily

upwards without a halt, amidst and around some enormous crevasses and magnificent masses of snow, without on the whole deviating much from a direct course to the summit, or encountering any really serious obstacle, we stood on the highest point of the final arête at 9.27, just seven hours and three quarters after quitting Trafoi. We had been actually on the march for six hours and three quarters, and had, in fact, lost more than half an hour in the wood; so that our progress had been rapid, considering that the difference of altitude between Trafoi and the Orteler Spitze is 7,733 feet.

Let me here guard myself against the imputation of 'doing' mountains against time, a system which is, I fear, becoming not uncommon. It may be retorted that I have just dwelt on the comparative rapidity of our own ascent of the Orteler, but to this I would reply that the narratives of almost all our predecessors describe the expedition as a very long one; that we were attempting a new route, and, not knowing the nature of the obstacles we might encounter at any moment, could not venture to linger much on the way; and, lastly, that in order to effect a junction at Pontresina with the rest of our party on the following evening, it was essential that we should get back to Trafoi reasonably early.

The highest ridge runs from NNE. to SSW., and looks like a gigantic snowdrift blown up by the wind to a thin edge, capped on the NW. by a *corniche*, and sloping rapidly on the SE. to the fearful precipices which sink away towards the western head of the Sulden Glacier. It might not inaptly be compared to the keel of a boat turned bottom-up and broken-backed, so as to allow of the stern portion being tilted up. The foot of the rudder-post thus reversed would represent the highest point at the NNE. extremity, and the convex bottom of the boat itself, sloping away on all sides, would be no unfair illustration of the great dome-like mass of snow and névé which clothes the broad shoulders of the mountain. The arête subsides into the general surface at its SW. end, beyond which and in the direction of the ridge dividing the Sulden and Unter Trafoier Glaciers, there is a second and inferior elevation.

We struck the *kamm* at its lowest point, and turning sharp to the left proceeded along its gently-inclined profile, which presented no sort of danger to heads free from dizziness. The day was a lovely one; there was not a particle of wind, and as the sun shone warmly down upon us we resolved to take our fill of the enjoyment of the glorious panorama which our position commanded. This was the more needful, as our stay on the Königsspitze had been brief, and we were desirous of atoning for the haste rendered necessary on that occasion by the intense cold.

Truth compels me to confess that the first portion of the two hours spent on the summit was devoted to the commissariat department, but hunger appeased, we set busily to work to make the most of the time. Clouds were already beginning to roll up here and there from the valleys, so the first thing to be done was to secure a sketch and a photograph. During our progress up the slopes of the névé the legs of the camera had unfortunately slipped from the fingers of their bearer, and gone flying downwards over the hard-frozen surface, disappearing at last over a brow suspiciously like the upper lip of a crevasse. All our efforts failed to recover them, and so the future local New Zealander may some day fish them out from amidst the fragments of avalanches in the Tabaretta Thal. A stand was improvised for the occasion by driving three axes side by side into the ridge and piling snow upon their heads, which when pressed down formed, thanks to regelation, a level and stable support. Two stereoscopic slides, including the Monte Cevedale, the Königsspitze, and the Klein Zebru, with portions of the ridge between the first and the Tresero, were at length obtained by E., and very successfully, as the result has proved. In the opposite direction a wonderful array of peaks met the eye. It began on the W. with the summits of the Grisons, followed in succession by the Bernina group, the mountains of the Middle and Lower Engadine, and the still more distant Vorarlberg. Next came the remarkable depression through which passes the route of the Finstermünz, connecting the valleys of the Adige and Inn. The Malser Heide—its broad green expanse diversified by the lakes

and bright-looking villages scattered over its surface, and
traversed by the long reaches of the white road—was seen
as on a map, bounded on the E. by the glittering snows
of the Weisskugel (12,620 feet) and other giants of the
Oetz Thal.   Less familiar forms succeeded as the eye
ranged over the peaks of the Stubayer, Duxer, and Ziller
Thal groups to the broad snowfields of the Venediger,
and finally rested on the sharp outline of the Gross
Glockner, south of which a perfect forest of jagged
aiguilles indicated the position of the glorious Dolomites,
which stretch from Botzen on the W. to Villach on the E.
Still nearer, the fine forms of the outlying members of the
Orteler Group which cluster round the valleys of Sulden,
Laas, Martell, Ulten, and Sole, would have attracted yet
more attention if the superior charms of the monarchs of
the ice-world had not dwarfed their pretensions.

Besides the mere extent of the view and the beautiful
grouping of the elements which composed it, there was on
this particular day an indescribable charm of colouring
which I have scarcely ever seen equalled.   The atmosphere
seemed to invest every object with the most wonderful
·harmony of tone, softening all asperities, subduing harsh
contrasts, and blending the whole into the perfection of
repose.   Time flew rapidly by, and we could willingly
have lingered; but much remained to be done, and at
11.10 we reluctantly quitted the summit, after securing
an aneroid observation, from which, by comparison with

They descend in triumph !

Great applause! Ah! So!! these English !!!

Aosta and Turin, the height comes out 12,799 feet, or 15 feet less than the result of the Kataster Survey.

At 12.35, after a fruitless hunt for the lost legs, we reached the level surface of the névé at the head of the Tabaretta Thal, and running rapidly down the ice took to the moraine on the right bank of the glacier at 12.50. Here all doubt and difficulty were at an end, and we felt justified in halting for a pipe till 1.30. The wood was reached at two o'clock, the Heiligen drei Brunnen at 2.25 (the *Legföhren* now doing good service, as we swung rapidly down by their long supple arms), and Trafoi at three o'clock. Goodnatured Mrs. Ortler received us with warm congratulations, gave us an excellent dinner, and started us at 5.30 for Prad, which we reached at 6.45, after undergoing an examination of passports, and quitted at seven o'clock. The Orteler rose more and more grandly behind us; but the light was waning fast as we drove into Mals at 8.30. Tea was welcome, and the prospect of a long ride in the dark to Nauders did not look tempting. However, it was useless to grumble, as the exigencies of our compact with our companions would not admit of our yielding to the seductions of Mals. Conscious misery was at least spared us, and I believe it was with a feeling of agreeable surprise that we found ourselves turned out at 1 A.M. into the road at Nauders before a gloomy rambling locked-up house, which for a long time gave no sign of life.

R

Thus ended our campaign in the Orteler district. Thanks to the almost uninterrupted fine weather and the able assistance of our guides, Christian Michel and Franz Biener, we had on the whole cause to be satisfied with the results attained, considering how short a time we had been able to devote to this object. It must not be supposed, however, that nothing remains to be accomplished, that the harvest has been more than partially garnered by us, or that there are not plenty of objects left for the explorer and lover of novelties, and still more for those who are wise enough to believe that mountains are amongst those 'things of beauty' which 'will never pass into nothingness,' and are not unworthy of their attention because some one else happens to have previously trod their summits.

Table of Heights.

Date	Hour	Station	Aneroid	Air	Aosta	Turin	Mean	Probable
				c				
Aug. 1	9.45 A.M.	Madatsch Joch . .	20.49	5°	10850	10826	10838	10750
,,	11 A.M.	Monte Cristallo . .	19.97	5°	11583	11570	11576	11370
,,	5.30 P.M.	Zebru Pass , . .	21.15	9°	9871	9945	9908	9700
,, 3	8.30 A.M.	Königs Spitze . .	18.91	4°·5	12603	12621	12612	12648
,,	10 A.M.	Königs Joch . . .	20.17	5°	11060	11067	11063	11000
,, 5	10.45 A.M.	Orteler Spitze . .	19.05	3°·5	12722	12876	12799	12814

APPENDIX.

THE earlier attempts to ascend the Orteler Spitze are detailed with considerable minuteness by Schaubach ('Deutsche Alpen,' B. IV. pp. 19–26), and in the second volume of the 'Mittheilungen des Oesterreichischen Alpen-Vereines,' Herr Pegger, our immediate predecessor, has appended to his personal narrative a short account of previous expeditions; but as both these works are comparatively unknown to English readers, I venture to think that a brief outline of the results of former attempts may not be without interest.

The summit of the Orteler was reached for the first time on the 27th September, 1804, by a famous chamois-hunter, named Joseph Pichler, with two natives of the Ziller Thal, at the instigation of the Archduke John. They were only able to remain four minutes on the top, or just long enough to obtain a barometrical observation, the accuracy of which is, however, more than doubtful, as by comparison with Glurns it gave for the peak a height of 14,412 French, or 15,860 English feet! Herr Gebhard, an officer charged with the investigation of the topography of the Ober-Vintschgau, was prevented by indisposition from accompanying the expedition, but in the following year, with indefatigable zeal, he effected the ascent no less than three times. He seems, however, to have left no account of his adventures— at least I have been unable to meet with, or hear of any.

More than twenty years passed by during which we hear nothing more of the Orteler Spitze, but on August 20-21, 1826, it was again ascended by the Austrian officer of engineers Sche-

belka, with Pichler for leader, and Fidel Timel of Sulden, Johann
Brunner of Gamphof, and Michael Gamper of Agums as subordinate guides. 'The attack was first made from the side of the
Sulden Thal, whence Gebhard's attempts were made, but enormous masses of ice barred all further progress at about five-sixths
of the height of the mountain, and the original route from Trafoi
had in consequence to be selected.' From the concluding words
of this statement, which I extract from Schaubach, it would
appear that Pichler had started from Trafoi on the occasion of
the first ascent, but why he afterwards adopted the Sulden Thal
as his starting-point when 'accompanying Gebhard is not explained. Be this as it may, Schebelka and his companions slept
on the night of August 20 in a ruined hut, which is probably
the one referred to in more recent narratives as situated near the
summit of the wood between the Orteler Glacier (Unter Trafoier
Ferner) and the Tabaretta Thal. Quitting this at 4.30 the next
morning, they gained the summit at 3.30 P.M. Here they found
the remains of Gebhard's pyramid, but in the interval since its
erection the summit had increased in height three *klafter* (18.67
English feet). A storm unfortunately coming on, obscured the
view, and compelled them to beat a precipitate retreat. At 1 A.M.
they reached the first trees, 'still two and a quarter hours above
the hut,' a statement which seems inexplicable, unless the darkness of the night or their excessive fatigue rendered their progress extremely slow. Finally, it was not till 10 A.M. on the 23rd
that they returned to Trafoi.

The next and best-known ascent was effected by Professor
Thurwieser in 1834, and is minutely described in the 'Zeitschrift
des Ferdinandeums, 3 Bändchen, Innsbruck, 1837,' pp. 89-163.
I have not been able to consult the original publication, but a
detailed *résumé* of the paper is given by Schaubach, from which I
extract the following particulars :—

Pichler, now 70 years of age, with his son Lax and Michael

Gamper, acted as guides. The party left Trafoi at 2.30 on the afternoon of the 12th of August, and following the path to the Heiligen drei Brunnen, thence ascended the 'Bergl,' the spur or buttress partially clothed with wood, to which allusion was so often made in the foregoing paper. In the hut at its summit, which was reached at 6 P.M., they took up their quarters for the night at a height of 6,327 Paris, or 6,743 English feet. A start was effected about four o'clock on the morning of the 13th. 'A ridge descending from the Orteler to the Trafoi Thal separates the summit of the "Bergl" from the lower Orteler Glacier (Unter Trafoier Ferner) which pours down on the right. This ridge had to be climbed round, in order to reach the upper portion of the glacier, where its surface is more level.' From this passage it would appear that Thurwieser and his companions attacked the Orteler from the W. instead of on the side visible from Trafoi, which has been selected by succeeding mountaineers. Whether he merely followed in the track of Schebelka is not stated, but I think we may presume this to have been the case, as the same guide (Pichler) led on each occasion. At 5.15 the lower Orteler glacier was reached, and 'the first of the four sections of the ascent was thus successfully accomplished.' The ice was at first almost concealed beneath the masses of débris which had fallen from the cliffs of the Orteler on the left, but soon became purer. Proceeding upwards, at first in a southerly and then in a south-easterly direction, the glacier was found to be more and more dislocated, and considerable difficulty was experienced in forcing a passage. This obstacle surmounted, a more.level portion was reached, which was, however, intersected by long and wide crevasses. The course was now altered, and they made straight for the cliffs of the Orteler itself, which were reached, not without difficulty, at 7.30, after two and a quarter hours' walk over the glacier. The second division of the ascent was thus accomplished, and the height was found to be 1,200 Paris (1,279 English) feet above the hut, or 7,527 Paris (8,022 English) feet above the sea. The rocks above appear to have proved formidable, but thanks to the skill of the gallant old Josele, and the discovery of a couloir whose upper and lower portions are known as the 'Schneerinne' and 'Untere Schneerinne,' a sort of elevated gully was reached, very steep, and only about two or three *klafter* (12 to 19 feet) broad, called by Thurwieser the 'Obere Schneerinne.' At nine o'clock, after a short halt, the travellers proceeded upwards, over a succession of perpendicular rocky steps, named 'Wandln,' from twenty to sixty feet in height, and divided by intervals, named 'Stellen,' which proved scarcely less troublesome. Finally, at 11.7, the edge of the Upper 'Orteler Ferner' was reached, after a scramble, which had now lasted four hours. Its inclination is stated to be 60°–65° (?), and its surface consisted of soft snow overlying névé, beneath which was hard ice. Some steps had to be cut, but after traversing a short portion of the ice, a level stony tract was reached, falling away in perpendicular precipices on the SW., and from which the snow had disappeared. The altitude was found to be 10,700 Paris (11,404 English) feet. A little further on the glacier (névé) was again entered upon, and at 11.19 they stood upon its first elevation or plateau. Here the giants of the Oetz Thal were descried over the ridge to the N., but the dome-like form of the névé still concealed the summit of the Orteler, and it being impossible to proceed straight in the direction in which the latter was supposed to lie, a detour was made to the right. The heat and light reflected from the brilliant surface, and the increasing inclination of the latter, proved too much for poor old Pichler, who was therefore left behind, after pointing out to his companions the route to be followed. The leadership was now assumed by a certain Strimer, of whom no mention had previously been made, but who appears to have been on the summit before, and is probably the same man as the one previously spoken of under the name of Gamper. The crevasses, though not numerous, were of enormous dimensions; but at length the goal appeared in sight, and they stood at the foot of the wind-heaped snowy arête, whose north end formed the actual summit. Here a bergschrund all but brought their further progress to a stand, but it was at length successfully traversed, and the arête ('Schneide') attained. This was blown up by the wind into a mere knife-edge, along which it was necessary to pass. On the side overhanging Sulden there was a *corniche* formed by the action of the west wind. Finally, at 12.36, they stood on the highest point—a snowy pyramid with sharp angles elevated from 26 to 32 feet above the dome-like expanse of névé stretching away to the N. and NW. The barometer gave a height of 12,044 Paris (12,836 English) feet, whilst the thermometer indicated + 4° Réaumur or 41° Fahrenheit, a temperature which rendered the halt on the summit extremely agreeable. There was not a breath of air, and the party were able, without inconvenience, to dispense with their coats.

At 1.30, Lax having been previously despatched to look after his father, Thurwieser 'followed with Strimer.' At two o'clock they rejoined the Pichlers, who had lighted a fire close to the foot of the upper névé at a spot the height of which was found to be 10,739 Paris (11,445 English) feet. Halting here till 2.42, they then proceeded down the 'Wandln,' slightly varying the route selected in the morning, and reached the lower Orteler Glacier at 5.12 and the hut on the 'Bergl' at 8.15. The next morning the Heiligen drei Brunnen were reached in one hour, a *Dankmesse* was performed in the little chapel, and the whole party then returned in high spirits to Trafoi.

In all the expeditions which have just been described the actual summit was attained, but no one, I believe, had since succeeded in getting beyond the foot of, or at most half-way up, the final snowy arête or Kamm until we once more planted our bâtons on its highest wreath.

The upper Orteler Ferner was reached by a party from Prad (including a girl of sixteen) and the 'Grat' itself by Dr. Von Ruthner and Herr Karner on the 25th August 1857 (see 'Eine Ersteigung der Ortelerspitze,' Mittheilungen der k. k. geog. Gesellschaft, 2 Jahrgang, 1858), by Herr Specht of Vienna in 1860, by two Irish gentlemen, Messrs. R. Jacobs and J. Walpole (who were so unfortunate as to be benighted and have to camp out on the névé) in 1861, and by Herr Egid Pegger of Innsbruck on the 29th July 1863.   Anton Ortler of Gomagoi and Josef Schöpf of Beidewasser seem to have generally acted as guides on these occasions; and, so far as I have been able to ascertain, the latter appears to have given entire satisfaction to his employers, whilst the former is spoken of in more doubtful terms.

I will conclude this historical sketch with a notice of the last-named expedition, which is briefly described by Herr Pegger in the second volume of the 'Mittheilungen des Oesterreichischen Alpen-Vereines.' The party, consisting of Herr Pegger and the guides Josef and Alois Schöpf of Beidewasser and Franz Hofer of Tartsch, left Trafoi at five P.M. on the 24th of July, and followed the route taken by Thurwieser as far as the summit of the wood on the 'Bergl,' which was reached at 6.30 and a bivouac at once organised.   A start was effected the next morning at 3.30, and proceeding across some slaty slopes and up a talus of débris from the northern cliffs of the Orteler, they stood at four o'clock at the commencement of the long snow slopes with an inclination of 38°, above which commences the steep 'Pleis,' which constitutes the main difficulty of the expedition.   At this point the weather suddenly changed, and a fearful storm came driving across from the opposite side of the valley.   They had just time to cross a small glacier and reach an overhanging rock before the tempest burst upon them, and as it was followed by steady rain, nothing remained but to make the best of their way back to Trafoi, which was reached in an hour and a quarter.

At 4.45 on the morning of July 29 they once more stood at the entrance of the ' Pleis.' The latter is a very uniform glacier or broad ice-filled couloir, some 2,000 feet in length, with an inclination of 35 to 45°, and usually consisting in autumn of hard slippery ice (*Glatteis*) which in the present instance was still covered with snow. In a quarter of an hour the ' Burg-stall,' an isolated ridge of rock cropping out from the ' Pleis,' was reached, and a halt of similar duration called to put on the *steigeisen* or crampons. Keeping close to the rocks on the right, up slopes which increased from 38° to 42° and finally to 45° (when a few steps had to be cut), they gained at 6.45 the summit of the ' Pleis.' The height of this spot is about 9,000 Vienna (9,334 English) feet, and its position is just at the commencement of the upper Orteler Glacier. This latter appears to have presented no difficulties, and at 9.15 the party stood on the final arête of the Orteler, twenty *klafter* (124 English feet) distant from and about eight feet below the actual summit.

Herr Pegger states that since Thurwieser's visit the arête and the summit had much changed, and that the latter appears to have become about three *klafter* lower, and to have shifted about four *klafter* farther to the E., judging from the position of the pole which had been there since 1834. After working along the arête for some distance, the travellers were reluctantly compelled (apparently by the want of proper axes) to abandon the attempt to gain the highest point. Unfortunately, great masses of cumuli lay on all the surrounding peaks, and the view was therefore almost entirely concealed. How long they remained is not stated, but by five P.M. they were once more back again at Trafoi.

It will be seen by a comparison of this account with the

narrative of Thurwieser that the upper Orteler Glacier or névé
was reached by the northern instead of the western face of the
mountain; and I believe the other recent ascents have taken
place in this direction, which was discovered by Anton Ortler
of Gomagoi, and adopted for the first time by Dr. von Ruthner
and Herr Karner, in 1857. An attempt made on the same day
from the Sulden Thal by Herr H. Wolf, a geologist, accompanied
by some guides of Gomagoi, proved unsuccessful, but the party
reached a height of 11,000 (Vienna) feet, and Herr Wolf attri-
butes his defeat to the unfavourable weather alone.

For further details on this subject as well as of more recent
ascents, I would refer the reader to the interesting papers by
Dr. Mojsisovics, in the volumes ('Mittheilungen') of the Austrian
Alpen-Verein, and to an article by Lieut. Payer, in Petermann's
'Mittheilungen' (Ergänzungsheft, No. 18).

A TALE OF THE ROAD.

———✦———

' Thus my Italy
Was stealing on us. Genoa broke with day,
The Doria's long pale palace striking out,
From green hills in advance of the white town,
A marble finger dominant to ships,
Seen glimmering through the uncertain gray of dawn.'
                                    E. B. BROWNING.

A TALE OF THE ROAD.

MANY a page has been written on the Corniche, that great highway along the coast of the Mediterranean, and narrow path between Italy and France, with its antique towns that seem like mere gatherings of tumble-down buildings that in old times grew up around a caravansary of the road, or a robber stronghold, under whose shelter galleys were moored in the harbour, or bandits swarmed along the shore; but lately there has been a fancy for old tales—'stories retold'—legends of the road, and such like histories; and a plain recital of how four English people drove from town to town, the way their horses galloped, the exact distance they made in a given time, the costumes of the people, the wayside inns, and the thousand and one small incidents that make up a pleasant week's travel, may have some slight interest a few years hence—say six or seven—when this article may be regarded as a rather valuable relic of the past; and the next generation, who will consider themselves by that time old enough to criticise their elders, will smile over the small adventures, the glimpses of a quiet rural antediluvian life which to them is a mystery of a bygone age.

That direful giant, steam, with its strong iron feet, is preparing to tramp with defiant snorts and much of noise
and smoke over that pleasant land; there will be a railway hotel possibly, somewhere where a grove of palms
rises now in quiet security, or a *buffet* at a station, and a
little French official will shout, ' Dix minutes d'arrêt !'—
and young England will eat hurriedly, and then, returning to his comfortable corner of the carriage, sleep
through the tunnels to Genoa, rejoicing in getting there
in time for the six o'clock table d'hôte, and in the knowledge that he has *done* the Corniche, and that really
distances are a mere nothing. ' Came from Nice this
morning—capital smooth line—slept the whole way :
there's such a lot of tunnels on this sort of coast one
can't read one's paper in any comfort, so I took a nap,
and didn't try. What an awful bore travelling must have
been in the old times, when people absolutely drove the
whole way, and were six days getting here, sir—six days
of twelve hours apiece, and had to lodge as they could on
the road, and of course always came to grief with springs,
or horses' knees, or a drunken cocher, or something ; and
yet people used to call that pleasure ! First-rate ale at
the buffet at St. Remo ! I shall be back in a week, and
mean to do the little distance by night. It's rather a *sell*,
you know, if one can't manage to vary one's sensations.
I've got rather a new thing in a reading-lamp, and mean
to get up a review article going home.'

And so our tale of the road comes to be written; there is but a little breathing time left us before some great capitalist or company comes on the ground and makes sad certainty of our fears. Just now the railroad is in a mess, and at a standstill; for the last two years, and longer for aught I know, there have been vast excavations, mounds of earth flung up, tunnels begun and sometimes completed, and at one little fishing village there is a stack of iron rails, an ominous parallelogram, looking out of place, stranded there on the sand amongst the fishing-nets, like a relic of San Lorenzo that may have been miraculously floated and washed ashore. Very ugly ' salvage' the poor *voituriers* think as they smack their whips and drive jeeringly past. The railroad is insolvent, and no one seems to know what items of humanity represent it; there was once an Italian company which failed, and there is supposed to be a mysterious understanding existing with the *crédit mobilier*, which has no observable effect. Here and there at long intervals upon the road you encounter an engineer and a man with a book or a chain, and I have even seen labourers at work, and watched them with a vague wonder as to whether they were real, and were actually paid by somebody on a Saturday night, and would be put on again the next Monday morning.

The *voituriers*—the mail-coachmen and postboys of the road, nod their heads gloomily over their own future. It is the old story over again; very pathetic, to my mind.

I remember a mournful history of the end of an old post-chariot, written I think by Mr. Charles Dickens, in which he tracked man and vehicle to their last resting-place, and found the latter robbed of its glory of wheels and shafts, grounded in a patch of cabbages, and the aged post-boy living inside. If such should be the fate of the carriage in which we made our triumphal progress from Nice to Genoa, Carlo Bassetti will be able to advertise it as a two-storied house, and let lodgings; for it was wonderful for size and general convenience and comfort, could be closed or open, with the usual amount of glass windows, fitted in between the woodwork, and hidden away in all directions in a marvellous manner unknown to English builders; there was a *coupé* which of itself would make a bathing machine, and a great place behind for luggage which, with the addition of a tarpauling roof, would be an admirable outhouse. It was white outside with the dust of ages, but that was part of its respectability. Its owner would have scorned to clean it, looking on such traces of antiquity with much the same pride as that with which a butler would cherish the cobwebs that decorate the cork of some especially choice vintage. And the driver was the owner, that was its crowning recommendation ; he could drive his well-bred wiry little horses as he pleased, and fortunately for us that was ‘ steadily up hill, and give them their heads when they reach the summit.’

How poor all written words seem to describe our pleasure : the big carriage lumbering up to the door of the
hotel, the luggage strapped on by busy porters, a great
basket lifted in well stocked for picnics by the way, great
bunches of red and yellow roses filling up the corners and
resting against a perfect hedge of orange blossom on the
back seat. We mount to our places; a light overcoat,
dust cloaks, muslin covers to the hats, white sunshades,
French chocolate, pale ale, pâté de Strasbourg, bread and
cheese, and stores of bonbons, books, English newspapers
(our ' Saturday Review ' has not arrived, has been stopped
in Paris, alas, on account of a critical and Imperial
analysis), sketch-books, and endless etcetera ; our *cocher*
draws the long whip through his fingers, uncovers to the
company, who, assembled under the verandah, watch our
start with sympathising interest, the secretary congratulates
us upon the weather, we compliment him upon the admirable arrangement of his hotel, men spring apparently
out of the earth and touch their caps insinuatingly and
then with delicately graduated shades of appreciation, the
cocher mounts to his box, gathers up the long reins, carefully sits on the end of them, cries ' *avanti* ' to his horses,
and with a cheery *bon voyage* from the verandah, we
wheel round the corner at a quick trot, and with gay
smackings of the whip and jubilant outcries from the
driver, and a glad chorus of little barkings from the very
small dog who sits up on his tail on the topmost trunk

behind, trying to look like a chasseur, we make a good
start in the pleasant afternoon sunshine.

There had been a sudden shower, which had laid the dust
and washed the great shining lemon leaves, and cooled and
freshened the air, and here and there the scarlet geranium
blossoms were scattered across the path as we passed open
gateways or light railings, that made pleasant breaks in
the stretch of high-walled gardens, and showed us glimpses
of villas, and beds gay with flowers, houses that for the
most part were settling into a state of summer somnolency,
with firmly-shuttered windows closed till the next season
for the flight of birds and humans southwards, left under
the care of sunburnt cheery old women, who sat on the
lowest step of the terrace by the big orange tree in the
green tub, their heads tied up in red handkerchiefs, and
with a snowy *fichu* drawn across the shoulders, the withered
fingers busy with their knitting, never stopping in their
work, though they look up and nod with a bright *buona
sera* as we rattle past.   Oh the high balustrade, a few
yards further, is a pretty group, rich enough in its brilliant
colouring to beguile a painter for a long day's work in the
sun, a bright brown face laughing down on the child
crowing at the horses, and askant at us, with innocent
happiness in the great black eyes.   The masses of wavy
hair are almost blue in the light, and the woman sits with
an indolent grace, full in the sunshine, which strikes on
her uncovered head, and makes deep sharply-cut shadows

across her neck and hands, and the white wall against which she leans, her scanty dress draping itself in soft folds, of a deep warm colour, like the tint of an Etruscan vase or fresh bright earth, wonderfully in harmony with such a head. These women love strong quiet-toned colours, as though their eyes needed the rest of such amidst the glare of white stone and marble, where earth and sea and sky seem scintillating with light. April was drawing to a close, so these pleasant-faced *concierges* were fairly in possession, and their little children watched us under perfect bowers of roses and clematis, that grew about the gates. As we mounted higher, the valleys and hills surrounding Cimier looked most lovely in the afternoon warmth and light, and far away in the distance the Col di Tenda shone white and glistening with snow. A fresh turn in the road, a steep bit surmounted, and a whole range of snowy peaks came into view. Our *cocher* gave an exultant smack with his whip, and cried, ' *Voilà les Alpes maritimes.*' The horses sniffed the clear mountain air, which came to us in great gusts, blowing through their manes, their heads held up to meet it with little glad neighings of delight, and the travellers turned eager eyes towards the mountains, welcoming them as old friends, and drinking in the delicious air, *le vent frappé*, which came to them across the ice-fields, with happy remembrances of glacier expeditions, and cool tramping through the snow. The hill was surmounted, and after the hot climb it was pleasant to

s

dash round the long curves of the road in a good canter,
feeling our spirits rising with every new peak that came
into sight, and every fresh little burst of the horses, who
were ready to race anything and everything on the road,
and dashed recklessly past a staid old curé in a gig, and
muleteers descending towards the shore, and the small
ragazzi of the road, who gave us cheers, ironical or con-
gratulatory, as we passed.

Still higher and higher, till Nice was hidden from view,
which we had been looking down upon round an inland
corner. The sea once more came into sight, not the
brilliant emerald of the morning, but a peacock blue and
green, almost as deep in tinting as the dark little Tyrol
lakes, and apparently floating upon it, far below us, was
the grey promontory beyond Villa Franca, lying like a
great flat oyster-shell out on its travels. The hills were
all grey and crumbly, with violet shadows, which are
sometimes almost of an inky blackness. The little town
of Esa was hardly to be distinguished from the stones it
grew out of; our road led us between broken bits of rock
where vegetation seemed to have died away, and a romantic or melodramatic mind might revel in the knowledge
that somewhere hereabouts there was once a murder,
sacrilege committed, a papal ban following, and an ecclesiastical malediction, beneath which flowers faded, crops
perished, and the stones were allowed to have it all their
own way. But even such a wealth of interest and legend-

ary lore did not tempt us to linger. We met flocks of goats, who seemed to find the excommunicated grass rather poor living, women and children, travellers on foot and in carriages, and found palms, pines, olives in every hole and cranny, when once the more desolate hills were left behind, and, above all, flowers everywhere. Each little three-year-old beggar on the road had roses in its hand, and it took some time to harden our hearts against such poetical mendicity :—a pair of lovely eyes lifted pleadingly as you pass, and a bunch of red roses held out in silence. They look like little St. Barbaras, or sweet young Saint Elizabeths of Hungary, and it is only the constant repetition of such groupings that, like the ubiquitous properties of relics, restores the Protestant mind to its proper tone of calm common sense.

As the shadows lengthen, the sea breeze begins to blow. The little green lizards, who have been basking in the heat, scamper up the high white walls, and vanish amongst the lemon trees, which grow more and more frequent, and are gay with their ripe fruit and thousands of blossoms, richer and brighter in their tintings than the white orange-buds which bloom amidst their great golden balls. The falling dew seems to make them exhale a fresher, deeper perfume. The air is intoxicating with their sweetness, and it is almost more than is good for us and the insects. After our two weary days' journey through France, we seemed suddenly to have entered upon a new existence, and to be nearing those enchanted gardens of the Hesperides, looking, as Jason did, upon

> ' A place not made for earthly bliss,
> Or eyes of dying men, for growing there
> The yellow apple and the painted pear,
> And well-filled golden cups of oranges
> Hung amid groves of pointed cypress trees;
> On grassy slopes the twining vine-boughs grew,
> And hoary olives 'twixt far mountains blue,
> And many-coloured flowers, like a cloud
> The rugged southern cliffs did softly shroud;
> And many a green-necked bird they saw alight
> Within the slim-leaved, thorny pomegranite,
> That flung its unstrung rubies on the grass,
> And slowly o'er the place the wind did pass
> Heavy with many odours that it bore
> From thymy hills down to the seabeat shore.' *

The green frogs sit under the bulrushes, and make a great deal of noise, each having much to say, and all croaking at once. We descend rapidly by wonderful curves, and cross high narrow bridges, and feel we are indeed nearing Italy, as we see the steep slope before us terraced with the utmost care and gardening toil. It looked in the distance as though some burly giant had built himself an easy flight of steps to the shore, thinking a little sea-bathing might be good for his constitution.

At about six o'clock we drew near the first villas of Mentone, anticipating with fond security at least two good nights' sleep, and a day of happy exploration among

* Morris's *Jason*.

the hills; but, unfortunately for our hopes, there was a
canker at the root—that is to say, an insect in the air (a
fact to be multiplied by thousands!). Some one had
warned us against one of the bays. We were quite satisfied
so far, but there our information ended, and we could not
recall which was the right one.* Not that there was much
choice; for at this season Mentone was preparing in hot
haste for its summer repose. We encountered but one or
two stray travellers in the streets as we drove through the
little town, and thought ourselves fortunate in seeing the
windows still open of the Hôtel de la Paix, and a waiter
sitting on the doorsteps contemplating the sea. Here we
could have rooms, and the society of a *famille anglaise*,
who formed the *table d'hôte*. We were soon established in
capital quarters, and made acquaintance with the English
family of two, who told us the hotel was to have been
closed that day, and would probably be so on the morrow,
and that they thought we should find the provisions
were at an end; but we decided that, as the family were
there for their health, they naturally took a morbid
view of things, and that it would all come right;
and we made enquiries as to donkeys for the morrow,
and laid plans for a picnic, which our father regarded
sceptically. The dinner was objectionable, both as to
quantity and quality, coming suddenly to an end before

---

* The Mosquitoes are said to be entirely confined to the bay of Mentone,
nearest Genoa.

we were at all prepared for such a *dénouement*; but we were still hopeful, and made the best of everything. The English family was to start early the next morning for Paris and Dover, and after the dinner they said good-bye, adding mournfully, they hoped we should not find the mosquitoes troublesome! How any invalid could have supported for weeks the life of bersaglieri conflict we endured during that one night, and lived, it is impossible to conceive.

Feeling a little uncomfortable after such a warning, on reaching our rooms we instituted a search; the walls were literally lined with an army of invaders, and for the next two hours the battle raged fiercely; there was a slipper, a handkerchief, a high-heeled boot, and the courage of despair on one side; on the other, the immensity of numbers, and a spirit of daring utterly reckless of consequences; the slaughter was terrible, but the mosquitoes remained virtually masters of the field. Of course we would not allow that we were beaten, and we did lie down and even tried to sleep, trusting feebly in the protection of our gauze draperies, and then the enemy had their revenge; under the cover of night they made fresh approaches and prepared to destroy us by wholesale consumption. Had sufficient time been given them, they might have succeeded in their object, but with the first dawn of day we reasserted ourselves and sat up—feeble indeed and exhausted, but with sufficient strength to pre-

Our first attack !

The enemy rally and charge again.

Carrying down the Lemons. Mentone.

pare for flight. Of course another such night was not to be thought of, and we arranged to start in the afternoon for San Remo, devoting one morning to seeing what we could of the nearest hills above Mentone and the little town itself.

The people look poor, and their houses are dirty and poverty-stricken, as in so many of these fishing villages, where the women are almost always thriftless and untidy, and the houses grievously ill-cared for. Much has been done for the people by many good charitable souls, schools established for the children, and earnest quiet labour persevered in for many years to help the poor mothers, morally and spiritually, but there is still sore need for more. Gladly and thankfully recognising the vast amount of good already effected by many strangers and inhabitants, we may be allowed to plead for yet greater efforts and individual work amongst the people of these winter homes in Italy. This beautiful little town has grown up very suddenly, almost called into existence out of its old life as a fishing village by the needs and affection of the English. We have signified our pleasure in the place, and houses and hotels and shops have sprung up as a natural sequence, and we rather pride ourselves on spending a good deal of money there, and doing a great amount of good to the people. I often wonder whether that is true practically, whether these poor honest-faced dirty southerners are any the better for our

coming and building houses on their fair headlands
and big hotels in the little streets. We settle down
with home newspapers, and pleasant picnics, and almost
fraternise with these picturesque peasants over our sketch-
books, and feel we are setting them a very good example
by our conduct in general, and our English Sundays in
particular. It is a good, pleasant, harmless life enough;
but surely there is better stuff in us, an infinite power
of helping and teaching, and plenty of will to do the
work, if only we would stop to think about it. These
moralisings will hardly fit into our story of a drive along
the shore, but we and our horses need halting-places, and
if there is no time for such action as we are pleading for,
there is often time for a wonderful amount of thought.
Lady Herbert has written on this subject words that are
so good and true, that we must venture to repeat some of
them here. 'Let us ask ourselves why it is that, among
the many English who yearly go abroad to seek for health
or enjoyment in a southern climate, so few are found to
devote any portion of their time during those winters to
the care of the sick and suffering poor around them?
They do it gladly at home; in their own villages it comes
as a matter of course. Why is it then that they shrink
from doing it abroad? Is there not everywhere suffering to be relieved, kind and soothing words to be spoken,
little and comparatively costless pleasures to be given?
. . . This short time devoted to God's poor will brighten

and sanctify their lives; will give them an aim and a
purpose unknown to the desultory pleasure-seekers around
them; and the very dullest residence will become to them
at once invested with an interest and a charm which no
worldly amusement can afford; while their memory will
live in the hearts of the grateful people, and a mutual
love will spring up between them which neither time nor
distance will efface.'

Up, by a steep winding path, we mounted slowly in the
hot noon-day sun, seeking the little English burial-ground.
A terrace, bounded by a broad stone balustrade, crowns
the hill and looks down upon the sea; a little spot, a mere
strip of earth, but dear and hallowed to how many hearts!
There are but a few graves, but they have been tenderly
cared for, and are beautiful with pure white crosses and
broad slabs of stone, half hidden by the masses of the
purple passion-flower, of red roses, of sweet-scented lilies,
that cluster at their feet and wind their tendrils clingingly
across the carven marble; signs and emblems of so
many things—of faithful human love, true and unfor-
getting, of young lives that have faded in their noon-
day sun, and in all the beauty of their bloom; and, above
all, rose and passion-flower, emblems of Love and Death,
mysteries the deepest and the most divine, *Christus Salvator* written upon every leaf. Here, where the scented
air is heavy with the perfume of orange blossom and
musical with the hum of happy insect life, those who were

weary, and maybe somewhat heavy laden, have lain down
to rest, very quietly, with folded hands, waiting the last
glad Evangel.   Far below them, softened as it nears the
shore by a veil of silver-leaved olives, the sea lies green
and still, stretching far away to meet the deep blue of the
sky.   Bells from the old church towers half-way down
ring matins and vespers to the sailors on the water, and
the dwellers in the little town, where houses are piled one
against another in picturesque confusion, each gaining as
best it may a doubtful foothold on the steep hill-side,
their deep red roofs making pleasant bits of colour amongst
the grey woods and the golden lemon orchards.   This
little burial-ground is not hidden away from human hopes
and sympathies and daily life, is neither lonely nor de-
serted, only 'set apart,' lifted above the turmoil and the
care, and lying in the sunshine.   And so He giveth His
beloved sleep.

       *   *   *   *   *   *

   The *mistrael* was blowing as we drove away from Mentone; a wind most undeservedly belied, we thought, as
we welcomed the cool fresh breeze from the sea.   Almost
every one knows the road, so there is little need of re-
capitulating a list of all its charms and interests.   It
resembles an old mail-coach road in England in one
respect only, that it is kept in thoroughly good repair,
and differs from it inasmuch as it is rich in many a mile
of rather tumble-down old villas, in glorious eastern palms,

in hedges of green and prickly pear, in little shrines to the
Madonna, in crowds of beggars waiting with an Italian's
lazy patience at lonely corners, and catching a *diligence*
at a long hill, in Spanish-looking mules, and Murillo-like
boys who cry for *soldi*, and in the general absence of
turnpikes. Our stage was a short one again and quickly
over, the little horses doing their work merrily and rattling
their bells at the beggars, whom they left gasping far
behind. The laws of the road are as binding as those of
the Medes and Persians. No two-horse carriage may pass
one with four, as long as it is in motion. We had a fifth
horse, but we should have scorned to make the most of
that small advantage, or to have attempted to distance a
voiture à quatre chevaux with which we had a speaking
acquaintance, if it should so happen that that *voiture*
should start some fine morning before us. As it was, it
was just one day behind. But there was always the *diligence*; a *diligence* going to Genoa, and one to be met on
the way, and the law says that the *diligence* may pass
anything. These enactments are not, I believe, to be
found on parchment, but they certainly do exist, either
written in the dust on the carriage or stamped on the
consciences of the drivers, and sorrow comes invariably to
those who attempt to evade them ; at all events, we nearly
came to direful grief after setting them at defiance, as my
tale will show.

There was one carriage on the road with four English,

who went slowly and steadily forward, getting up early and always making a long day's work of it; we learnt to know their faces, and once when they overtook us while we were lunching and feeding two small boys with cakes and oranges, we longed to indulge our impulse to extend hospitality to our countrymen, feeling intuitively that they must be hungry; but the fear of the 'world's dread laugh' at such a solecism, and their probably well-bred astonishment in the remembrance that we had not been introduced, deterred us, and we had to fall back upon a brother and sister in a landau who were younger, and with whom, having fraternised previously at Nice, we were in a position to share a biscuit without indiscretion.

At five o'clock (two hours from Mentone), we drew up at the Hôtel Victoria in pleasant San Remo. How Romulus and Remus were ever canonised it is difficult to imagine; but tradition tells of an archbishop of Genoa of the ninth century, a St. Romulus, in whose honour the little town of Matuta was built; but faring badly under his auspices, and being roughly handled by the Saracens, who cared little for the saintly benediction, the inhabitants retreated to the hills, and tried their fortune once more under the same august patronage. A hundred years later a band of enterprising citizens descended once more to the coast, and rebuilt the fallen houses of Matuta, to which, says Mons. Élisée Reclus, 'on donne le nom de Sanremo, pour indiquer ainsi la fraternité des deux cités

voisines;' the saintly prefix being a delicate touch of
southern sentiment and national vanity, gratifying at once
to the small town itself, and to the feelings of the younger
of the old Roman brothers. San Remo is certainly under
the especial patronage of one of the first Roman prince
bishops (if ecclesiastical history decides to regard the
great Twins in that light, being always a little vague and
shadowy as to times and seasons), and flourishes accordingly, being a bright, cheery, cleanly place. Old San
Romulus has a few houses somewhere near by, but he is
merely looked upon as a poor relation, hardly to be recognised by San Remo in its prosperity.

The visitors here, too, were mostly gone, though there
were many idlers under the chestnut avenue, carriages
driving home, and sweet-faced English children, talking
little broken French sentences to their *bonnes*. At the
hotel we were 'monarchs of all we surveyed,' or at least
sole tenants-at-will. There was plenty of time for a walk,
so the ladies of the party started on a voyage of discovery,
the success of which looked doubtful, as only the youngest
traveller could speak a word of Italian, and her Italian was
the language of Manzoni, and unadapted to the questions
and remarks incident to common life. The others usually
adopted a system, very simple, but sure in its results;
they always went straight to their point; if a church
was the object desired, they said '*chiesa*' or '*basilica*,'
feeling so far safe, and then added the name of the par-

ticular church, or its patron saint, interrogatively. This
always elicited a voluble reply, which being unable to
comprehend, they waited till the native was exhausted,
and then pointed, still interrogatively, to the four points
of the compass; one being indicated, and a clue thus
given, they instantly seized it and started, and wherever
the path became two or even three, as paths are given to
do suddenly in a totally unexpected and aggravating
manner, they would stand patiently and point again.
But this language of signs was scorned, as belonging
simply to the infancy of nations, by the youngest traveller,
who conscientiously endeavoured to unravel the remarks
of the inhabitants, and to follow their advice, which
sometimes led the party into the perplexities of a watercourse, or a *cul de sac* amongst vineyard walls.   In the
present instance, we were bound to the Church of La
Santa Annunziata; as it was on the summit of a hill, and
most of the paths went up steps, we rightly supposed
that one or other staircase would land us there at last,
though sometimes we appeared to go through the very
houses of the townspeople, and into second stories of the
buildings, where it seemed impossible we could come out
anywhere but on the roofs.   At last, however, the stairs
came to an end, changing to stones and pebbles; and
then olive trees grew again on grass slopes, and we met
women laden with baskets of lemons, and men and boys
with goats and mules, preparing to go down the stairs,
and finding their stables somewhere on the third or fourth

stories of that queer heap of old tenements. The view from the plateau above was very fine, but we feared to linger, as twilight was deepening, and there were some very rough-looking people to be passed on our way down under the dark arches. One old crone, fearful to look upon, with eager eyes, and scanty grey hairs, and withered hands held out as if to grasp us, begging for *buona mano* vociferously, and with angry declamation, and a dark handsome woman with a wild face followed us muttering excitedly, and only half willing to let us go by. Out in the open air again, we ran down a dry old watercourse, exchanging good night with the peasants returning from the fields; one with a sheep and lamb fastened by a cord, one bending beneath a heavy load of fresh grass, and with a goat that followed bleating, while she gossiped with a handsome-faced *contadino*, who, with his dog and gun, lingered at her side. There was a paper on the church door above, granting plenary indulgence to all visitors; on the strength of which, no doubt, the old women on the staircase exact their dole of charity.

On the following morning we tried to get to the top of an olive wood, but found it hard work to ascend a hill monotonously terraced, to keep the earth, which is always carefully prepared and manured, about the roots of the trees, and with a series of steep steps and broken piles of stones designed for the use of man; very rough stepping-stones we thought them for the poor bare-footed girls, who came down so heavily weighted, that they could not pick their way, and must have often suffered cruelly in the descent. Here, again, our father wisely sought shelter and repose *aux bords de la mer*, while the three other travellers began their toilsome climb. An olive wood in theory, and to a certain extent truly so, is a very beautiful thing, but it was noon of a hot summer's day, the sea-breeze had prudently remained below also, and the top boughs of the olive trees alone caught any air that was going that way ; the staircase seemed to go on for miles ; it was like a very early and rude representation of Jacob's ladder, the top whereof was lost in the clouds. We gave up in despair our hopes of looking down on the highest olive trees, seating ourselves instead for a long rest in the grass, and tried to paint their silver leaves, and the fair green sea that lay smiling far below us, and the blue light above our heads, and then scrambled down again to San Remo, with handfuls of wild flowers of a rare beauty, as our reward. Very welcome was some *vin du pays*, in the shape of lemonade made from the fresh fruit cool and scented as its blossoms.

A thunderstorm gathered later over the town, the lightning flashed, and there were growlings and mutterings amongst the hills, and then the heavy drops fell with a dull plash, faster and faster, and a great sheet of water dashed against our windows and darkened the leaves and earth. A pleasant storm, soon over, welcome as summer rain always is, and followed by sunshine that was reflected from each little bead of light hanging on the flowers, or glistening on the harness of our good little beasts, who, standing at the door, pawed the ground impatient to be off again. Some of the last day's dust had possibly been washed away in that sudden flood, and made some dirty little muddy pools amongst the baggage; but during the course of ages the dust on a real old 'campaigner' is either ingrained or veneered; it is an indurated white covering, composed originally of a pulverised conglomerate, a 'deposit' which in time adheres so closely to its receptacle that it forms part of the whole, and it would be difficult for the most skilful analytical chemist to say where leather ends and where dust begins.

What perfect happiness it was, perched up in the *coupé*, to look down on those fine good little steeds, who took kindly to the road as though they enjoyed the fun as much as we did, to watch the way in which one would sham fatigue and give up pulling, and how a little reproachful word from the *cocher* touched its conscience in a moment, and sent it into a repentant gallop at the next hill. How perfectly he had them in hand, and how well they knew him! A low whistle would check them in a moment at the greatest speed, and as for the whip, that was simply used as a musical accompaniment, Bassetti looking ferociously around as we clattered through the queer little towns on our route, lashing out right and left in a way

T

that imposed on nobody. No one who has not driven a mail-coach through the narrow alleys about the Seven Dials, or any other well-known and populous retreat, would be qualified to take the place of an Italian *voiturier*; the highway becomes in a moment the width of your carriage, and the old houses topple over threateningly, only prevented from falling on you by great beams, that prop them up, and arches that rest between their upper stories; suddenly, your road narrows, if that were possible, and goes into a tunnel; it is like driving through a drain, with humans instead of rats clinging to the walls to escape your wheels; and rags, and fish, and miserable merchandize of beans and polenta, filling up the openings to the dwellings where the poor creatures congregate in crowds. Here the whip has enough to do, and twists itself into a little agony of warning shrieks to any carriage or *diligence* that may rashly enter the tunnels at the other end. A queer fact this to be realized, that a road between Italy and France, after all that has been said about 'the march of civilization,' 'the high road of nations,' 'the progressive advancement of humanities,' has to creep through the afore-mentioned drains literally or metaphorically, however proudly it may set out on its travels. It is a pity, surely, that somehow it has left so little trace of its progress in any change for the better, for a small matter of eight or nine hundred years!

Travelling on, we turned a headland and came upon

Porto Morizio, a grand pile of buildings, churches, chapels, houses, with rows of arcades and open *loggie* rising one above the other, and towering over the sea. A mile and a half at an easy canter, and we are at the handsome suspension bridge, with its two marble arches, that leads to Oneglia, where we and our horses are to rest for the night. Porto Morizio is a modern affair as compared to Romulus and Remus, a mere eleventh century town, but boasting some 6,000 inhabitants; Oneglia lies on the low land beside the sea, and, according to our old friend Reclus, the former offers 'an aspect superb,' the latter is simply 'gracieuse!' In both, work being over for the day, the streets were swarming with people, and on this coast, as Mr. Dickens says of some nearer home, a good many men seem to earn their livelihood by looking at the sea. At the *arc de triomphe* of the bridge was a toll-bar, necessitating a slight delay, a huge *diligence* painted black and yellow and looking like a collection of gigantic bees that had just swarmed and brought their luggage with them, stood heavily freighted, but with a good team of six horses, waiting while the driver, who had descended to pay, fumbled for his change. We saw a gleam of delight in the eye of our *cocher*, and cried 'Avanti!' under our breath: flinging down a coin without drawing rein, he gave the horses their heads, the *diligence* driver rushing wildly to his place, and only regaining it as we dashed by, and then for seven minutes and a half there was almost a neck

T 2

and neck race, the two great lumbering carriages swinging frightfully from side to side as we dashed through the town. Our leaders once bolted across an open piazza, jamming us however in such a manner that no one could pass, and we managed to hold our own and make a fresh start, townspeople and salesmen, carts and carriages drawing hastily aside, and with a gasp of content we drew up at the Hôtel Royal, winners by a length !

The evening was glorious, and after securing rooms, the feminine portion of the party was tempted by the rich sunset light to linger in the open air, while our father returned to the hotel, and ordered supper. The ladies wandered round to the port at the back of the town, making small sketches of Porto Morizio in its ' *aspect superbe*,' of a cart and two great sleepy, mild-eyed, dun-coloured oxen, of women and babies, who also lingered on the quay, enjoying the coolness and rest. Some few sailors and *sous-officiers* gathered round, and pleasant-spoken peasants, who criticised the drawings and politely expressed their pleasure over the sketch-books ; but gradually a plague of small boys began to darken the air : first one or two, like the scouts of the mosquitoes, hovered near, then, growing bolder, they signalled to their fellows, and the gnats began to swarm. They were tolerably respectful at first, keeping at a moderate distance, and acting almost as a *garde d'honneur*, conducting the ladies to the Mole, where they lingered rejoicing in the great waves that

Standing at bay!

Defying the Military.   Oneglia

dashed against the narrow wall, bringing a gusty smell of the sea, and flinging a pleasant briny spray upon their faces. But the *ragazzi* of Oneglia were unable to comprehend the enjoyment of the English in standing to be wetted with salt water, and evidently believed they must have some secret reason for their excursion on the Mole, that, if known, would prove to be of vast interest. The impression spread that something must come of it, and more boys arrived each moment, till the 'following' became somewhat troublesome. The youngest traveller enquired, in her choicest Italian, whether they had never, on any previous occasion, encountered wild or unknown animals, to which the most intelligent of the mob gravely replied, 'Signorina, never.' Four of the boys went in front, the mob always keeping the necessary space clear, and executed somersaults in the hope of extracting *sous*, and about sixty constituted themselves a body-guard. It was impossible to disperse them, and as fresh arrivals swelled the numbers every moment, and none of them really knew what they were looking at, they took to cheering as a lively exercise, which they seemed to find so beneficial that the performance was unanimously prolonged.

The ladies having vainly requested to be left in peace, walked in dignified contempt, three abreast, towards the shelter of the hotel, afraid to laugh, and disdaining to run, and were conducted to the very door amidst ironical *vivas!*

About one hundred and fifty boys and girls immediately took up a position in the narrow street beneath the windows, from which safe elevation their victims placidly regarded them; but the officials of the hotel, considering the demonstration a little too popular, rushed to disperse the mob. An active waiter, armed with a napkin and a large carriage-whip, did his best; but the incorrigible little animals retreated for the moment, only to take up a more secure position the next. Then the military were called out, and one infantry soldier gesticulated and shrieked at the boys, who made faces at him in return, till seizing his sword (in its sheath), with both hands he made a desperate charge, and the mothers at that moment coming to his assistance, turned the enemy by a flank movement. A small creature was captured, and chastized then and there, and a general stampede followed. One persistent girl with a big baby alone held her ground, and I think we may consider it was a drawn battle between her and the military.

We were early the next morning, breakfasting at seven, and making a good start before any of our companions of the road were moving. Our stage was to be a longer one than usual, and we were all in good heart for the work. The weather was glorious, the colouring of sea and distant hills radiantly beautiful in its varying tintings of green and blue, pink and violet, with snowy summits rising at times over the nearer ranges on our left, and Genoa with its

15 miles an hour!

forts and lighthouse growing ever more and more distinct out of the purple and grey haze that shaped itself into far-away hills resting on the water.

Our road led, by a gradual climb, and then by a steep descent, sometimes steady, sometimes precipitous, along the edge of the rock. Always, nearer or farther below us, the waves fretted against the stones, and here and there a landslip showed where the road had given way, or it turned suddenly, almost at an acute angle, and one could look down an infinite depth with no foreground of protecting wall or fence to break the view!

As we were quietly walking up a long hill, a distant sound came to us which acted magically on our *cocher*, a noise of horses' feet and of one driving furiously. Bassetti drew his reins together, stood up in his seat, and gave one long anxious look behind; then shook his ribbons eagerly, cried in an agony of appeal to his horses, and settled down to his work. The good beasts perfectly understood his feelings, which was more than we did at the moment, and rose to the occasion; there was no hanging back about any of them, in three minutes they had gained the top of the hill, and were going down the slope as fast as they could lay legs to the ground; and there round a corner, almost on top of us, came the great black and yellow *diligence*, and we understood it all, with a half shiver of terror: for these southern fellows are utterly reckless when their passions are

roused, and between Carlo and the *diligence* driver it was
combat à outrance.   Knowing it was useless to remon-
strate, and dangerous even to speak, our father held his
peace and waited, and the other occupant of the *coupé*
confesses to a quiver of alarm, and an anxious watching
of each fresh piece of road that came into view, for at the
headlong speed at which we were going, it would have
been utterly impossible to have pulled up the horses suddenly, and had we encountered any great waggons on the
road, or other cart or carriage, there must have been a
horrible smash, and the big *diligence* would have fallen
on top of us ! It was certainly a mad gallop, down hill
on such a road, at the rate of fifteen miles an hour, but
it was a wonderful sight to see ! The way our *cocher*
turned the corners, thundering down the slopes, one
wheel almost on its side as we edged round a sharp rock,
the carriage swaying as though it must topple over, the
wheels spinning over the stones and the great whip
cracking and whistling to the echoes, the thud thud of
the pursuing feet, the wind that blew against us, the
danger that gave an edge to our enjoyment, the terror
of what was coming, and the pleasure in our success,
made that half-hour on the Corniche a bit of travelling experience not soon to be forgotten ! It is an uncertain way of seeing the shores of the Mediterranean,
but that race was to us a combination of delights one
does not often secure in this matter-of-fact world, and I

Hotel Reale Genoa

On the road again!

only hope the travellers in the *diligence* enjoyed it as
heartily.   Of the feelings of their driver we know nothing,
as of course we won in a canter when we once reached
the level, and dashing through the little town of Lanona,
where his stage ended, we left our rivals far behind.

I must not linger to describe one midday halt, and the
queer cookery that accompanied it, or our more steady-
going progress during the afternoon, towards Savona with
its pleasant hotel and flowery garden, and the broad quays
where vessels are filling and unloading all day long, and
piles of lemons, bags of corn, and crates of bottles and
earthenware crowd the pavement; of the moon, very faint
and young as yet, that shone upon the sea; of our drive
to Pegli through a southern land of rich cultivation,
vines and chestnuts, lemon and orange orchards, and other
green things pleasant to the eyes and good for food; of
the blind beggars who always saw the exact number of
people there were to beg from, and who appealed to each;
of the beggar with one arm, who had a second gracefully
but partially concealed by a piece of drapery; of more
fishing villages, and of people going and coming throng-
ingly upon the road as we neared Genoa.

There is little space left in which to tell of our visit
to the Villa Palavacini, whose princely owner makes
strangers welcome; where, in the language of the ancient
poets, ' nature and art go hand in hand,' and where accordingly there are all the sweetest flowers that ever bloom

in the sunshine, classical temples, fountains, Chinese pagodas, stalactite caves, a lake, islands, temples, a swing, secret *jets d'eau* that play upon the unwary, a merry-go-round with a wooden pony for the *Marchese*, and a *char à banc* for the *Marchesa*, and three more steeds, and three more carriages, for the Palavacini guests; a magnificent palace; and a terrace, standing on which one looks across at Genoa as she lies with her fair arms outstretched, smiling at the sea.

There is no time to tell of the dusty way that led to her, or how we passed under the guarded gateway and trotted merrily through the streets; how we paused in the Piazza della Annunziata and had our leaders taken off, the angles of Genoese streets being somewhat sharper even than those of the Corniche, and their width about three yards across; how in a dark alley we did in a manner come to grief, and make an ignominious end of our triumphant progress, for at the very corner of the Albergo Reale the near horse slipped and stumbled, and in its fall knocked over its companion; how we looked down on the débris from our vast elevation, descending at length literally into the arms of the Genoese; how the good steeds picked themselves up again, and were none the worse, but ready as ever for a fresh scamper on the old road, where we would hope many of our countrymen may be fortunate enough to fall in with those five clever little horses, and our worthy Carlo Bassetti of Arona.

MOUNTAINEERING IN TYROL.

—◦—

APPENDIX.

APPENDIX.

———◦◦———

MOUNTAINEERING IN TYROL.

———

HAVING obtained a tolerably complete knowledge of
Tyrol during five consecutive visits to different parts
of that country, in 1863–4–5–6–7, and being inclined to
think that the exquisite beauty of its scenery, and the
very moderate cost of travel will lead to its being visited
every year by an increasing number of our countrymen,
I venture to offer, for the information of other mountaineers, a sketch of an eight weeks' tour which I believe
will be found to embrace the chief objects of interest
throughout the principal mountain groups. I assume
that the Tyrol is entered at Landeck in the upper Inn
Thal, which may be reached viâ the Vorarlberg either
from Zurich or Constance, in about three days from
London ; whilst in returning from Bormio a great variety
of interesting routes offer themselves to the traveller's
choice.

1. Thursday. From Landeck by the Finstermünz Pass to
(a) Reschen and the highest available quarters in the Langtau-
ferer Thal, or (b) to Mals and the châlets at the head of the
Matscher Thal.

2. To Vent (or Fend) in the Oetzthal by (*a*) the Langtau-ferer Joch, or (*b*) the Matscher (Hintereis) Joch, ascending, in the first case, the Langtauferer Spitz, and, in the second, the Weisskugel *en route*.

3. Ascend the Wildspitz.

*4. At Vent, and stroll down to Sölden in the afternoon.

5. By the Winacher Thal and Pfaffen Ferner to the summit of the Schneide or Zuckerhütl, and then by the Pfaffen Joch and Sulzenau Glacier to Graba and Neustift in the Stubay Thal, whence Schönberg and perhaps Innsbruck may be reached the same night.

6. To, and at Innsbruck.

7. At Innsbruck, and by rail to Jenbach, and *voiture* to Zell in the Ziller Thal.

8. Drive to Mayrhofen, and thence proceed up the Zemm and Zamser Thal to the chûlets at the entrance of the Hörpinger Thal.

9. Ascend the Hoch Mösele Spitz, and proceed by the Mösele Ferner and Mühlwalder Thal to Taufers; thence drive up the Ahren Thal to Steinhaus, or farther if time will permit.

10. By the Vord, or Hint Thörl, to Pregraten in the Virgen Thal.

*11. At Pregraten, and thence by the Dorfer Thal to the Johanns Hütte near the foot of the Dorfer Kees.

12. Ascend the Gross Venediger, and descend by the Unter-sulzbach Kees and Thal to Neukirchen in the Pinzgau; thence drive to Mittersill.

13. Drive to Zell-am-See and Saalfelden (*a*) or Frohnwies (*b*).

14. Cross (*a*) the Steinernes Meer to Königssee and Berchtes-gaden, or (*b*) proceed to the same place by the Hirschbühel Pass and Ramsau.

15. At Berchtesgaden.

16. Ascend the Jenner Spitz; cross the Torrener Joch to Golling; and thence drive to Salzburg viâ Hallein.

17. Drive to Ischl viâ St. Gilgen and the Wolfgang See, or quit the carriage at St. Gilgen and ascend the Schafberg to sleep, proceeding to Ischl the next morning.

*18. At Ischl.

19. Descend the Traun by boat to Ebensee, and then take the steamer to Gmunden on the Traun See, returning in the same way, or by carriage to Ebensee, and driving back to Ischl, whence Alt-Aussee may be reached by *voiture* the same evening viâ Laufen.

20. Visit Aussee and the Grundl See, and then proceed to Hallstadt viâ Ober Traun and the Hallstädter See.

21. Visit the Rudolfsthurm, and returning to the village, proceed to the Wiesen Alp (Almhütte) to sleep.

22. Ascend the Dachstein and descend (*a*) by the Hoch Gjaidstein Joch and Schladminger Kees to Ramsau and Schladming in the Enns Thal, or (*b*) to Hinter Gosau.

23. Drive (*a*) to Radstadt, St. Johann (im Pongau), and Lend; or (*b*) over Pass Gschütt to Abtenau and Golling, and thence to Werfen, St. Johann, and Lend, if time permits.

24. To Wildbad Gastein, per *voiture* in either case.

*25. At Wildbad Gastein.

26. Cross the Stanzer Scharte to Bucheben in the Rauriser Thal, and then the Schütterriedl to St. Wolfgang and Ferleiten in the Fusch Thal.

27. Cross (*a*) the Pfandl Scharte, or (*b*) the Bockkar Scharte, to Heiligenblut in the Möll Thal, in the latter case ascending the Breit Kopf. The first is the easier, but the second is by far the finer route.

28. At Heiligenblut, and to the Leiter Hütte to sleep.

29. Ascend the Gross Glockner, descend to Kals, and proceeding to Huben, drive thence to Lienz.

30. Drive to Sillian and Inichen, and over the Ampezzo Pass to Cortina and S. Vito.

31. Ascend the Antelao viâ the Forcella Piccola, and returning to the Pass descend by the Val Oten to Calalzo and Pieve di Cadore or Tai.

*32. At Cadore or Tai, and in the afternoon to Forno di Zoldo in Val di Zoldo.

33. Cross Passo Coldai (ascending Monte Civita en route ?) to Alleghe and Caprile.

34. Visit the gorge of Sottoguda in Val Pettorina, and then, crossing due S. to Forno di Canale by a pass between Monte Pezza and Monte Alto, proceed up the valley to Gares.

35. Ascend the Palle di S. Martino (if possible) or Cimon della Pala by the Valle delle Comelle, and returning to Gares, cross the Gesurette Pass to the Valle di S. Lucano and Agordo.

36. To Caprile up the Cordevole Valley viâ Cencenighe and the Lago d'Alleghe, and thence on to Pieve by the Livinallongo Thal.

37. Cross viâ the summit of the Monte Prelungei (Zissa Berg ?) to Corfara in the Gader Thal, and from thence proceed up the valley to the Grödner Jöchl, and, skirting the head of the Grödner Thal, traverse the Sella Pass to Campidello in Val Fassa (Fleimser Thal). Ascend the valley to Alba or Penia, or even some higher sleeping-quarters if time permits.

38. Ascend the Marmolata and return to Campidello.

*39. At Campidello.

40. Viâ the Duron Pass and over the summit of the Schlern to Bad Ratzes. Thence viâ Völs to Steg in the Eisack Thal, and to Botzen per *voiture*.

41. At Botzen, and per rail to Trent and Roveredo, and thence to Riva at the head of the Lago di Garda per *voiture*.

42. Drive up the Val di Sarca to Alle Sarche, and thence walk to Molveno.

43. Cross by the Bocca di Brenta (ascending the Cima Tosa on the way), to Pinzolo in Val Rendena.

44. At Pinzolo and to the Bedole Malga in Val di Genova.

45. Ascend the Adamello and return (*a*) to the Bedole châlet, or (*b*) to Pinzolo.

*46. At (*a*) the Bedole Alp or (*b*) Pinzolo; in the latter case proceeding in the evening to the Nardis Alp to sleep.

47. Proceed (*a*) to the summit of the Cercen Pass, thence ascend the Presanella, and returning to the col drop down on the N. side to Vermiglio, Fosine, and the Bagni di Pejo, in Val di Sole. Or (*b*) ascend the Presanella from the Nardis Alp by the Glacier of the same name, and descending by the opposite arête upon the Cercen Pass, proceed thence as already suggested (*a*).

48. By Val del Monte and the Glacier at the head of the Val Piana (or Val Umbrina?) to the ridge running S.W. from the Pizzo della Mare, ascend the latter, and returning to the col, traverse the névé of the Gavia Glacier to the summit of the Pizzo Tresero, whence Sta Catarina may be reached very directly viâ the Tresero Alp.

49. At Sta Catarina.

50. At Sta Catarina; ascend Monte Confinale.

51. Cross the Passo di Forno to the highest châlets in the Val della Mare, perhaps ascending the Vios, or Viozzi, Spitz *en route*.

52. By the Glacier of La Mare to the saddle between the two highest summits of the Monte Cevedale or Fürkeli (the Zufall Spitz of the maps of Lombardy and Tyrol), ascend the latter, and dropping down in a N. direction upon the Cevedale Pass, and skirting the head of the Langenferner (which descends into the Martell Thal) to the Janiger Scharte, traverse the latter to Gampenhöfe and St. Gertrud in the Sulden Thal viâ the Sulden Glacier.

*53. At St. Gertrud.

54. Ascend the Orteler Spitz and descend by the Trafoi route to Trafoi.

55. At Trafoi; drive to Gomagoi in the afternoon, and stroll up the Sulden Thal to St. Gertrud and Gampenhöfe.

56. Cross the Pass between the Orteler Spitz and Klein Zebru, ascend the latter, and then proceeding to the Orteler Joch, traverse the Unterer Trafoiferner to the Heiligen Drei Brunnen and Trafoi (viâ the 'Bergl'?), or, keeping away to the left, cross the lower portion of the Ober Trafoiferner and gain the Stelvio road by the slopes of the Madatsch Spitz.

57. Cross the Stelvio to Bormio per *voiture* or on foot, and if desired, Tirano may easily be reached the same night, and London in four or five days, either viâ Chiavenna and the Splügen, or by the Bernina, St. Moritz, and the Julier or Albula, to Chur and Zürich.

The following suggestions on the subject of maps, guide-books, and guides, in connection with the foregoing route, may be found serviceable.

MAPS.

For Tyrol in general.

1. Mayr's 'Karte von Tirol.'   Munich; *or,*
2. Mayr's 'Atlas der Alpenländer,' sheets 2, 3, 5, and perhaps 6.

For days 1–4.

3. 'Special Karte der Oetzthaler Alpen,' by K. von Sonklar and H. Berghaus.   Gotha, Perthes.

For days 5 *and* 6.

4. 'Special Karte der Stubaier Gebirgsgruppe,' by L. Pfaundler. Innsbruck, Wagner.

Or (*less detailed*) *for days* 1–6.

5. 'General Quartiermeister-Stab, Karte der gefürsteten Grafschaft Tirol etc.,' $\frac{1}{144000}$; sheets 7 and 8.

For days 7–12.
The same, sheet 9.

For days 12–16.
Mayr 1 or 2 will probably suffice.

For days 17–26.
The same.

Or for days 17–22.

6. 'Special Karte des Salzkammergutes,' by J. J. Pauliny, $\frac{1}{144000}$. Vienna, Lechner.

For days 27-29.

7. The map of the neighbourhood of the Gross Glockner, by Keil, appended to Dr. von Ruthner's 'Aus der Tauern,' is by far the best.

For days 30–36.
Mayr 1 or 2 ; or

8. 'Topographische Karte des Lombardisch-Venetianischen Königreichs,' $\frac{1}{80000}$. Milan, 1833–8. Sheets F. 1 and 2.

For days 37–41.
Mayr 1 or 2 will probably suffice.

For days 42–48.
No. 5, sheets 16 and 19, for general purposes, and, for details of 44–47,

U

9. 'Die Adamello-Presanella Alpen,' by J. Payer, $\frac{1}{58000}$. Gotha, Perthes. (Appended to a paper by Lieutenant Payer in Petermann's 'Mittheilungen;' Ergänzungsheft, No. 17. November 1865. Gotha, Perthes.)

For days 48–51.

No. 8, sheets D. 1 and 2, *and*

10. A map accompanying a paper by F. F. Tuckett in the 'Alpine Journal' for December 1864 (vol. i. p. 384), with corrections in the number for September 1865 (vol. ii. pp. 145–7), and that for September 1866 (vol. ii. pp. 352–7).

For days 51–57.

No. 5, sheet 16, together with

11. The map accompanying 'Die Ortler Alpen (Sulden Gebiet und Monte Cevedale),' and 'Die westlichen Ortler-Alpen (Trafoier Gebiet),' by Lieutenant J. Payer. Petermann's 'Mittheilungen,' Ergänzungsheft, No. 18 and 23, 1867–8. Gotha, Perthes.

GUIDE-BOOKS, ETC.

Murray's ' Southern Germany.'

„ ' Knapsack Guide to Tyrol.'

Schaubach's 'Deutschen Alpen,' 2nd edition. Jena, Frommann. Vol. iii. (Salzburg, Salzkammergut, &c.). Vol. iv. (Central and Southern Tyrol).

'The Dolomite Mountains,' by Messrs. Gilbert and Churchill (a most charming book). Longmans & Co.

' Guide to the Central Alps,' by J. Ball.

' Guide to the Eastern Alps,' by J. Ball.

' Jahrbuch des Oesterreichischen Alpine-Vereines' (five volumes of which have already been published).

The Alpine Journal' (of which three volumes have appeared) also contains scattered papers and notices on various portions of the Austrian Alps.

GUIDES.

1. Matscher Thal. The Jäger at Matsch.
2. Langtauferer Thal. Blas in Mallag.
3. Vent (Oetzthal). Cyprian Granbichler.
4. Mayrhofen (Ziller-Thal). Förster Hochleitner; also Samer (*vulgò* Josele) at Ginzling, and Bartl and Jackl, either there or at Breitlechner.
5. Pregraten (Virgen Thal). The Brothers Steiner, and the smith of Pregraten.
6. Berchtesgaden. Josef Grafl and his brothers, &c.
7. Hallstadt. Wallner, Loydl, Stocker, and Zauner.
8. Fusch. Anton Hütter.
9. Heiligenblut. Wallner, B. and C. Lackner, Breimisch, Veit Bäuerle, Granegger, Eder.
10. S. Vito. The Cacciatore Ossi.
11. Caprile. Pellegrino Pellegrini of Rocca, and for the Marmolata the brothers Dimaj of Ampezzo.
12. Campidello (Val Fassa). J. B. Bernard, 'Waldaufseher.'
13. Molveno. Bonifazio Nicolosi.
14. Pinzolo. Förster Suda (?).
15. Cogolo. Binder, Framba, and Domenico Venere.
16. Sulden Thal. Pinggera of Sulden, or Janiger of Maria Schmelz in the Martell Thal.

Our route of 1866 is given below under the idea that it
may prove useful to some inexperienced travellers who
wish to explore those parts of Tyrol that are easily accessible and well adapted for ladies. It might be condensed
in many ways and with advantage, as in our case it had
to be modified from time to time to suit the weather and
the mountaineering plans of some of the party.

1. Paris to Basle.
2. Basle to Schaffhausen.
3. Schaffhausen to Constance and Lindau, and thence to Im-
    menstadt by rail and to Hindelang by carriage.
4. Hindelang to Lermos by carriage.
5. Lermos to Nassereit and Innsbruck by carriage. Hôtel
    d'Autriche, excellent.
6–7. At Innsbruck.
8. By rail to Wörgl, thence post to Waidring.
9. Waidring to Lofer, Reichenhall, and Berchtesgaden by car-
    riage. Hotel zum Watzmann, good.
10. To Königs-See and back, &c.
11. To Salzburg by carriage. Hotel Nelbök, very good.
12. To Ischl by carriage. Hotel Goldenes Kreuz, excellent.
13. At Ischl. Excursionized.
14. At Ischl.
15. To Aussee and its lakes, by carriage.
16. To Hallstadt and return to Ischl. This is an easy excursion
    to and from Ischl direct.
17. To Ebensee and Gmunden, to and from Ischl by carriage, or
    boat down the Traun.
18. From Ischl to Salzburg. The Schafberg, 5,703 feet, may be
    ascended *en route*; the view is very fine, and there is an
    inn on the summit.

19. To Berchtesgaden by carriage.
20, 21, 22. At Berchtesgaden and to the Königs-See and Wildbach Klamm ; a wonderful cascade under the rocks.
23. From Berchtesgaden to Zell am See by carriage, 12 hours over Hirschbühel Pass.
24. To Krimml, carriage, 12 hours including halts.
25. Krimml, inn rough but clean, to Gerlos on horseback, 4 hours ; on to Zell in Ziller-Thal in bergwägen, 4 hours.
26. At Zell and to Karlsteg and back, carriage and horseback.
27. From Zell to Jenbach by carriage, and rail to Innsbruck.
28. At Innsbruck.
29. Innsbruck to Zirl, Telfs, and Imst, carriage, 11½ hours.
30. Imst to Landeck and Finstermünz, 12 hours, carriage.
31. Hof Finstermünz to Nauders and Zernetz, 12 hours by carriage.
32. To Pontresina by carriage.
33. At Pontresina, Gredig's hotel, good.
34. Ditto, and in bergwägen to Sils Maria; good cookery at the Alpen Rose.
35. Ditto.   Service at St. Moritz.
36. Ditto, to the Roseg Glacier.
37. Ditto, to the top of the Bernina Pass.
38. Ditto to the Morteratsch Glacier.
39. Ditto.
40. Ditto.   Ascended the Muoters.
41. Ditto.
42. Ditto.   Service at St. Moritz.
43. Ditto.   Ascended the Piz Languard.   Walther, Flury, and Jenni are the principal guides.
44. To Samaden and over the Julier Pass to Chur, 12 hours by diligence.
45. Chur to Zurich by rail.
46. Zurich to Basle and through the night to Paris.